A HOUSE BY THE SEA

A House by the Sea

SIKEENA KARMALI

ESPLANADE
Books

THE FICTION SERIES AT VÉHICULE PRESS

Published with the generous assistance of The Canada Council for the Arts, the Book Publishing Industry Development Program of the Department of Canadian Heritage, and the Société de développement des entreprises culturelles du Québec (SODEC).

Esplanade Fiction Series editor: Andrew Steinmetz
Cover design: David Drummond
Special assistance: R. Bruce Henry and Rosemary Dardick
Set in Adobe Minion by Simon Garamond
Printed by AGMV-Marquis Inc.

CATALOGUING IN PUBLICATION
Karmali, Sikeena
A house by the sea / Sikeena Karmali
ISBN 1-55065-176-5
I. Title
PS8571.A843H69 2003   C813'.54   C2003-903244-2
PR9199.3K375H69 2003

Véhicule Press
www.vehiculepress.com

CANADIAN DISTRIBUTION: LitDistCo Distribution,
100 Armstrong Avenue,
Georgetown, Ontario, L7G 5S4 / 800-591-6250 / orders@litdistco.ca

U.S. DISTRIBUTION: Independent Publishers Group,
814 North Franklin Street,
Chicago, Illinois 60610 / 800-888-4741 / frontdesk@ipgbook.com

Printed in Canada

For my parents, Kulsum and Amir

Read in the name of your Lord ... Who taught by the pen.

–Surah of the Ovum Cell, *The Holy Qur'an*

Stop the words now.
Open the window in the centre of your chest, and let spirit
fly in and out.

–Mowlana Jalluddin Rumi

Acknowledgements

I am not sure this book would have seen the light of day without the assistance of my editor Andrew Steinmetz who was able to see and understand what I was trying to do with my writing. I owe him respect and immense gratitude for helping to make it happen.

The writing of this book has taken the better part of a decade. I wish to thank all of you who believed in it and who provided love, support, a place to stay and a warm meal: Wa'il Qattan, Paula Hacopian, Susanna Doyle, Jessica Doyle, Wayne Barret, Casper Grathwohl, Lina Hourani, Shaun Ferguson, Henrietta Hely-Hutchinson, Yasmine Ahmed and Françoise Sullivan.

I would like to thank Anne Henderson for introducing me to Véhicule Press and everyone at Véhicule Press for their encouragement, help and support, especially Vicki Marcok and Scott McRae. I would like to thank Simon Dardick for having the courage to publish fiction that is unconventional.

Lastly, I owe the world to my brother Shafiq Karmali for continuing to believe in me, against all the odds.

Contents

Zahra's house by the sea in decrepit Stone Town has been abandoned for almost half a century. The mashrebeyya of the windows and arches is clouded by years of dust and grime. A surface layer of slick greyish-green slime has gelled in the basin of the fountain in the courtyard. The wooden bench is missing most of its teeth. Only the skeleton remains of a swing under the mango tree. The wide arches have begun to decompose. The interior walls are crumbling. The garden is untended, the charm overgrown into a natural passion, impassable. The house is empty, vacant, like a ghost. It faces the sea, looking for its memories of life.

Khatak

Khatak, like all classical Indian dance, has its origins in the temple. Where the more popular Bharta Natyam illustrates the mythic tales of the Vedas, Khatak usually unveils a moral or spiritual understanding.

Khatak consists of eight basic beats: *tha, thai, thai, thet; ha, thai, thai, thet.* They are repeated to form a rhythm in sixteenths. This rhythm is broken by three half-steps: *dhi, thi, thi.* The dance is rooted in chakras, circles that are stepped by breaking the pattern of eight into fourths. The dancer wears bells, junjuru, tied around her ankles. When she spins, the music of the junjuru keeps rhythm with the tabla. A dancer is judged by the grace of her eyes and hands, and by how frantically fast, and wilfully slow, she can spin.

GHULSHAN AND ALI

My mother's eyes shine. Her pupils swim. Her lashes flicker. When she smiles, the corners light up and they sparkle. I have never held her gaze. But she holds mine. I carry her eyes with me. My mother lives inside me.

I am forever searching for her in the eyes of others. When I find her, I shake. The earth quakes and all my puppets crumble. You see, I myself am a puppet. Born of my imagination. It is my imagination that inspires my twenty-four-year-old mother to walk to work at the dentist's office in Moshi. My half-caste father follows her in his car. His is the only new, ivory-coloured Opal sedan in Moshi. He drives it with more pomp than his ancestors riding Arabian steeds from Samarkand to conquer the villages along the Gulf of Kutch. So he pursued her. Red roses igniting scarlet blood. Her bare bronze legs tucked into a pair of white pumps, swaying on tottering heels and convincing her hips to follow. Ghulshan and her Ali. They have now become legend. Braver than Leili and Majnoun, Romeo and Juliet, and Tristan and Isolde. Tragedy, so jealous of Romance, has plagued them. Born of their joy, I imagine their sorrow.

Come along. You must imagine with me. My mother and father, Ghulshan and Ali, have gone to Zanzibar. Have finally agreed, at my insistence, to take a holiday. To return to East Africa. They would not return to the Kilimanjaran slopes of Tanzania. So I suggested the breezy, not quite African, seaport island of Zanzibar. Zanzibar, now, after thirty-seven years of marriage, contemplating a divorce from Tanzania. *Talaq. Talaq. Talaq.* Convenient, no? Soon she will be free. Heady freedom, with price not negotiable. Can Zanzibar afford to pay?

Tomorrow I will board the plane to join them.

ZAHRA

Here I am. Recruiting your imagination, fully aware that you are looking for me. This is the story of my desire. Shall we escape? Return, and run again. I wish to stop running. To take my home off my back and lay it down, here, lay my burden down and sort through it.

Tomorrow afternoon at 1:20 I will leave cold, grey England and return to Zanzibar, not-so-ancient garden of the Omani Sultanate. An island of merchants, of men who trade, bargain for their lives, gamble with blood. Zanzibar was their ballroom, their khottha. Will you dance? Stamp your feet! Wail and scream.

Tha, thai, thai thet
right, left, right, left
ha, thai, thai, thet
left, right, left, right.
Dhi, thi, thie
full, half, half
dhi, thi, thie
full, half, half
dhi, thi, thie
side, side, down.

Chakras winding, slowly at first, teasingly composed. Arrogant grace infiltrates you. Kisses of the flute drowned by thundering tablas, her junjuru screaming in unison. Chakras whirling in the wind. The raga changes. A new season slapping your face. Her bleeding feet beat infinity. *Panj tden pak.* The hand of Fatimah raised. Sharp turn of the head, once, twice, thrice, and the bells died. Discomfort imbues me, but I dance all the same.

I am going to Zanzibar to melt in the warm embrace of my mother's bulging arms, drown in her watery eyes. It has been thirteen guilty months since I have seen Ghulshan and Ali. My home is their shifting abode, perfumed not with roses but with the pungent smell of affliction. I have left the ends of the earth to return to them. They have gone to the ends of the earth and waited for me to come. I always take my own footsteps home.

Seven a.m. Woken from sleep by England's weak sun. No passion, just duty. I have a plane to catch in five hours. Haven't finished packing. I need to shower. Leave keys in post-box. Turn off gas. Stop at Lloyds Bank cash-point. Take out £700 sterling. Quick stop at Boots chemists, get contact lens solution, Kotex, deodorant, sun block, lip balm, cigarettes. One dozen Cadburys for Ali and me and some Crunchie bars for Ghulshan. Nothing beats English chocolate, so rich and creamy. Yes, we like it milky. Diluted.

Stop at Piazza Café: cappuccino, orange juice, pain au chocolat. Tell Franco, the Sicilian manager who fathers me, I won't be around for two weeks.

Piccadilly line or mini-cab to Heathrow? Mercury mobile phone. One, two, one. Phoning cab service. Fifteen minutes later.

"Miss Zahra? What terminal you going to?"

"Four."

"Going on holiday?"

"No. Home."

"Where is that?"

"East Africa."

"Yeah?" He is interested. "I'm from Sudan. You Muslim? You don't look African. Your family from Kenya or something. I know lots of Asians from Kenya. They don't call Africa home."

Did you know I was a princess? Yes, I was a princess. I used to ride in large black cars with seats as wide as your bed, feet dangling, laughter dancing as I watched the sun drip upon the chauffeur. Now I ride the Underground. The rain drips upon me.

At Terminal Four the driver asks for £25. I pay him, find a trolley for my luggage, and run towards the British Airways counter. I am late.

"I am sorry Miss. These are company regulations. EVERY FLIGHT BY EVERY AIRLINE COMPANY IN THE WORLD IS OVER-SOLD. This is why we ask you to arrive early or pre-select your seat twenty-four hours prior to flying."

I have paid £650 for my ticket but cannot get on the flight. I must be experiencing a momentary lapse of reason. Five minutes later I am screaming in the face of a manager who tells me, Queen of Patience, to wait. So, I wait. Bless the names of Allah, Ali and all his descendants. Devour a Cadbury's Flake bar. At my last mouthful, the manager returns.

"You are a very lucky girl! We have one seat left and the couple ahead of you is refusing to be split up. You will be flying first-class!" His face is beaming. "Hurry along now, dear, otherwise you're going to miss your flight!"

Thank Allah. Off I go to customs, next stop—the official has a problem with my visa. Over a decade and Heathrow has not changed. But I have become bigger and smarter.

"Why do you have a working visa for the United Kingdom, Miss?"

"Because I work in the United Kingdom, Sir."

"And what is it that you do?"

"I am a lawyer specialising in immigration," I lie.

I am accustomed to long flights. I have formulated an equation for stuffing myself and my belongings into narrow partitions of space that swallow whatever dignity may have remained intact through the process of checking in and clearing customs. First-class comfort comes as a pleasant surprise. The seats are as wide as a love-seat. A button on the armrest allows me to unfold and recline, bottom pushing forward as the back falls and legs rise. Stewardesses are accommodating. I am offered a choice of champagne: pink or white. There is a real menu. A white tablecloth is arranged on my large pull-down table, with real silverware. Magazines plus the British Airways in-flight bulletin are stuffed into a side pocket. I have a mini-television with satellite channels that doubles as a telephone. On the leather seat lies a vanity case packed to the brim with goods advertised in *Elle* magazine. And right beside it, a still-life of luxury, airline-style: British Airways stationery and pen, two fluffy pillows and a large, soft, woolly blanket. I will kill you if you fall asleep.

RUMINATION

In the sky my thoughts wander. I become anxious. Why have I chosen to believe in this fantasy to the point of living it? Is this a fairy tale, where I am going to waltz into Zanzibar and land in my grandmother's house, then magically reclaim it and live happily ever after? Am I just a starry fool? Simultaneously, I am intoxicated with apprehension at meeting Ghulshan and Ali again, and at coming home.

DELICIOUS DREAM

I love to come home, wherever it may be. My mother prepares for my homecoming. She makes my favourite foods: khichadi, kheema mattar, ndizi na nyama, plantain chips, Persian pilaff, aubergine bhurto, and of course yellow Uganda toast. My father stocks up on chocolate and fruits. My mother buys me new soaps and shampoos. She prepares my room, changes the sheets, vacuums the carpet, hangs my favourite clothes in the cupboard, lays out my new things on the bed. My father selects from the additions to his music collection new records for me to hear. I can never sleep the night before I am going home. I arrive haggard and tired, soliciting compassion, which I always get. Nestled into my alcove on the plane, I can already smell my mother's kitchen. Feel the warmth of her arms around me, taste the salt of her tears.

When I arrive, I see my mother behind the railings anxiously searching the faces of strangers. Then she sees mine. Her eyes light up. Satisfied, she stands where she is, waiting for me to come to her. My father helps me with my luggage, usually complaining about how heavily I travel. My father is tall and he walks very quickly. He pushes the trolley to the car and my mother and I follow behind him, arm in arm.

I sit in the front seat with my father. The new collection of ghazals on the stereo charms me. My mother, from the back seat, asks me if I want to eat first or shower. I always arrive at night, I always eat first. My mother sits with me, giving me news of family and friends, the latest gossip, panchaat. My father sits in his smoking chair and waits. After eating, I take my cup of tea and go to him. I sit very close to him. He asks me if I like the new music. Then he makes a tape of it for me. I peel and cut some fruit and eat it with him. When we have finished, my mother joins us and I place my head in her lap until my father rises to go to bed. Then I shower. When I emerge from the bathroom, I find my mother waiting in my room. Usually, she has sifted through my bags and her eyes ask a thousand silent questions as she watches my body move from the towel through nakedness into her newly-bought cotton nightie. I hate this, but stand for scrutiny. In my home, there is little sense of privacy. I sit on the bed with her. She combs my hair and plaits it, and we talk.

I tell her my stories. Who I met, who I didn't meet, always censoring for her ears. Now and again I release a restricted detail. She never reacts immediately. Not until the day after tomorrow, when I have fought with her about her unrelenting self-imprisonment in the name of duty—her martyrdom to the exacting tasks of a good Indian wife—will she mention this tiny detail. She tells me her stories, spinning decades of living, transgressing, in limbo from one world to another, but never comfortably settled. Weaving these into the thread of her tangled voice, she tells me her stories. And I listen. Usually with some kind of rage. She tells me not to be angry. Who can we blame? After all this is life and we must live it. Then we lie on the bed. Sometimes I put my head in her lap again. Sometimes she leaves. Sometimes she stays all night.

In the morning, I sit with my father while he has his tea and pound cake. Then, when he leaves for work, I run upstairs to my parents' room and crawl into bed with my mother. Soon she will wake up. I stay in their bed until noon. I dream. My dreams are always so sweet; I hate to leave them. Eventually, I do. I join my mother for lunch. We have bitings, maybe even sandwiches or soup. I hang around the kitchen until she gets fed up with me and kicks me out.

My father returns home and we have dinner. I help my mother wash up. We join my father. They watch a Bollywood film while I read a book and follow the film.

On Friday evening we go to prayers at the Jamaat Khana set up by the immigrant community, with the help of His Highness' Institutions. Then we have tea with an aunt or cousin. But first, my father will have to be convinced to take an outing.

On Saturday we go to the local Little India established by Punjabis when they came to Vancouver, or to London or Arusha or

Nairobi at the turn of the century under the auspices of the British Raj. My mother and I shop for saris and shalwar qamise. We usually argue and disagree, such different tastes. *De gustibus non disputandum est.* Then we look in the jewellery shops. We have tea, pakoras and delicious, saffron-coloured, fat-drenched, oohey-gooey hot-hot jallebis. After we have shopped for groceries, my father comes and collects us. We take some jallebis for him. In the car, much to his dismay, I refuse to shut up. I talk non-stop until we reach home. I wonder if he listens. My mother has no problem shutting me out.

On Monday, I stay home with my mother and learn how to make cucu-paka—East African-style chicken curry in coconut sauce. On Tuesday I take the bus into town, visit my father at work and wander around bookshops and boutiques. I stop at a café and come home with Ali for dinner. Next Friday I will have lunch with my cousin Yasmine, and attend evening prayers with her. Then she, her husband, their two sons and her mother—my father's sister Kulsum—will come home for tea and bitings. The men sit slightly apart and talk about Allah knows what and we women gossip at the kitchen table. My father intrudes and gives us his look of scorn. We pretend to feel shame and shut up. He leaves and we laugh. I love my cousin Yasmine.

My mother always cries at the airport. She cries when I arrive and cries when I depart. I love coming home, but it is never for long.

GOODBYE

I have always wanted at the end of a performance to beg the audience to stay. They always leave.

There is a new interactive theatre on Lady Margaret Road, London NW5. There is only one performance. The tickets cost everything you own or nothing. It lasts until eternity. The audience is not free to leave unless permission is requested during the intervals. There are four intervals every year. Emergency intervals may be called at anytime. Ten emergency intervals are allowed per participant. All children born in the theatre are required to pledge to it some token of allegiance. It is a travelling theatre. The piece opens on the sea.

Births and marriages are scene stealers. Executed in the most auspicious, painful detail. Deaths are ethereal, transforming only mood. Love, pain, joy and sorrow are shared. Hatred is tolerated, laughter celebrated, tears are consumed. Age is immaterial, responsibility paramount. Everyone wears red, and blue. Gold and silver. Black and white. Blood is sacred. Scarlet.

The most ingenious scenes take place over fax and telephone. Videos and letters are used to 'remember'. Yuck. There are two pet elephants. Samia and Alain. They mate in the desert and beautiful Nina is born. She falls in love with the clown. They spend endless hours riding under the moon. During the day he sleeps and Nina basks in the sun. Chatting with everybody, offering her infantile affections. And they advise her.

Yasmine went, unannounced, to the theatre and never returned. I was always jealous when she was allowed to go out without me. I suppose I knew she wouldn't return one day. So I went and slept in her bed to smell her. I can still smell her. Jasmine powder, amber soap, coconut oil, damasked skin and mangoes.

Goodbye darling, my mother awaits in Zanzibar. When Yasmine went to the theatre, they were performing Sir Andrew Lloyd Weber's *Evita*. The truth is she never left me.

ZANZIBAR

The stewardess wakes me with an offer of coffee. I accept and attempt to sit up in my bed. I have missed my first-class breakfast and we will be landing in twenty-five minutes. Oh my Allah. Coffee spills. I get up, squeeze through the bed beside me into the aisle where I reach up for my bag, gracefully yank out the vanity case and head for the toilet.

My hair closely resembles an upside-down mop. I have two new pimples, black clouds under my eyes, and bad breath. I run the cold water, pull out my British Airways toothbrush and British Airways toothpaste and brush my teeth. Then I rinse the sink clean. I find some face gel, lather with my fingers and wash my face. I repeat this, this time with a flannel, and I scrub. Pimples are gone but there is a small amount of blood. I pat my face dry with paper towels and apply talcum powder. This dries and congeals the blood, and now I may gently pick off the scabs. I find some moisturiser and massage it into my face. And this is the moment I look myself in the eye, gaze for a few minutes. Deciding it was a bad idea, I scramble for my make-up. I use some loose powder to hide my black clouds. Next, I sweep my hair to the back of my neck, and twist it into an upside down figure eight. I fasten with a clip and return to my face. One coat of mascara applied to upper lashes, "Bordeaux" blush swept onto cheekbones and dusted on chin, tip of nose and forehead. The stewardess knocks on the door to tell me I have to return to my seat. I quickly spray some perfume behind my ears and on my wrists, shove everything in the bag, take out a lipstick and return.

The lipstick has a metal case so I can see the reflection of my lips. I pull out the lipstick, no. 79, turn the case horizontally, and paint my lips. Opening my purse, I drop the lipstick in, take out some hand-cream, smooth my hands, replace the cream, shut the purse and shove it back under the seat in front. The man beside me, the one who didn't notice me tripping over him on the way to the toilet, now introduces himself.

"Hello. It seems we have both slept for the entire flight."

"Yes. *And* we missed breakfast."

"Jah, jah. Do you like to breakfast?"

"It is my favourite meal."

"Oh, really. Perhaps, then, we shall have the opportunity to share a breakfast in Zanzibar."

"That's unlikely." Was I flirting?

"Well you never know what can happen. My name is Derek Van Horne, from Berrleen, West German part."

The head steward announces that we have arrived.

"Welcome to Zanzibar, Mr. Van Horne."

Once we have landed I become anxious. Filing through a chaotic mass of people and duty-free shops, I hear all around me Swahili and the familiar strangeness of a colonially blended English. Newsagents, smoke-shop, currency exchange. Currency exchange. I change £200 into two hundred thousand Tanzanian shillings! The money has inflated. One-shilling coins or notes are not to be found. I remember my weekly pocket money of two shillings that I never managed to spend. Yasmine and I had a stash of socks under our beds that were filled with half-shilling coins. My expenses now are staggeringly different. This is a new country and I have lived abroad for over a decade. Two hundred thousand shillings!

"Jambo." The customs officer greets me in Swahili and, looking at my Canadian passport, remarks loudly that I was born in Nairobi. *Where are you coming from? Why you are here? For how long? How much money you have got with you?*

He lets me through after examining the return portion of my ticket.

At the luggage conveyer, I find myself, as usual, despite my impatience, horrified by the eagerness of tourists, Zanzibaris and businessmen who behave like a berserk nest of bees. I sit on a bench, allowing others to pass before me. When I spot my mammothic, bulging bag, I too run to the luggage belt and shock the crowd by hurling the bag, and half my body with it, off the conveyor and onto my trolley. So much for grace.

Wheeling my trolley through a corridor of downhill curves leading to a second set of Customs, I realise there is a reason why I don't drive cars. I smile as sweetly as possible, unleash my hair, and hope to be successful in casting myself as the westernised airhead who wants to know all about the exotica from which she hails, and announce, before they ask me, that I have nothing to declare. It works. The customs men smile, examine my behind with more interest than my bags, let me through and slip a card into my hand, should I need help getting around Zanzibar.

Eagerly I search the crowd. A mass of faces from vanilla to almond-fudge to chocolate-cocoa—and then I see him. Our eyes meet, his face swoons, eyes become deeper and he comes towards me. She is behind him, gives a nervous twitch, straightens her back, looks up and flashes a smile which lights up her face, bringing shame to the cover-girl of this month's *Elle* tucked under my armpit. She waits for me. I run into my father's embrace. He no longer towers above me but chest is still firm, arms like iron around me and the beloved earlobes, which I kiss, still long and loopy. Sunken eyes, and those silent scars I can barely face. But he is smiling, taking the trolley from me and leading me towards Ghulshan. She doesn't move. I am in side-kicking pain and fear as they approach, drumming-up my heartbeat. My vision blurs. Self-pity and longing threaten to overtake my resolve. Zahra, be strong. Guilt and desire may yet burst into thunderous rain which will shake my body with convulsions until hands beat upon my chest, pull at my hair, and I become the wild-haired witch-angel, head raised in a broth of ecstatic agony. Yeah Allah, give me strength. The need to spare them brings me the resolve to hold off the thunder, reserve it for my own climate. I approach her. She raises her arms. I descend into them. My mother embraces me. She holds me. Pushes me away, to raise her swimming pupils. I have never held her gaze. But she holds mine.

I have not seen Ghulshan and Ali in thirteen moons. Since the day after I returned from that fateful visit to Fatimah-Fui. And I have not set foot in East Africa in fifteen years. Neither have they. I have come home to Ghulshan and Ali, home to my earth, my sea, this land upon which we were born. We are to have a holiday by the sea.

The ritual has not changed. It is night-time. Ghulshan and Ali are staying at a rented cottage by the seashore. Ghulshan has cooked ndizi na nyama for me, Ali has discovered a new blend of Swahili music and is eager for me to listen to the cassettes, already in the rented car, on the drive from the airport.

In the morning, we walk along the shore. Ali walks with his hands clasped behind his back. He recounts for me his memories. He has a gold tooth in the corner of the left side of his mouth. I forget how he lost it. As he smiles now, the sun glitters on his tooth. His skin has taken the honeyed colour I have not seen in the decade of his absence from Africa.

We return to the cottage. Ali watches the local news on the television. A refreshing experience for me to hear Swahili television. I go to the market with my mother. We buy bread, some vegetables, fish and mangoes for lunch. I also buy a necklace of wooden beads carved with lotuses for myself and a red and yellow khanga for my mother to wear around the house. We spend 5,000 shillings.

An old friend of my father's comes for lunch. He has been very hospitable. Ghulshan and Ali have met his family. He has introduced them to the local community and taken them to evening prayers at the Jamaat Khana last Friday. His name is Amir Karmali.

We have a delicious meal of maachi bhat, fish in coconut curry, rice, vegetables fried with tomatoes and coriander, and sliced mangoes. I help my mother with the washing of bowls, side plates, tumblers, pots, spoons and knives while Ali and Amir Uncle converse on the veranda. When we have finished, Amir Uncle returns to his office and Ghulshan joins my father for an afternoon rest. I decide to go for a swim. After ample prayers and warnings from my mother, I set out with sunglasses, sun-oil, magazine, bottle of water and my mother's new khanga tied around my waist.

The sea is relatively empty. A German couple frolic on the shore. Some children are playing. Others are selling roasted peanuts. A woman seated by a display of bamboo and wicker baskets, weaves mats and hats. I untie my khanga and spread it on the sand. I sit with my knees bent towards my chin and stare at the sea.

Rising up I step to the edge of the waves. The water is clear and warm. My feet sink into the creamy sand, the colour of ancient linen. The day before I left London I visited an Iranian salon in Hampstead and asked a middle-aged lady with strong well-formed hands to remove the hair from my legs and arms with hot depilatory wax. The water is soft; it soothes my still-tender skin. I step forward. The sand becomes rocky and the stones pinch my feet. I decide to pour myself in. I extend my arms, stretching my back and legs until I am submerged. My body thrusts forward and I float into a vortex, my back arches and I come up with my hair in my face.

I attempt to read, and lie in sleep's seduction, embraced by the sun.

"Zahra."

Ghulshan is sitting beside me, eyes still clouded from her rest. She has come to wake me with a glass of cool guava juice in her hand. It refreshes me. I place my head in her lap. She caresses my hair, tracing with her fingers her tales upon my scalp, etching indelible routes from my head to my heart. Labyrinths of recognition. Finally, Ali joins us. We pass the rest of the afternoon under the spell of lazhuward.

After tea, we sit on the veranda and play rummy with British Airways cards. My father, master of skill, servant of luck, keeps Ghulshan and me at the losing end. It must be said however: with no small amount of difficulty. We, mother and daughter, have united our forces: red roses feeding scarlet blood.

In the evening Ali drives us into town in an old Peugeot 504 he has rented from Amir Uncle. He parks in a lot belonging to the local Jain temple. We walk along the streets into the principal meydan. My father buys warm roasted peanuts wrapped in a conical newspaper shell. He strikes up a conversation with the old man selling them. Both smile jovially, perhaps remembering nuances of their pasts.

My mother and I stop at various stalls and sift through knick-knacks. We exert ourselves. I have to exercise the most disciplined temperance to keep from adding to the museum of my flat. Hungry, we sit at a table in a joint that could be placed, in our contemporary semiology, at the periphery of traditional coffee house, urban kebab stop and bourgeois café. My mother and I are the only women. Ali is at his chivalrous blushing best. We dine on mishkaki kebabs and fried mogo cassava sticks. Drink tea, are watched by the other patrons. We also watch people and we talk about the people we watch. I have more to say than anyone else. Ghulshan eventually tunes out and Ali remains confounded. Poor man.

"When are you getting married, Beti?"

"Never, Mummy."

"Hai, hai. Don't say that. Some nice man will come and take you. But you must look after yourself. Wear nice ironed clothes, brush your hair, put on some lipstick and stop this vagabond-floating-around-in-gypsy-style-frocks business."

Nomad ness. No mad ness. If you want me, come and take me. Spirits of the earth, unhitched and roaming. Cigarettes for the hungry. Sirens to the blind. Gagged by the hand of reason, we light torches in the wind. I have a friend who eyes pregnant women with green envy. Every month she prays for her blood to come.

Angels won't you come?

My ayah's name was Betty; she had joined the East African

Christian Orthodox Church. Sometimes I went to mass with her on Sundays. She was always telling me stories of Jesu Christos. In England, there are also many stories of Him. I liked Betty's stories better. I even went to mass once in London. It was very different from the Swahili mass I attended at the church in Arusha. They are different worlds, Africa and Britain. Betty used to sing me a lullaby. It was called "Malaika."

Malaika	Angel
nakupenda Malaika	I love you, Angel
Malaika	Angel
nakupenda Malaika	how I love you, Angel
nami nifanyeje, kijana mwenzio	What could I do for you, oh my young love?
nashindwa na mali sina we	Fate has not blessed me with riches,
ningekuoa Malaika	I would have married you, Angel
nashindwa na mali sina we	If Fate had blessed me with riches
ningekuoa Malaika	I would have married you, Angel
Malaika	Angel
nakupenda Malaika	I love you, Angel
pesa zasumbua voho yangu	Riches are wrecking my soul
pesa zasumbua voho yangu	Riches are wrecking my soul
ningekuoa dada	I would have married, oh sister
ningekuoa mama	I would have married, oh mother
nashindwa na mali sina we	If Fate had blessed me with riches
ningekuoa Malaika	I would have married an Angel
Malaika	Angel
nakupenda Malaika	I love you, Angel

ZANZIBAR

Days spent by the sea with Ghulshan and Ali. Crimson. Wounds begin to bloom like roses. Jarring memories rise.

I have scrubbed and bathed. Washed, oiled and soaked. Tamed and cooled. My old cotton gypsy frock comforts, envelops and, yes, floats. It is azure in colour. The skirt ends just above my ankles. The sleeves are short. My hair is swept up and tied. Unobstructed by cosmetic vanity, free to the wind and exposed to the sun, I leave the house in a pair of malapas with my new wicker basket. It was a bargain at 500 shillings, and the woman has become my friend. I wander the streets, the markets and the squares. Alone. I stop for several drinks, hot and cold. By midday, I can no longer resist the smell of barbecued fish. The harbour drowns in its own life. Polluted. Frantic. Frenzied vertigo. The fish is delicious. Crisp, charred, cumined and lemony skin gives way to lush flesh. A balm for the tongue.

I must ask myself why I have come to Zanzibar. Well, you and I, we both know why I have come. It is the search for home. I have come in search of a home where history allows me to belong, where I can claim a heritage. I suppose there are other places I could do this, but this one resonates. I have decided upon Zanzibar. I want that cradle of warmth; I want to be led through Ghulshan's womb, into Zahra's.

Zahra. Shakespeare said a rose by any other name smells just as sweet. Well, I think Shakespeare lied. He never smelled Ghulshan's perfume. Poor man. But I know and must convince the world. Mother-daughter me. That burden of carrying a name, I have decided to swallow whole, digesting the nine yards. Do I have the stamina? That strength of spirit to endure my own history?

ALI

My father has a beautiful voice. When he sings, his eyes swell up with tears, like my mother's. His voice is soothing, like honey. Clear and dense, thick, round and melodious. He sings very softly. I hear it like the baby who upon glimpsing water remembers the comforting fluids of her mother's womb. My proud father has so beautiful a voice that he becomes humble when he sings. He sings only in devotion: to Ghulshan, to Zahra, to Allah and Ali.

Every time my father sneezes, he recites half the Qur'an, the ninety-nine names of Allah his prophet, and all forty-nine Imams from Ali onwards. When he sneezes in public it becomes an embarrassing liturgy. When one sneeze follows another I cannot control my laughter. And then I begin to hiccup. Between the ages of two and eleven, I thought my father was King of the World. Seven breaths away from Allah, and only one breath short of the Imam.

Ghulshan and Ali live alone now. After seven years they left London for Canada searching for a less morose climate. They lived by the sea. They were aliens, misfits even in the immigrant community that had gathered in Vancouver. Like farmers living in the city, Ghulshan and Ali are astonished by their own community. The emptiness of suburban life. The crass lack of elegance, of nuance, confidence, wholeness, of meaning. Pimps and whores of consumerism. All this, in a beautiful city, flanked by the ocean, cradled by mountains, infused with greenness.

Eventually, Ghulshan and Ali left Vancouver. Orphans of the sea. Spirits of the earth, unhitched and now roaming. They will find another valley—cleaner, smaller, more cordial, less urban—nesting at the foothills of another mountain. They will live as they have lived for decades.

Their son Sultan is in New York, married and working. Their daughter stayed in England, at university and then at work. She is employed by international organizations that aim to better the world through education.

Ghulshan and Ali live alone. Ghulshan cooks feasts. Ali doesn't eat all day so that he can come home and enjoy them. Sometimes Ghulshan takes a bus to the nearby shopping mall. Still in high-heeled English pumps, still vain and, yes, still beautiful. But the heels no longer totter. She wanders through the mall. Buys biscuits and underwear on sale at Marks & Spencer, the new Estée Lauder anti-ageing cream, plastic gadgets for her kitchen and a new nightie for her daughter Zahra. She shouldn't spend so much money. Oh well, she will keep the receipts and maybe return an item. Slowly she walks to the food court. She makes two rounds of the kiosks. Finally, she decides upon a cinnamon bun and coffee. Ghulshan sits and eats her bun and sips her coffee. Watching the people around her, she realises they are no different from her. Thus comforted, seeing that she is really just another drop in the sea, she takes the bus home to finish cooking and clean up before Ali arrives back home.

On Sundays their daughter telephones from across the ocean. She misses the omelets and parathas. Why must she stay so far away? Always leaving them. Running away. Tragedy—she is too weak. Hungry—what are you hungry for? Don't you see dear? What you crave is right here. Inside this cocoon. Your scarlet blood, ours. Stick to your own kind. The world will dilute you.

Having run once from a burning farm, I keep running.

CAIRO

India, Africa and Arabia. Three worlds unite, inhale the air and depart. Leaving to us one unforgettable breath that we spend the rest of our lives trying to catch. Miming the three-way dance. Ménage à trois. It is unnatural, darling. The forced act of a humanity dissatisfied with its fate. Unnatural, like drinking blood.

I spend a year in Egypt ostensibly studying at the American University in Cairo, but really coming into my own. Cairo embraces me with the comforting arms of a mother embracing a pitiful orphan. I fit in. I have an Indian face but jet-black wildly-curly hair that is characteristic of Egyptian women and which they alone know how to tame. My skin is the same colour as theirs. For the first time in my life, I look like everyone else, not a spoilt, privileged, brown-skinned aberration in the sea of black Africa, nor a dirty, spicy immigrant in the land of raw flesh and linear bodies.

Home? Is this home? But how could it be? The Egyptians assume I am one of them, a member of the westernised élite perhaps, that is until I open my mouth and betray three years of classical Arabic instruction without a word of contemporary usage. My first day at the market, the vegetable women taunt me, laughing as I speak. I laugh back, securing good humour and bargain vegetable prices. They cannot bear to cheat me, these women friends. I will learn to buy Cadbury milk chocolates from Sunny's supermarket in Zamalek and distribute them among their scattered, dusty children who squeal in delight at the taste of that creamy cocoa. I become known to them as anissa al shocolat, the chocolate woman. As soon as I emerge from around the corner of the Twenty-sixth of July bridge, with my pink plastic vegetable basket, they spot me and begin to dance in delight, shouting my new title to the world until the Sunny's shopping bag appears and the chocolate has been distributed. I kneel with them at the edge of the pavement. I always remember to buy one for myself, and we unwrap and delicately consume our treats. The children's mothers produce a glass of dark rich tea from somewhere amidst the baskets of belongings covered with bright cotton throws. I share with them my chocolate, and they stuff my basket full of delicious tomatoes, eggplants, zucchini, onions, garlic, cilantro, long green chillies, crisp white cauliflowers, fresh leaves and a bit of whatever else happens to be in season. Soon, I am expected, and they refuse to take my money. So I try to bring along something useful that they will enjoy, something slightly luxurious that they will never buy themselves. Sometimes I bring cheese or delicious pastries from Simmond's. The women wrap the pastries in clean cotton strips to keep them warm. They take them home to share. When I have a taxi, I take a sack of rice or flour. If I have forgotten the chocolate or haven't found the time to buy some compensation for payment, then I don't dare show my face. Instead I buy expensive vegetables from the greengrocer.

I become acquainted with the sizeable expatriate community in Cairo that mingles intimately with the élite. Some of them attend the university with me. We share taxis and class notes. I often skip classes that are for the most part rather rigid and formal, preferring instead to visit my favourite haunts. I wander through the dusty, old, cobbled alleys of Fustat, discovering each day a new twist, a forgotten gate—seeing anew the glory of the majestic minaret basked in the white light of the desert. I discover for myself the shrines and mausolea of Sayyida Zeinab which pay homage to the little-known female saints of Islam. I wander, sometimes encumbered and protected simultaneously by the veil, through the Old City. I sit in the shade of the courtyards, walk between those famous gates, climb the minarets and gaze with wonder at the domes. While munching on roasted nuts bought from the street vendor, I buy trinkets. As I wander alone through the Khan el-Khalili, stopping to look at everything that catches my fancy, sometimes returning to buy, I feel the titillating thrill of a consumerism that is rooted in colonial exoticism.

I stroll along the corniche of the Nile and watch the brazen sun sink into its waters.

What I do not know is that this is the homeland of my grandmother
Zahra, my beloved namesake.

I meet women in Cairo who teach me who I am. How to be strong
without relinquishing my femininity. How to avoid a feminism that
recasts women into male idioms. How to be modern, living in the
western world without losing my history. How to love a man without
succumbing to him.

I find my place among a throng of expatriates, rootless or refugees
just like me. I begin to learn that I am not so much an alien, just a
little off centre, on the peripheries, as it were. A new kind of belonging, but unstable still.

Cairo, city of chaos. City of dirt and dust. City of fifteen million
people and an unrelenting spirit. I learn Egyptian dialect at school
and in the bazaars. I spend days in Sayyida Zeinab. It is attached to
the ancient site of Fustat. Most of my time here is spent recording
the twisting arabesque flavours of the mausolea. I lug a bulging black
bag stuffed with tools: a Canon 35mm camera, packets of Kodak
film, rolls of flimsy tracing paper and a box of charcoal sticks. Sayyida
Zeinab is a sanctuary of the holy to comfort the paupers. Children
clothed in rags of mud and dust swim in the sewers. Hollering a
flurry of exclamations, they race past each other and run in wild
whirls around me and my foreign equipment. Escorted by this dele-
gation, I navigate through narrow colonnades and under the shadows
of arches. The music is of donkeys' hoofs, the bells of Italian bicycles,
the hooting of Datsun trucks and screeching black and white Peugeots.
It is accompanied by the drumming of the children's naked feet.

They think me mad, the people of Sayyida Zeinab. Me with my
pale threadbare jeans and dirty Adidas sneakers. I wear my brother's
abandoned large cotton shirts and wrap flowery scarves around my
voluminous hair in an effort to hide my provocative charms. My
mission consists of fastening flying sheets of tracing paper onto the
ancient walls. And all for what? To delicately trace the designs of
their ornamentation! Copy the arabesques: squiggly lines, cur-
vaceous flora and opulent vines. Calligraphy etched along the borders
and an epitaph hidden here and there. Surely there must be better
things to do at the university! However, they get used to my presence,

these people. Men, women and children who shuttle about their daily lives battling the impossible odds for survival in an ancient city, congested with human life and choking on its own history. They bring me a glass of tea now and again. Around lunchtime, they share their kusherie with me. When I am away for a couple of days, they ask after me.

I have found an accomplice. She is one of the hundreds of women who float through this magnificent city. A mistress of every twisting niche; custodian of a millennium of secrets. One of the women who scurry in black flowing robes tied over long frilly cotton frocks. A matching headscarf that escapes the high knot tied at the back and falls over two large gold hoops and into the eyes circled with legendary kohl. These women govern the streets of Cairo. Her name is Sahar. Every morning she meets me at my taxi, smiling. We drag my things out of the car and she invites me to share a cup of sweet tea. We sit at the steps leading to the door of the one-room flat she shares with her husband, three children and mother-in-law. I chat with her about my life, which in her eyes appears totally whimsical. She tells me about her daily travails, most of which involve ferocious battles with her mother-in-law for power over the household.

One day, Sahar gives me a talisman: a small rectangular package the size of my thumb. Scraps of paper are wrapped in plastic cellophane and secured with red thread. What? I ask. Something to protect you, she says. The evil eye has winked in my direction and I must undo its curse. I don't want to believe her, of course. I take the amulet, secure the red thread around my neck and look away. I continue with my work, scrubbing the walls of the mausoleum of Sayyida Sakineh, stripping her naked of history. I am washing the walls of dust and grime so that they will gleam iridescent in photographs. Sahar takes a cotton rag from my plastic bag, drops it into my bucket of water and lemon juice, rings out the excess moisture and joins me.

Throughout the morning I cannot concentrate. I stand for long minutes clutching a soaking rag, wetting my clothes, motionless. At lunchtime, I give Sahar some money and she brings us boiled eggs and tamia and ful sandwiches from the canteen around the corner. As we eat, perched on the steps leading to the minaret of Qait Bey, I ask her about this curse.

"It is from a woman who is your relative. She does not share your blood but has married in."

"Why would anyone want to curse me?"

"Jealousy. Women will always be jealous of you. You must protect yourself. Do not underestimate jealousy, it is the most evil of the deadly sins."

"Who is it?"

"I cannot tell you."

"You cannot or you will not."

"Whichever you prefer."

"Oh for God's sake!"

"If you want to undo this curse, you must seek the protection of God. He is the only one who can help you. You must believe. You must have absolute faith. Then you will be strong. Then God will protect you like a veil. Seek the protection of He who is Majestic. But you must believe. Without faith there is nothing."

She instructs me to light a red candle in a bowl of water and let it burn to the core. Then I should wash my feet in the water of the bowl. This I should do for seven nights.

"But you must, must pray!"

Communicate with the Divine. In whatever form I choose.

"It does not matter, meditation, recitation of His name on the sibah, zikr or salat. But you must pray. Zahra, aziza, you must pray."

She will also pray for me.

Unsettled by Sahar, I return to London. I accept a job in the education department of the Aga Khan Foundation. I still think I can change the world by educating it. Before beginning my job, I visit Ghulshan and Ali in Canada.

FATIMA-FUI

During this time in Canada I go to visit my father's second-eldest sister who raised Ali after Zahra died, and told him stories of Zanzibar where family secrets lie, waiting to be exposed. She migrated to Canada, following her eldest son who works as a systems engineer.

Fatima-Fui calls me Ma-Beti: mother-daughter, after my name. She has made my favourite fried cassava mogo sticks and imbli, tamarind chutney. Horrified at the unshiny dryness of my hair, she sits me on the floor with a plate of mogo, a bowl of imbli and a cup of tea. Having disappeared into her cluttered bedroom that smells of East African Vicks Vaporub and halud, she returns with a tin of almond oil, a black wooden pick comb, and a blue and green towel spotted with white and yellow daisies. She sits on the sofa, spreads the towel over her lap and yanks my head towards her. Unfurling my ratted ponytail she asks if the mogo is fine. I emit a "very fine" between mouthfuls, and, satisfied, she continues with her business of combing and oiling until my hair no longer bears any resemblance to jeethra. In this fashion, pulling together the scattered bits of her memory, she unravels for me her fateful tale.

"You know, Ma-Beti, Maji's father has very beautiful house in Zanzibar. Very beautiful, very big. Many trees and courtyard. Even view of sea. When they leave Zanzibar, just before British, they leave with new hope, even when imports business is so good. When they leave Zanzibar, Maji's father, I don't even know his name, they say it is Sultan something, he leaves house in her name. He feels bad for his daughter. Allah knows, maybe someday she will need something. You know, they give her nothing for marriage. So, before going back, he leaves beautiful house in her name. But your Maji, you know, she is very proud. She never keeps touch with family. No. And she passes from this world, they do not know. Anyway. Your Bapaji, Vilayat Khan, is also very proud. Does not accept gift when authorities notify him. No, he will not take property of stolen daughter. Everybody so proud.

But then. Then, you know what happened? Maji's elder sister, before dying, she leaves house for your father! In his name, Ali Vilayat Khan! How did she know? Allah, so mysterious your ways. So now, where is this house? Must still be there. Don't you think, Beti? Maji's house must still be there, no? Is in name of your father, not in Maji's name or Bapaji's name. Maybe government took when they take everything else. No, no, must still be there, no? It is last bit of Maji. It is everything we have left, no? I am right no? Anyway, Allah knows."

ZANZIBAR

The smell of barbecued fish draws me in again. I amble towards the market. It is bustling with the spirit of entrepreneurship. Peddlers have set up their goods in every available space and busily hawk their wares. Every imaginable item from food to ceramics, to clothing and hardware, from books to spare car parts, is for sale here in this suqoni.

I follow my nose towards the pungent smell of fish roasting in cumin. Near the edge of the market, the end which falls in the midst of large rocks and industrial debris into the sea, sits a row of fishermen selling fresh, live and cooked seafood. The fish is cooked over a rectangular cast iron pot standing on two legs that holds hot coals. It rests on a mesh bed of criss-crossed twigs. The skins are charred black. I ask for two. The fisherman lifts them off the grill with his grubby fingers. He places them on a sheet of newspaper and asks me if I would like salt, lemon and chilli. I say yes to all three. He sprinkles them generously, wraps them in a second sheet of paper and hands them over. The weight of the fish intensifies the heat, so that through the thin sheets of paper my hands are scorched.

FATIMA-FUI'S TALE

"You know, none of us can find Maji's house. No. We are only old-fashioned, married with first husbands and now sickness to keep us at home. Your father, maybe he could find but he lost himself. Now who will go to Zanzibar just to find out about house? And certificate with Ali's name must be required. Maybe house is not even there, finished like everything else. Such a beautiful house. Who would want to plunder? Oh Ali, what shame! What you think, Ma-Beti, you are educated girl?"

My Fui-ma only speaks English when the matter is important to her, and she speaks only in the present tense. I was choking on my bitter-sweet imbli, desperately trying to remember if my birth certificate listed my father's full name.

A house in Zanzibar by the sea. Reluctantly, I savour the aroma of conspiracy.

ZANZIBAR

I wrap the fish into the skirt of my frock and, with legs shamelessly exposed, carry it to the other side of the harbour. Settling onto an empty bench on the boulevard, I spread out my lunch. The crunchy skins lift off exposing a flesh which is snow-white and succulent. Abandoning etiquette, I indulge with gusto. Fishy, lemony, cumined juice drips all over my fingers, from the corners of my mouth onto my chin and across my bodice. The sun shines bright and strong through the boulevard. It heats the mass of my black hair forming droplets of sweat at the back of my neck. Sunlight induces the sea, to sparkle like a royal jewel. Licking my lips and fingers, I raise my head into the blinding embrace of the sun. The world ceases for a moment. It is replaced by a blaze of white light. I have forgotten my sunglasses and must cover my brow with my hand before my vision clears.

A Property Law sign hangs inside the third-floor window of what looks like an old residence converted into offices. Instinctively, I rise from the bench and cross the street to the building. A heavy carved door blocks my path. I push it open with some effort and find myself climbing up three flights of wide, red-carpeted, chipped wooden steps, to arrive on the third floor.

The door is ajar.

"Can I help you?" An immaculately groomed, pretty, not too thin, caramel-skinned woman sits at a desk in the reception area. She speaks the Queen's English.

"I would like to see the solicitor."

"Do you have an appointment with Mr. Zamakhshari? Are you a client?"

"Not yet."

"Excuse me, Miss. This is not a drop-in clinic."

A door opens behind me. I feel the air lift, and turn around.

"Hello."

A man stands in the doorway. He is holding a sheaf of papers. The sun is looming behind him. Hanging, as if waiting. A chaperone. His skin is tanned. Not too dark. Honeyed like Ali's. His frame is tall, not too broad. Thighs are just thicker than mine. Champagne linen trousers hang on a flat waist. They sit on polished cinnamon shoes with short leather laces tied in a crisp bow. His meticulous cotton shirt, stiff as virginity; unbuttoned at the neck. The face is gazing at my azure frock and unpainted toenails, sitting flat on malapas and peering from a leather noose. His full lips curve into a crescent, mint-coloured eyes are sparkling. Mountainous cheekbones form a valley and fall into a cleft. Tea-stained cloudy hair is ruffled. Hands are wide, long fingered and sculpted. Wedding ring is shining like the sun.

He stretches his arm, offering me the unringed hand. I meet it with my own sticky, sour equivalent.

"Oh, goodness. I'm sorry, I've just eaten some fish from the harbour."

"Delicious. No?"

"Yes."

Drowning in cliché. Since when do I exclaim "oh goodness" instead of "shit"?

"Have you been helped, uh—"

"Zahra."

"Mrs. Zahra?"

"Miss Zahra. No."

Under the evil eye of Miss This-Is-Not-A-Drop-In, I follow him into his office where he gives me a tissue for my hands. *Nos morituri te salutamus.*

The view of the harbour is symphonic. Standing before the window, I can hear the adhan. It is very loud, piercing and full-bodied. The voice enters my veins and flows through my blood, slowing its tempo until it is calm. Then it begins slowly to rise, echoing those calligraphic curves, lingering here and there, repeating. Breaking the rhythm only to mend it again. Its repercussions immeasurable. Encircling my blood until it mounts, overtaking me, my heart beating in accompaniment at the edge of combustion. The adhan. The muezzin's voice pierces the world to embrace it. It infuses every leaf, seed, tree, fruit. Every crawling, swimming or soaring creature. Land, sea and sky. It enters the veins. Uniting until everything, all life beats the same rhythm. The adhan rounds up these creatures embracing them until they choke. All become One.

Watching the harbour from the solicitor's window, I tell him as briefly, cleverly and honestly as I can about my grandmother's house. He is either listening intently or dreaming. I cannot be sure.

"What can I do for you, Miss Zahra?"

"I want to find the house. And if possible, claim it in my father's name."

"That house may no longer exist. If it does, how are we to know which one it is? There are hundreds of houses in Zanzibar with sycamore trees and courtyards, Miss Zahra. You have no address, a vague family name. Nothing. Just a rough description. The Sultan's properties were huge and widespread. Dozens of houses were let to Europeans before, during and after the fall of the Oligarchy in 1960. Is your father still alive? Even if we do find the house, claiming it is almost out of the question. You would have to buy it. I suggest you take a holiday and enjoy yourself. Zanzibar can be a lovely place for a young woman with no attachments."

But I am longing precisely for an attachment. Am tired of being free. Freedom is not free at all. It has a hefty price. I want an anchor to the world. Upon leaving his office, I am sure that he was listening, not dreaming. Angels, where are you?

That evening, we are invited to dine with Amir Uncle and his family at their home. I have painted my eyes, lips, cheekbones, finger- and toenails. Sculpted my hair into a perfect sphere at the nape of my neck. Wrapped my body into a silky sari. Slipped my feet into delicate silver sandals with a latticed noose around my big toe.

If you want me. Come and get me. Take me, away.

We are joined at Amir Uncle's house by a Ugandan Gujarati couple and their delicate bachelor son who is studying business in Paris and is roughly my age. Studying business! Amir Uncle's daughters, it is pronounced, are away at college in America. As if America were a city! To one and all Amir Uncle announces that we are to have the charming company of Zanzibar's most prominent

lawyer: an Arab who has married a fair-skinned local Gujarati girl—
after all, we are all Muslims. They are Mr. and Mrs. Hussein
Zamakhshari.

Who would not recognise such a name? I have been mesmerised
by his memory all afternoon and well into this early evening. But
alas prince and princess charming have arrived and Mrs. "Auntie"
Karmali, a decorous woman who my mother vaguely remembers
from her hostel days, is leading them towards the enclosed courtyard
where we happen to be seated. So my heart cannot leap, as I have to
work fast to call upon Allah to bless the Prophet and all his descendants before I immerse myself in conversation with the business-
studying bachelor. To no avail. Mrs Karmali, as a result of the sin
she is about to commit, will never be addressed by my heart as
"Auntie". She shall remain forever the wife of Amir Uncle Babu
Karmali. She has decided to parade the couple around the room,
introducing them to each and everyone, individually.

"This is Zahra, daughter of Ghulshan and Ali."

I stretch a polite hand into her jewel-clad paw and smile
graciously, avoiding his gaze. He has coated his virginal shirt with a
champagne jacket to match his trousers and render him suited.

Cursing whoever entered this 007 into my numerological chart,
I do not notice the dinner. Mrs. Karmali politely asks Ghulshan if I
am watching my figure. She has the same problem with her presumably anorexic daughters. A gamble in presumption, I agree. But likely
not to be far from the truth. Mr. Hussein Zamakshari decides to
look at what I should not be watching. Against my most prudent
impulse, I shift legs, contort buttocks, stretch midriff and thrust bust
to ensure that he will be pleased by what he sees. Ali seems to take
notice of Mr. Zamakhshari's lack of shame but luckily not mine.

When Fate beckons, I always follow.

The lawyer's wife is adorned with a black chiffon slip dress that
ends at mid-thigh and allows her breasts to sprawl. Her hair is short,
cropped and coiffed. Layers of gold burden her neck, ears, wrists
and fingers. Her bare legs teeter over a spike-heeled, open-toed,
crocodile-skin contraption, but not the way Ghulshan's once did.
She is flirting expertly with the business-studying bachelor. He is
discussing investment tactics for the Zanzibari economy, while she

presents a prelude of her sexual skills. Whetting the young boy's appetite for a main course he will never taste. Or will he?

I have wandered into the garden. I feel secluded, like an Olympian runner who in midrace abracadabras out of sight, refreshes her steroid input and returns anew with just enough testosterone to see her finish the race and then collapse.

"Miss Zahra, I hear you are involved with His Highness's institutions in London."

Pause. I turn around. He has followed me. Minty eyes are twinkling, this time in moonlight. "Rest assured. I am a very discreet man. Please ring my office tomorrow." He slips his card into my hands and vanishes.

The moon shines like a smile in the sky. One hour and forty-seven minutes later, I am lying in bed, having peeled off my sari and painted face. Ghulshan enters my room and sits at the edge of the bed with two glasses of water. We talk about Hussein's wife. My mother thinks she is a bit loud—read improper—but fair, and with a fine figure. These are the kinds of girls men like. Very glamorous. If I put in half as much effort, I would find a husband in no time. He is a good catch. Charming and handsome, and with personality. But be careful. Ghulshan has heard rumours. "Don't meet him again, dear. Mrs. Karmali was telling me such stories. It seems they live in separate houses. And married not even a year! I tell you, young people nowadays. Did you see her dress, as if she forgot the rest of it at home!"

I have the instinct to glamorously attack the lawyer's wife with my scarlet nails. But I will not, not now. I could wake up and pray. I would have to wash myself of this evening first. So much energy, tangled into a knot of apprehension, lies dormant inside me. I explore its dimension. It overwhelms me. Makes me numb. I choose, then, to stay here in bed and sing my devotions.

I rise to the sun's early-morning embrace and a rippling breeze from the sea. My sleep has been consumed. I lie in a lull, my mind swims lazily. I feel suffused with desire. Reminiscent, caressing lightness and the sound of resplendent laughter cacophoning in my memory. Sweet, timid happiness and wondrous fate. Ten thousand names but none as resonant as yours. Purple passion turns crimson.

The blushing sun hides, sending the moon, mistress mine.
Often I remember Africa. The majestic Kilimanjaro, proud, erect and piercing, but also enigmatic and mystical. Calm under the burning sun. Surreptitious branches of the baobab tree, satanic in its implications. Birds that wail. Sad, brooding elephants. Ten thousand miles of jungle, veiled in mystery, chastised by its keeper. Golden glorious lions. Only to be raped by empire, impregnated by history, sending to the world its weeping bastards. Orphans of the sea. Beauty raised her head, blessed my soul, breathed fire into my veins, only to be silenced. Despoil and disease. Rage. The sun still burns, empty passion. The unkissed moon—no longer virgin—moaning for pleasure, but scathed. A dance of the lips, melody to the fingers, symphony without orchestra. Imagine the moon at orgasm. Can you hear her cries? Still barren, this earth of mine. I want to grow cherry blossoms that will whisper mischievously to your magnolias. So much more beautiful they must be. I prefer cherries all the same. I want you and the moon together in one equation. Paradise now and again. Silence. Screaming in your face. Take mine. Offered delectably, in small doses. Around and around, until roses fall, thorns bleed and the sun, it melts. Leaving to us the cool moon. Still moaning for pleasure. La Luna, mother of the devil, sister of Fate. I implore you, smile. Cradle me in your crescent. Silver light, golden love, shimmering tresses of the earth. Can you look? Do you dare?

Unrested, I stumble into the kitchen and join my father for breakfast. Ghulshan is still sleeping. We both sip blessed water, aab-e-saafa. He cuts a papaya in half, scrapes out its seeds and places one half on my plate and the other on his. He brews coffee with a pinch of salt for flavour and finally wins a standing ovation from me for his piping hot vitumbuas, that come straight from the pan of the lady in the market place who fries them every morning. But I cannot eat the delicious meal, appetite has flown away. "Papa, do you remember where Dadi-ma's house was? I would like to see it."

Ali is surprised in an expecting manner. "It has probably been destroyed. I don't quite remember, somewhere to the southwest of the city."

"Maybe we can look for it. One day."

"Yes. Maybe, but perhaps it is better to let sleeping dogs lie."

45

I decide to go to the shore, for the fish and for him. With the exception of the shell sari and a scarlet shalwar qamise—in case we go to Jamaat Khana—I have not brought proper clothes to Zanzibar. I arrive on the third floor in a pair of crisp, white, newly ironed, fitted trousers and one of my father's equally crisp white cotton shirts. Feet clad in same silver sandals, eyes and lips painted, hair unleashed and brushed. Very glamorous, hardly, but half as much effort has dutifully been put in. Miss This-Is-Not-A-Drop-In does not recognise me until I tell her my name. Her nose crinkles, eyes open wider and rotate up and down. I try to flash Ghulshan's smile.

"Is he expecting you?"

"No."

"Just one moment please." Eyes drop, eyebrows rise, mouth frowns. She picks up the telephone.

"Miss Zahra is here to see you." Pause. "I shall send her in?" Then looking at me with a bewitching smile: "You may go into his office."

Hussein is already standing.

"I asked you to telephone me."

"I lost your card."

"I am just about to have lunch. You will have to join me."

We walk across the street past the fateful spot along the square by the shore where I sat yesterday auspiciously licking my lips and fingers only to gaze at the third floor. Avoiding the musical harbour, he leads me to a quiet enclosed veranda. Picturesque, one would say. The tables here are escorted by wooden chairs and dressed in white. Elegant stems with locks of blushing virgin petals languidly recline in the shade of blue glass vases. Porcelain dishes and sparkling cutlery attend in patient arrangement. But the fish is off the same grill as at the polluted, frenzied shore. I like to eat rice and potatoes. I hate deciding between the two. Agony. I imagine the other to have tasted better. I am always in anguish of being deprived that real pleasure. Which do you prefer? Ultram bibis? Aquam an undam?

"It's a new menu," he says.

"Oh yes," she replies.

"Perhaps a glass of water then?"

"Make that two," he adds, mischievously looking up at the waiter, knowing full well that he shall receive his usual cold German lager. He eats sexually, avoiding the cutlery and indulging his fingers, bestowing upon the fish the honour of being consumed by him. He arranges the skeletals in vertical order before rinsing off the lemony juices into a bowl of hot water and wiping his fingers with a steaming towel. Thus sterilised, he lights a cigarette, leans back into his chair, cocks his head forward and smiles at me. Missing the irony, I destroy it by asking about the house. He expels smoke.

"I have found your beloved house, darling." Smiling crescent. I am on the verge of volcanic eruption. Somewhere in the back of my mind I know that this quest for my grandmother's house is more about me than about my father's love for the mother he never really knew. Nor does its association with me end at my curiosity to learn more about the woman I have been named for, about whom so much still remains a mystery. I know that it is about my desire, the need for a space called home. A place totally mine, allowing me to belong as it resonates my dispersed beings—collecting those scattered bits of my spirit for which I am forever yearning. Perhaps somewhat stupidly, I have imagined that if I live in this house upon the flanks of Africa, nourished by an ocean that I make more comfortable by calling a sea, and gazing upwards, glazed by the sun, towards that still enigmatic continent India and her mother Asia, perhaps then I will become whole: unite my world like the voice of the muezzin who calls the adhan. For the moment however, I must ignore all this and focus on the task at hand. Taking these footsteps of mine, one at a time. "The house is not in your father's name, nor in the name of his mother."

Everything, all desires which I chose to ignore, are resurrecting from somewhere in the centre of my being, crawling up my insides through my stomach towards my ribcage, upon which they hinge, hanging, circling my breasts and threatening to choke me.

Hussein has a friend who works in a building that houses the government's archival papers. He is an askari. The security guard slipped into the government building last night and quite easily located the chronological records of property because they sit in dusty piles on bent shelves inscribed with year, name and description of purchase, rental or sale. So, for example, "1915, Ahmed Sultan,

Imperial Property, behind the House of Wonders". He found a house in Stone Town, at a corner, the northwest wing facing the sea, entered under the name of an Arab family that arrived in Zanzibar on March 21, 1915. In 1982 the house was transferred to a certain Mrs. Khan. She rents it to the government which uses it as a warehouse. My mother is Mrs. Khan. So is Supria, my brother's wife. But neither is the said Mrs. Khan.

Here I am having yearned for a Resolution. Ending and beginning. All new, without the chaos of the past.

"At what date do the records begin?" I ask Mr. Zamakhshari.

"Hmm?"

"At what date do the records begin?"

"1695 AD. Do you know who this woman Zeenat Khan is?"

The brazen-haired witch rises. There is no masquerade, no pretty innocent princess, no pious holy virgin, no blushing bride or blooming mother. No angelic redemption. This time it is in-your-face. Exasperated, livid rage where the world becomes a brew of slimy, creeping dust-licking lizards who want now to be God with holy-virgin-mother-wife as accessory and tool. Teeth and tongue are stained scarlet from the aperitifs. Get a new tie darling, the season's colour is yellow.

"Can you take me to the house?"

I will commit suicide if he refuses or if the moisture that fills the sockets of my eyes threatens to drip. Allah help me. Unpainted cheekbones and nose-tip are red. Moisture is drip-dripping, voice has become strangled, hands are quivering, nose mucous is flowing like a river and potential adulterer-solicitor is driving me to Dadima's house. But I am crying for my mother. For Ghulshan. And I have nothing with which to kill myself. Does he know? He must know. My father? Why? How am I going to forgive him?

He telephones Miss This-Is-Not-A-Drop-In and takes me to his car. I, a crescent, am cradled in the front seat, restricted by seatbelt, shivering under the burning sun. We drive towards the harbour, away from the city centre, on narrow labyrinthine streets and past crumbling buildings that pay tribute to the mishmash of Portuguese, Arab, Indian and British civilisations that have assembled the history of what is present-day Zanzibar. The car is causing a commotion, obstructing pedestrians, raising a cloud of dust. He parks near the Old Fort. The sea is alive. We can hear it crashing along the shore. He comes around and opens the door. Leads me out of the car and we proceed on foot. Children in tattered rags scurry along with their palms held out. I fish into my pockets for some change and he laughs at me, making me feel like some European colonial lady taking pity upon the natives. I hand them some shillings all the same and they are ecstatic, beaming with those beatific smiles that belong exclusively to children. I am no European lady but I decide against reprimanding him. We walk past the ruins of the Old House of Wonders and behind the Royal Baths. I stop still as I hear the haunting adhan. Oh God, bless us. We continue walking, away from the harbour now but still following the shoreline. We pass the People's Palace and he turns right down a narrow street, then left and then right again. Gargoyles are swimming in my stomach, which is perched perilously at the nape of my neck. Lips are as dry as the Sahara. Hai-Hai! What he must think!? I really can't afford to care. Nehi, nehi bhaiji. Adultery is sin. Zinnah. Fahishah. Immoral conduct. Disturbing the peace. Thou shall not rage. Savage beasts. Do not indulge.

Calmness overcomes me. I become numb, like a fever that burns so high it ends in shivers. A blade so sharp, it becomes painless, overcoming anxiety by surrendering. Fate has her own dance. We are merely alibis. Hussein turns left for the last time. Slowly we approach Zahra's house. I can see it, recognising it easily from the street as the only empty-looking grand house in a cluster of neglected buildings that are occupied by the poor. There is a gate at the road. Hussein stops in his tracks and looks at me as if he has never seen me before. An askari approaches us. He asks if we are lost. The lawyer tells him we want to look at the house. He asks if we have a permit. No. The askari begins to explain that this is a government building. Hussein gives him a 5,000-shilling note. The askari slips it into his pocket and continues his explanation, commenting on the expenses of raising a family in this day and age. The scorching sun is glistening on his skin. Hussein takes out another note, gives it to him. The askari asks him to wait. Silence.

The gate is lined with sycamore and jacaranda tress. Their branches spin a web to filter the sun. The walls of the house are limestone, patterned by a shadow of eroded lattices. The askari returns. Continuing to ignore me, he addresses the lawyer, calling him "Sir". We may walk around the outside of the house, through the garden and courtyard, but we may not enter. Another askari comes and stands behind him. Hussein alleges that the house is for sale and that if we are to buy it, we must have a look at the inside. The two askaris are surprised. "But we have not been informed that the house is for sale." Hussein insists. They claim not to have keys for the house. I tell him that I will be happy simply to walk around the courtyard and jungle-like garden.

We walk through the gate framed by untended bushes of gooseberry perfumed with tall cascading clove and jasmine trees. I find my own pace, and he leaves me. The house is shaped square with the gate forming the fourth wall. There is a courtyard and garden. The round basin of a dry fountain sits in the centre of the garden flanked by a bench and an old-fashioned swing. The bench, cracked in half, faces the gate. The swing, with its rotten wooden seat, faces the entrance to the house. Its solid iron handles hanging from a concrete post shaped like a horseshoe. A swelling mango tree droops over the swing, embracing in its branches a younger tree in its first bloom of lycheees. Each of the three walls has an entrance moulded of iwan arches and ornamented with heavy carved wooden doors that swing open from the centre. Opposite the bench three wide steps lead to a veranda strewn with wicker chairs, an old wooden side table and the askari's cot. Behind the veranda looms the largest archway that rises to a cupola and finally a dome. The walls are tall. Roman arches form windows: two beside each archway. The windows are screened with geometric wooden grillwork, mashrebeyya. These are covered with milky spider webs.

I feel the queasiness of a deep conch somewhere inside of my stomach. Resonance. I want to sit on the swing, but I walk towards the bench instead. My eyes become misty, clouding my vision. The courtyard is plated with tiles patterned in green and blue arabesques. The foot of the basin lies at the heart of an eight-pointed star, a muqarnas. Blooming rose branches crawl around the fountain. I can smell jasmine in the air.

The wooden swing is cushioned in scarlet. An adolescent girl lies on the swing, turning her face to the breeze. I can feel her husband's presence but he is nowhere to be seen. Her face is my face, only fairer and younger, my expression, my confusion. I try to meet her, hold her gaze. She turns her face and looks through me, the corners of her lips tilting towards a smile. She knows, she knows. Yeah Khuddah! She knows! How can this be? This world? Why so disappointing? Cultivating desire so that you crave that which cannot be. This cannot be. I want to embrace the girl on the swing. To absorb her spirit, and seek from it my strength.

The girl looks up at me. She meets my gaze. Her look is kind, filled with love. She speaks in Arabic, Egyptian dialect:

"Do you know, every little bit, every breath helps. It helps to lead the way. Don't worry. You must believe my darling. Without faith, there is nothing. Nothing. Nothing to relieve, to exhaust. To confound and enlighten. We must believe. Otherwise we cannot even die."

She looks away. Her image begins to fade. The scent of the air changes. Then she whispers, "I am with you in each breath."

I am sitting on the bench with my face in my hands. The sun has left us to usher in the cool moon. He is beside me. I have no idea how long we have been here. Perhaps a century. He reaches across the bench, places his hand on my head, dropping it to draw the hair from my face. His other arm at my waist pulls me towards him and he places his lips just above mine so that his bottom lip meets my top one. I ask him to take me to the sea.

At the shore, I tear myself free of clothing and dive into the waves. He does not follow. Leaving me to my drama, but watching. He sits beside my white clothes. The water is lit silver by the moon. I want it to sweep me away. I want to see Yasmine. I need her embrace. The sea weeps with me. We weep with desire.

When I emerge from the sea, he comes to meet me at the water's edge. An imagined diaphanous boundary separating sand from sea. We meet at the edge. He reaches for me and I soak him with my wetness. We embrace. I cannot move. Keeping still, with closed eyelids, I surrender my skin to the urging desire of his lips, his hands.

I follow the beckoning finger. His touch is light and titillating. Throbbing. It resonates. Will echo within me in the days to come.

We sleep in the sand, entwined like serpents. I do not usually fall asleep in the presence of men I do not know. I awake to a coolness that brushes aside his warmth just before dawn. He takes me home. I steal into the cottage. Ghulshan is waiting for me, sitting at the kitchen table with a pot of steaming tea.

Tha
India

NOOR. GULF OF KUTCH. 1920

Noor was born in a small village along the coast of the Gulf of Kutch. Floods had drowned the farm again that year. The waters came sweeping from the glorious mountain peaks of Kashmir through the Punjab, cutting a corner in Rajastan and gushing into the Arabian Sea.

For three years the villagers' farms have been drowning. The wealthy merchants had the foresight and influence to farm on higher ground. The rest of the peninsula has fallen into the clutches of famine. The British East India Company has only exacerbated matters by patrolling sea routes into the Indian Ocean, forcing local fishermen either to risk their unworthy lives and fish at night, or to fish at high noon and sell their wares to the navy. The consequence of both options is exorbitant prices that only the merchants can pay. The poorer Muslim families have been reduced to eating the forbidden shellfish. Prawn, lobster and crab are added to sizzling fried curries, drenched with lime and covered with coriander in a vain effort to hide the flesh and overwhelm the taste.

Luckily Noor's brothers Sher Ali, Shamsh Ali and Karim Ali have found some work as woodcarvers and handymen for the local Nawab Sahib. The Mukhi Sahib recommended Noor's brothers to the Nawab. Some of Noor's cousins have found work on the ships of local merchants, who paid high sums in solid gold to win the blessing of a British stamp before setting sail for the Arabian Sea, across the Indian Ocean and to Mombassa. In the seaside markets of Mombasa, they will trade Indian spices, rice, cotton, gold and silver.

Noor sits in the courtyard with her sisters and cousins. Her elder sister Ferial and their new sister-in-law Dolat Bhabhi are sorting and cleaning lentils and rice to make khichadi for the afternoon meal. Noor stitches mirrors into a chori. She weaves them into lotus flowers, clusters of stars and flowers, cashew-shaped paisleys and peacock feathers. The chori is red. She has already finished the pachedi. They are for her cousin's wedding.

Just last week, Noor and Ferial had their arms, wrists and ankles tattooed with green ink. Their mother is preparing them for marriage. The family can no longer afford to keep young healthy girls at home. But they couldn't possibly afford a dowry. Any day now Ma will come to their room and whisper. Noor does not want to leave her family. She hopes she will marry one of the cousins who live in the same village. Noor was born at the time of Divali. Her mother thinks she must be at least twelve years old by now.

Two hours before dawn, Noor, Ferial, Dolat and their mother awake. They wash their faces, hands and feet with water collected at the overflowing well, that now sits cool in ceramic urns in the kitchen. Ferial takes a mat outside and unrolls it upon the veranda. The women sit together in prayer. They silently chant the name of their Guide. Their rhythms meet. Noor can never concentrate properly. Her eyes wander. They seek the coming dawn. She always wakes in a trance to find that light has come, her mother and sisters have risen, ended their prayers, put the tea on the stove and begun to roll the rotla. Ferial thinks that Noor is lazy. Noor shouldn't really care what Ferial thinks, but she does.

She spends her days puzzled over her fate. She seeks answers in everything she can imagine. She asks the sun and the moon, but fails to understand them. She asks the stars. Their language is sometimes more comprehensible, but she still doesn't understand. She asks the sand, the leaves, the seeds, grains of rice. But they are simple, and they can only give simple answers. Noor understands she is not simple like them. When absolutely desperate, she asks the cards. They tell her, but she is too scared to listen. Oh! If only Noor could live her life.

In the afternoons, before they eat, Noor takes some food to the Jamaat Khana. She offers it to her Imam and then gives it to the poor. She always prays for the poor. If we don't pray for ourselves who else will? Certainly not the ones who already have everything, so Noor thought. Noor returns home. Her mother recites the Bismallah and they eat.

One day their mother came into Noor and Ferial's room. She asked them if they remembered their cousins Qassim Ali and Razak. The boys had decided to make a life in East Africa. The English Sahibs were building a road for railcars and many local boys were going in hopes of securing a livelihood. Qassim Ali and Razak had written a letter to the family. The Mukhi Sahib had just come and read it to her. They are requesting brides for marriage. Their Mukhi emphasised that the boys had been kind enough not to ask for a dowry, only to send the girls by ship to Mombassa. Ferial and Noor are to depart in two months time. The Mukhi has promised to look after the passage. Many other brides will also be travelling. The Mukhi and his Sahiba will travel with them to ensure their safe arrival.

Noor's golden face turned pallid. The colour of a dull moon. Ferial scolded her and their mother advised them to thank their fates. But she forgot to smile. Oh whom we call Mother, you forgot to smile.

The following morning Noors and Ferial's engagements were announced. Neighbours and relatives came around to see the girls and congratulate the family. Mother had prepared ladhos and peras for the guests to sweeten their mouths. Milky sherbet, pink from the essence of rose petals, sweet and expensively saffroned, was passed around in glass tumblers. The elder women of Razak and Qassim Ali's families, who lived in a nearby village, set out on foot and donkey one morning to arrive in time for the afternoon meal and a viewing of the brides. Mother had sent her husband off to the seashore to buy some expensive fish. She prepared a sumptuous maachi bhat, fish curried in coconut cream, buttery rice, sweet bulgur lapsi, aubergines, cauliflower and peas in tomato curry, and fresh hot chapattis. Noor and Ferial were dressed up in their best clothes and asked to demurely serve the meal. Their in-laws had brought whatever silks and gold they could afford for the girls to sew into frock-pachedis to wear on their wedding day. The women spent the night, returning to their village early the next day. They would return after a week for the wedding rituals and ceremonies which would take place with grooms absent.

Noor and Ferial have both received the same gifts from their in-laws. Three yards of cream-coloured silk embroidered with gold thread. Four gold bangles, two for each wrist. A set of gold hooped earrings with dangling bells. A gold arabesque pendant, with the word "Ali" hidden in the ornate calligraphy, hanging on a gold chain, and a plain gold band for the ring finger. The sisters spread their wares before them. Ferial examines the silk to determine its quality and gazes up at Noor whose lip is now quivering. She comforts her sister and then begins to sob herself. The wedding is next Friday.

On Sunday morning, Noor and Ferial have been soaked, scrubbed and oiled. They are armed with wicker baskets which they balance on their heads. Sent into the fields to pick henna leaves, they are dressed in old cotton short-sleeved gypsy frocks with full skirts that end just above the ankles. They are covered against the sun, wearing pink and light blue pachedis respectively. Their feet are shod in toe-looped chapels. Ecstatic to have escaped the mundane household chores, the sisters skip along the path. Their chatter occasionally breaks off as they sing a gheet or two. They stoop over pungent henna plants and pluck them naked. Taking a rest by some old tree trunks they share a snack of an old chapatti wrapped over a ripe sweet banana.

They each return home gleefully with basketfuls. The henna leaves are to be lightly washed and then dried in the sun. After a day they will be ground with pestle and mortar into a powder. Tea water, crushed clove and a touch of oil will be mixed into the powder to make a paste, mehendi. Wedding preparations are in full swing. With the help of aunties, sisters, cousins and nieces. Mother is delegating the preparation of sweetmeats for the feast: green pistachio burfi fudge, badam almond in semolina flour pak squares, sweet, sticky, gelatinous carrot halva, round jaggehry ladoo balls seasoned with roasted poppy seed, to be accompanied by ghantia, chickpea flour fritters and sambar, a hot and sour pickle of mangoes, apples and carrots. Ferial cannot sew so Noor is furiously sewing both her own wedding dress and her elder sister's. Her cousin Khatoun helps her when she can. Ferial keeps the house in some kind of running order and makes regular trips to the market and the well.

On Thursday morning, after their meditation and a breakfast of chapattis, yoghurt and hot glasses of tea, Noor and Ferial are led back into the bedroom where the whole family sleeps, mother and father on a cot at the back of the room, Noor and Ferial on floor mats in a front corner, and the boys on mats in the opposite corner. The girls are surprised to find the room crowded with their female relatives seated in a crescent on the floor. They look at Noor and Ferial and smile. In the centre two white sheets are laid over bamboo mats, and beside them sits a large earthenware pot filled with boiling water. A small kerosene stove with low flames heats a pot of chaasni. The sugar and lemon syrup looks like honey. It is used to sweeten sweetmeats and to strip away unwanted hair. Noor's eyes are bright and alert. Mother motions them into the room and sits them down in the centre of the crescent, one on each sheet. She asks the girls to remove their clothing. They stare unbelievingly at her. Finally she yanks at their frocks, pulling the skirts above their heads. The girls undress and rub themselves clean with the boiling water and a cotton cloth. They wrap themselves in the white sheets and sit on the mats. Mother's elder cousin Sherbanu steps forward to do the deed. She attends to Ferial first as she is older. Noor watches their mother's cousin dip a blunt knife into the syrupy liquid and spread it in a thin film over Ferial's legs. Sherbanu takes a strip of cotton from a basket at her side and places it over the film of syrup. She vigorously rubs her hands up and down on the cloth for about a minute. She stretches Ferial's leg taut and rips off the cloth, taking hair from the root and a layer of dead skin with it. Ferial screams into the sky and Noor's eyes bulge with fear. When Sherbanu Massi turns towards her, syrupy knife in hand, Noor jumps up and bolts out of the house. She is caught, restrained, dragged back into the house, held down and made smooth as a seal.

The grooms' wedding party arrives that afternoon to be housed by generous neighbours and fed by their in-laws. They have brought gift platters of pomegranates, dried fruits and nuts, gunnysacks filled with rice, a live lamb and several chickens for the festive meal, and adornments for the brides. Noor and Ferial cannot go out to welcome or even see them, as they are busy having hands and feet laced with henna. The men will gather in a borrowed tent while the women will come inside to inspect the brides dressed in red frock-pachedis and wearing all the gold they own. They will form a queue in descending order of age and respect. Each groom's mother will be the first to place a gift in each girl's lap. She picks sweets from a tray held by a young relative and drops one into each bride's mouth. She gives her a sip of sherbet. She makes a rotating fanlike movement of the hands and fingers at her temples, and repeats it beside Noor and Fatima's side to wave away the evil spirits. Finally, she auspiciously cracks her knuckles at the brides. Each woman in the queue will bless the girls with this ritual. The bride in turn will smile demurely, with downcast eyes, careful not to touch her hands still wet with henna on anyone or anything.

After the grooms' women have left, the women of the bride's own family bless them in a similar fashion. Noor is thankful to have Ferial beside her through all this. She is tired of hanging her head down and wants to sit up straight, staring defiantly into the eyes of the family she will join but never get to know. After the ceremonies, chicken pilaff is served and the brides are allowed to retire to their room. Their mother and close female relatives bathe them with milk and honey. Noor and Ferial spend their last night at home on their parents' cot.

Noor cannot sleep. She wonders how Ferial has managed to slip drowsily away. Noor hangs and sways like a pendulum in a fit of anxiety. She does not want to get married and above all she does not want to go to Africa. "O heaven, help me," she prays as she stares out into the dark night.

Friday is the day of Noor and Ferial's joint wedding. They are allowed to rest past dawn. After the sun has appeared they dress in their cream-coloured wedding finery. The actual marriage ceremony is skipped, but all other rituals are observed. The brides are welcomed into the luncheon tent by their new mother-in-law. They do not step over sapatia as the husbands are not present to provide an equal competition, but Qassim Ali and Razak's mother, with a black badeni cloth over her head, welcomes them. She again slips something sweet into their mouths and gives them a sip of sherbet that they bend to receive. Her daughter holds a platter of rice, sweets, supari betel nuts and a yellow liquid, saffron soaked in water. Their mother-in-law dips her forefinger into the saffron and stains a yellow spot at the place of each bride's third eye. She gathers rice in her palms and presses it against the yellow dot. Several grains stick to the centre of the forehead and the rest fall away. Noor finds herself smiling sweetly at this somewhat wrinkled woman. She regrets that she will not be living with her. Holding a betel nut in her hand, to ward off evil the woman circles both the brides' full figures then hurls the nut to the East. Then she takes another, and in turn does the same for the other points of the compass. Finally she showers rice upon them and ceremoniously cracks her knuckles. The brides are welcomed into the festive tent. A tabla player will beat out quarter-rhythms and the men and women will gather in circles to dance a rasrah, led by the brides.

KHATAK DREAM

The walls of the tent are painted scarlet. A rim of golden calligraphy, etched by Ali, borders its upper edges. It is the Surat al-Noor from the Holy Qur'an.

Intricately carved silver elephants are poised at the four corners. Arabesque openings exhale winding breaths of smoke which perfume the room with sandalwood and myrrh. Baskets of lemon and jasmine flowers festoon the walls. Four crossed torches bring light and warmth. It is dusk. We are in the valley, having arrived earlier in the afternoon after a long journey across mountains upon wild horses. We have been bathed and robed and then guided to a tent, where we are asked to form a circle. A young girl arrives. She is dressed in long, richly-coloured robes, silver twinkles as she walks, a crown of orchids on her noble head. Her eyes are swimming. In her hands she holds a long flask with a soft rounded belly and smooth, spherical head. She is the handmaiden of those famous angels. She circles us, waving her flask to sprinkle us with the wetness of attar.

Two men follow her. They wear flowing white robes, skull caps and brightly-coloured shawls over their shoulders. They sit in the centre of the circle beside a pair of tabla drums and a santur. The tabla player begins a hesitant rhythm. As the santur's stringed lament responds, the beat becomes stronger and insistent, flows in waves over the assembled. The child-angel returns, offering cups filled with a liquid so deeply scarlet it is purple. It tastes full and fruity with echoes of saffron and cinnamon. We sit in silence and sip our drinks.

Two figures emerge from the lattice through which the tent breathes. They are clothed in flared, cascading skirts, fitted bodices, and trails of silk fall from their heads to the floor. The colour is the most extraordinary iridescent pearl white. It is the antithesis to the blue sea, the sandy desert dunes, the dizzying explosion of brilliance that is India. They meet at the centre of the circle, joining one set of hands and greeting us with the other, in a gesture that bends from the waist, allowing the head to fall and meet a hand that touches its forehead. Slowly they dance. Beginning with gentle taps of the foot, to be followed by the hips swaying in detachment from their waists. Hands gesticulating like the wind, fingers miming the opening and closing of lotuses, heads tilting gently like pendulums. Their movements escalate with the rhythm of the tabla: feet are now stamping, hips thrusting, hands shooting, fingers pointing, followed by piercing eyes and heads which rise in ecstasy. Their dancing erupts until they are spinning deliriously in the most graceful frenzy of nothingness. Soon they will embrace and laugh shamelessly, shrieking long, sharp, hollow ululations.

We are left mute. Having shared their rapture. They seem to be sisters of the moon. The world becomes One. United by a Single Spirit.

The child-angel motions us into another tent where we are seated upon cushions and see the pictorial stories of carpets from Bukhara and Kashgar. The sisters arrive, still enraptured, serving us a feast. Steaming wooden trays of hot flat breads cooked in the tandoor oven are followed by cumined pulses in copper bowls. A saffroned pilaff is served with chicken in a stew of apricots. Mint-roasted lamb is accompanied by glazed potatoes with cilantro. Silky coconut-creamed fish arrives wrapped in banana leaves and with coriandered tomatoes laced with onion. Pride of place is given to shining white, luminous, virginal grains of sweet succulent rice. The pastries are like organza. The meal ends in a rainbow of apples, a symphony of pears, sweetened lemon, figs, pomegranates, almonds and pistachio.

As we depart near dawn, the angels bless us with a kiss.

NOOR. THE SWAHILI COAST. 1932

On Saturday morning Noor and Ferial are escorted to the quay by their father-in-law. They will join about thirty girls, also recently married to ghosts, to board the ship to another world.

It is time for the gourthari, more popularly known as the crying ceremony, where the bride's family bids her farewell: pledging her to her husband. Qassim Ali and Razak's mother will try to compensate for Noor and Ferial's loss with gifts of gold and silver to their families. Noor stands with her sister at the foot of the dock and her brothers Sher Ali, Shamsh Ali and Karim Ali come forward to bid them farewell. Sher Ali, two years younger than Noor, is her best friend in games, her support when the world invades her sensibilities, and the one she sits with under the neem tree to laugh and cry and suck on bittersweet tamarind beads. His tears have risen and are now spilling. Their father envelops his girls in a warm embrace. Mother waves icily. Noor is sobbing hysterically, the black kajal that rims her eyes flows across her cheeks. They board the ship, Ferial drawing Noor along.

The Mukhi Sahib and Mukhiani Sahiba have reassured the families of all the brides boarding the ship they will be in the very best of care. Most of the girls like Noor and Ferial are from poorer families who could not dream of affording a dowry and who already have too many mouths to feed. Of these families some suffer twinges of guilt. Mothers' nights will be marred by dreams of their daughters in darkest Africa. They console themselves with thoughts of the good life the girls will have in a land bountiful with promise of harvest and success, with husbands gainfully employed. Fathers will crouch under the black canopy of night smoking a bedi, and ease their frowns with thoughts of the young, industrious men whose hard lives in savage jungles they have softened with the comfort of a wife.

The ship is a cargo ship, not intended to transport humans. The Mukhi and Mukhiani have a room with the crew on the deck. The girls are allotted a dark and damp room below deck. Thirty newlywed brides in one room, spread across the floor, sleeping on mats. They take their meals after the crew has finished, taking turns in the kitchen to prepare a bland dhal of dried pulses and boiled rice which they eat for breakfast, lunch and dinner. Sometimes they are given leftover scraps from the crew's meals, a couple of chapattis, an egg or two, but no fruit, no vegetables, no milk, no sugar, not even tea. The Mukhi and Mukhiani dine with the crew.

Noor becomes seasick, her nerves are a mess. She has lost her centre and cannot bear it. She refuses to eat or mingle with the other girls. She retires to a corner of their vast pit and stews in her distress. Her eyes hold a blank unseeing gaze. Ferial is fed up with tending to her weak little sister. She has been chatting with some girls who have received letters from their husbands describing East Africa. She can read and recites them for a crowd who shudder with fear and a touch of excitement. She has returned to check on her sister. She finds her huddled in a corner, praying with her tasbih. "Noorraah! No one, overwhelmed with pity at your long face, is going to stop the boat and take you back home! Why can't you stop being so painfully sensitive and just make the most of it like the rest of us? Dream of your husband, an unseen land, a new life! You better smarten up and become strong. Life is not a bed of roses and if you don't look out it will blow you away like a speck of dust!" Ferial thunders off and Noor does not know what has hit her.

After a week at sea, a young girl from the neighbouring village of Junagadh, overwhelmed by the anxiety of marriage to a man she has not seen and the prospect of a new life in an unimaginably exotic land, climbs up to the deck. She craves some fresh air and a soothing stroll. She walks along the railing and is sickened by the sight of high cascading waves. Leaning over the railing to retch, the girl is suddenly attacked by a coolie from the ship's crew. He carries her into a corner by the stairs that lead below, lifts up her skirts, tears open her blouse and descends crushing upon her. Stupefied she cannot find a voice to scream but the girls hear a commotion and rush up to find the man running off, drawing up his shalwars over an exposed behind as he scuttles along. The girl has found her voice and now screams violently, unstoppably. Two girls run off to the fetch the Mukhiani who arrives with her husband. The offender will be identified by the girls. He is found and indeed punished by the captain, who fires him. But he must remain aboard for the remainder of the journey and his salary will be paid so that he may feed his wife and children. The girls will now travel in packs and never come onto the deck except to take their meals in the canteen. And the raped girl, upon arrival in East Africa, will spill the truth to her kind husband, who, instead of sending her back to her family, disgraced, will keep her. He will also keep an African mistress.

Noor and Ferial arrived safely in Mombassa after two weeks at sea. They dressed up in their cream wedding frock-pachedis that hung loosely from their starved figures. Fear in heart, they went to meet their fates. Qassim Ali and Razak had come to the shore. The Mukhi performed thirty marriages on the dock. Noor wept because the ritual henna, celebration of womanhood and protection from tragedy and evil, had worn off her hands and feet before she was married. The husbands hired a hut along the inner shore but first they took their wives to a small restaurant housed in a shack two miles down the seashore. It is run by a Gujarati cook, his wife-assistant and their waiter son. Rickety wooden tables and chairs are strewn around the wet, dirty room that breathes its fragrant spices into miles of seashore. The brothers order a lavish meal of potato bhajias, meat samosas, goat biryani, yoghurt, cucumber and tea. The sisters eat ravenously, forgetting their manners. The men smile with pity. They take a walk along the shore, Qassim Ali and Razak walk in front and Noor and Ferial trail behind. They attempt conversation, speaking niceties and enquiring in turn about the journey and life in Africa. Finally they come to the huts, separate but huddled to-gether. The brothers bid each other farewell and Ferial gives Noor a knowing look. Inside the hut, Qassim Ali presents his wife Ferial with a gift of new linens for their bed and a small ivory pendant. He reaches awkwardly for her hair. She removes her pachedi and yields to him. Razak has also bought a gift for his wife Noor but she sits perched on the edge of the bed sobbing. He clears his throat and attempts to speak to her but stops himself. How could he pressure her? He can only imagine what she has endured. So he steps outside, leaving her to herself. He takes a mat and a sheet with him, settling down on the short veranda. The sea air is fresh and there is no point in rushing Fate.

Noor eventually became accustomed to Razak's gentle company. Occasionally she would smile and this soothed Razak's precarious consciousness. They travelled inland from post to post while Razak found various jobs with the British East Africa Rail Company. Finally, they settled in Moshi where a bigwig Gujarati merchant whom everyone called Mr. T employed Razak as a driver cum all-around multi-task man. Qassim Ali and Ferial settled in the nearby town of Arusha where he worked in a general goods store. They had better luck.

Noor managed to run a household. She substituted cassava for potatoes, used coconut milk for flavour and eventually discovered an Indian grocer whose wife she befriended. She took refuge in cooking wholesome meals for her husband and tending their small, two-room hut. She bore five children before the age of twenty-one: two sons, then a daughter, another son and finally the youngest daughter. Razak had decided to obey the advice of his Imam and educate their children. This meant that he did not have any help with his chores, and neither did Noor. He often took odd jobs to help pay his children's school tuition, for which he was perennially in debt. When the oldest son turned thirteen and entered secondary school, Razak began to work as a night lorry driver, transporting the Gujarati merchant's goods from German East Africa to British East Africa. At this moment Tragedy decided to raise her weary head and spread her looming wings over them.

The Second World War had begun. East Africa was a supply point and Razak was driving his truck of smuggled goods by night. Mr. T had failed to mention two crucial facts to Razak: first, he was crossing a legally closed boundary. Second, he was carrying British arms and currency out of German territory. Razak, who stuck fast to his principles, never poked his nose in other people's business beyond what necessity demanded. To snoop through Mr. T's goods was not necessary. Besides, the Mukhi had recommended and sworn by Mr. T some fourteen years ago. Touch wood, Razak had found

Mr. T to be a cautious and reliable man. In short, Razak happily, if somewhat tiredly, followed the forested backroads from Moshi through Kisumu to Nairobi, without question.

LETTER. ARUSHA, TANGANYIKA. NOVEMBER 26, 1938

My dear brothers,

Your daughters have all been honourably married and now live as the respectful wives of the new community we are founding here in this strange but beautiful land.

The railway has been built. Brides arriving by the shipload from Gujarat and Kutch have been husbanded. Children have been born, families inaugurated. The Indians have formed pockets of their own communities, scattered along the posts of the British East Africa Railway route.

Some wealthy Indian merchants have also come to exploit the commerce of the new trade markets. Indian managers are appointed by British companies. We Indians have become experts in the ways of the English. The arms and legs of their administration: middlemen. Not quite as fine as the British sahibs themselves but infinitely better than the Negroes. Our people have been imported not only to East Africa, but also to South Africa, the Caribbean Islands, the colonies of the New World, and even London, that bustling imperial capital.

The Pathans, esteemed warriors of the Punjab, are becoming staples of the British regiments, scattered across the empire upon which the sun does not set. Soldiers, fighting the battles of their conquerors. Hindus, Muslims, Sikhs, all together. We bring with us our ways, we Indians. Hoarding spices, layers of homespun silk and cotton, chunks of cone-shaped incense, and our Gods, all bundled up and tied in a gunnysack, to be housed on our backs until we find a place to set them down. We Indians preserve our ways. We will remain amongst our own. We do not mix, for interbreeding is a sacrilege.

And our women, they stay at home. Fertilising spirit, concocting feasts from grains and beans, listening to the wind, watching the moon and continuing to believe in the Fate that has brought them here.

*The Africans, where are the Africans? Sorry victims. Third in a
pyramid of England, India and Africa.*

NOOR. MOSHI, TANGANYIKA. 1940

Noor spent much of her time at home, alone with her two daughters
and youngest son. The two eldest were away, boarding at hostels.
Razak came home late in the afternoon, ate and went to work. He
came home again in the night, slept, awoke, ate and went back to
work. One night Razak didn't come home. Noor waited until
morning. Then she sent the girls and the boy to the local school and
went to visit Mr. T. She had consulted the sun and the moon, this
time she understood.

She arrived at the home of the merchant, twelve miles away, on
foot. "Where is my husband?" She asked a man who seemed to be
an askari guarding, or rather loitering, around the entrance to the
house.

"Honourable lady, I am not blessed with the omnipotence that
is Allah's alone, hence not knowing who your husband is, I can hardly
answer where he is."

"I am Razak's wife." As Noor announced her identity, the askari's
face paled and he led her inside the house. There was not a woman
to be seen. Some men were sitting on a low wooden cot, drinking
tea and conversing in grunts and moans. They were unshaven and
dirty. All eyes and heads turned towards her, unashamedly
contemplating her desirability, as if appraising a shank at the
butcher's. "I am here to speak with Mr. T," she said resolutely but
with downcast eyes.

"He is not here," replied a voice from the cot.

"Then I will wait for him," Noor retorted, gathering the folds of
her pachedi. She turned around and walked out of the room, onto
the two steps at the entrance. She lifted her skirt and sat on the first
step, tucking her legs beneath her. She reached for the tasbih which
was wound around her wrist like an attractive set of bangles,
unwound it and began counting the names of Allah and Ali. It was
half past ten in the morning.

At two o'clock, Noor, cooked by the midday sun and moistened by a sauce of sweet sweat, realised that she had to go home and feed her children who would have returned from the Aga Khan School. She turned her head, pulling the pachedi alongside and looked from the corners of her eyes into the room. She could smell the masalas of the men's meal, prepared undoubtedly by someone's wife, mother or sister, she thought. The men, who had not shifted from their positions on the cot, rose towards the small sink at the end of the room to wash their hands. Would they offer her some food? She decided to leave at once to save herself the humiliation of either imposing on their lunch or being deemed unworthy of a few grains of rice. Noor once again lifted her skirt, stood up and walked away without bidding farewell. When she reached home she told her children she had been visiting a friend from Jamaat Khana.

The next day, Qassim Ali arrived from Arusha. Noor's sister Ferial had stayed with the children: three boys. Over a cup of tea, Qasim Ali told her that Razak was in Tanga prison, having been caught by German authorities smuggling weapons to the English. Noor wailed and beat her chest. Qassim Ali left for the bus station to go visit his brother.

Noor started to embroider again. Her embroidery became famous: cashews, paisleys and lotus flowers adorned every bride wed in Moshi for the next five years. She also began to cook massive cauldrons of food: the lunch orders from the town's shops and offices and dinners of local male households. The meals were delivered in tiffins, tin containers stacked one on top of the other in groups of three to five, and supported by a metal frame and handle. While Noor worked hard and filled the stomachs of countless hungry bachelors, the children continued to attend school. They learned to become assistant chefs, delivery boys, lackeys and seamstresses. The eldest girl also learned to read, write and do maths.

Six months later, the youngest girl, Yasmine Razak, only four years old, caught a fever. It stayed for two weeks. Expensive doctors were summoned. Their medicine was bought. Mr. T paid. Two more weeks passed. Yasmine died in her sleep. Razak, in prison, was heartbroken. It was believed by all the people of Moshi who lived during Noor's time that beautiful Yasmine died of a curse of the evil eye. Many hungry families and lust-inflamed men were astounded by how well Noor was managing on a new continent, with a husband in prison.

It was Ramadan, two years later. The older boys were home from school on holiday. Razak was to be released from prison for the feast of Eid that broke the month of fasting, three days away. Spirits were soaring. Everyone was happy, even Noor. A few hours before sunset, the eldest boy Noor Ali, came home with his friends. He was famished. Noor told him it would be okay to break his fast now, he had already fasted the whole month. Her son refused. He said he would go swimming with his friends and by the time he returned it would be sunset. How impressed his father would be when he heard that Noor Ali had fasted the whole month!

Noor Ali and his younger brother Ahmed Ali, along with the rest of the boys in the neighbourhood, used to swim in the park just outside Moshi at the southern foothills of Kilimanjaro. The river was rocky and fast. Sped by its descent down the slopes of Kilimanjaro, it dropped thunderously into a waterfall that filled a sinewy, stony niche in the earth. It was not safe to swim here, but these were poor Indian boys from a struggling neighbourhood. No one paid much attention to them. Let them have their thrills. The boys jump and kid around in their shorts. The water is not very deep, it is cool and refreshing, but it has an undertow.

Noor is busy, happily preparing a Ramadan feast for her family. She has come to love her husband, although you would never hear such words from her mouth. She is anxious for his return. She is pleased that Noor Ali, her firstborn, the light of her eyes, has returned from school with his brother. How delighted Razak will be when he sees how much the boys have grown! She wants to finish cooking, laying the table and cleaning one hour before sunset, to have time to bathe and prepare herself to be seen by her husband.

The undertow pulls Noor Ali. He waves frantically and then shouts between gulps of water. He is kicking and screaming, manages to get hold of a high rock and hangs on. His younger brother Ahmed Ali dives into the river and offers his hand to his brother. But the river becomes ferocious, the undertow sucks him in and his brother's hand too.

At sunset, fresh and beautified Noor is called to the shore to meet the corpses of her two oldest sons. The river has taken the spirits but left the flesh. Noor looks pallid, but watch her. She walks, gracing the sand, tall and strong. Her sister Ferial's words are ringing in her ears, "Noorrah! You better smarten up and become strong. Life is not a bed of roses and if you don't look out it will blow you away just like a speck of dust!" Yes, Ferial, you were right. No bed of roses for me, no matter how much I dream. It won't come now. Too late. Wish I had listened before. Teach me then—now—how to take the next breath. How do I face another sun?

Razak comes home to bury his two sons. They are interred that very night. The funeral ceremonies are attended by the whole town. Eid becomes a sombre occasion. Even Mr. T does not feast.

Noor had a very dear, kind friend. She met her in the early morning hours at Jamaat Khana; they spoke in Swahili. Her name was Zahra. She lived on a cocoa farm with her husband and twelve children. When Noor's first daughter was a year old, she had taken her to Zahra to be blessed and pierced in the ears and nose. Noor's first daughter was called Ghulshan because she had cheeks like damasked roses.

Ghulshan was raised in a two-bedroom hut with seven people. Mother Noor, father Razak, brother Omar Ali, deceased brothers Noor Ali and Ahmed Ali and deceased sister Yasmine. There was a common room with a coal stove and water pipe. One corner was furnished with mats and a small table. Behind the stove, Ghulshan filled a large pot with water, hung a towel in front of her and bathed. When she was finished, Omar Ali followed. New water, same soap, same towel. Toilets were outside in a small straw hut. This was her life. She knew laughter and she knew carelessness.

Sometimes when Zahra came to Moshi with her two sons, she would ask them to take her to Noor's house-shop. She would greet Noor at the steps and ask her sons to come and fetch her again after a couple of hours. Zahra and Noor would retire to the back of the shop where Noor would make some hot, spicy, milky tea and choose some tempting treats from half-full tiffins to offer to her friend. Zahra would then unwrap her pachedi and unbutton her blouse to show Noor her most recent wounds.

Two decades pass. Noor and Razak continue to live in their hut-house. Ghulshan and the youngest son, only two left out of five, are growing up. They attend the hostel in Mombasa to be educated. Razak, however has become disheartened. Each morning he wakes to the image of his three deceased children. They hang close to him like long shadows obscuring the sun. He remembers all the time he spent away from them, on the road, working, and finally in prison. He was always running from them. Squeezing in an affection here, a smile there. Indeed he did not know his children. Never knew what Noor Ali liked to eat, or how fast he could run, never saw Ahmed Ali ride his broken red bike, never listened to beautiful Yasmine's sweet broken sentences. Razak, loyal, virtuous good man, kind husband, dedicated father. The image falls apart. He begins to touch that poison from which he had sworn abstinence. Razak falls to drink. He joins the sad, bitter men who could not bend to Fate's cruel iron hand and now lie broken. Razak drinks himself into a numb blindness. He drinks until his dead children's faces disappear. Then he goes home to Noor, mouth rinsed with menthol water. Noor's high cheeks have fallen, the sight of her once pious, now drunkard husband pierces her fragile heart. Noor has made up her mind to be strong. When Razak becomes diabetic and his medicines are expensive, Ghulshan chooses to return from hostel and begin to work. Loyal to her family, she sacrifices her own education. As recompense, Ghulshan buys a new dress every six months and saves her money to buy one bottle of Oil of Olay lotion every four months. She was free to hem her dresses shorter and shorter when they frayed. She was free to stain her lips with pan-juice and turn them into rose petals. She was free to sit outside under the stars all night and giggle with her friend Leila. When Noor scolded her, Razak came to her rescue.

With her rosy literate looks, she becomes a secretary at a fancy dentist's office. Omar Ali continues to school. Ghulshan pays for his tuition and her father's expenses.

Omar Ali used to write letters to his beloved mother, light of the heavens. They included a scaled diagram of the box-parcel filled with the food and gifts he fantasized she would have sent him, had she the means. Each item was labelled, wrapped and engineered into its place. Ghulshan tried to materialise these dreams. She only succeeded in providing what was functionally necessary: toothpaste, packages of daal, new undershirts, chevro made by Noor, maybe even a Cadbury's chocolate, but never expensive English biscuits and cologne, new shoes and trousers, fountain pens and thickly lined expensive books.

One day, Ghulshan was walking to her work at the dentist's office in Moshi. Her legs were tucked into white English pumps, swaying on spiked heels, her hips swivelled. A car—an ivory-coloured Opal sedan—followed her. Its driver offered her a lift. Much to Ghulshan's dismay, she accepted. Every morning after that she found the car waiting for her in that same spot, outside Babu Khan's bakery.

Eventually tongues began to flick. Noor took sweetmeats to Babu who sold them at his shop, keeping twenty-five percent of the profit. She heard the stories from him, about her daughter. Ghulshan's movements were now monitored. And when Omar Ali returned from school, he forbade his sister to leave the house after sunset. Ghulshan, overwhelmed by anger, slapped him and was never forgiven by Noor. Horrible enough not to marry until twenty-four, but to carry on like this was absolutely inexcusable, and with some car-driving, trouser-suit-wearing, cigarette-smoking playboy from Khuddah knows where! He would play with her to his heart's delight and then seek someone of his own creed. Yeah Allah, Ghulshan! Have you learnt nothing? Stick to your roots. Why not marry Babu the baker's son, Amir Karmali?

Ghulshan intoxicated many promising bachelors. She refused their hands. Her hand was for the fulfilment of Noor's, Razak's and Omar Ali's dreams.

Another day, when Noor went to deliver sweets to Babu Khan, he invited her into the back room for a cup of tea. Noor, fragile as she had become, was perplexed and refused. Babu insisted that he had the most honourable intentions, and that the matter was of great urgency. To protect her reputation, he asked his youngest son Amir to join them.

Noor sat perched stiffly in her wooden chair, one leg tucked behind the other, both under the chair. There was flour in the air, accompanied by the delicious smell of baking bread. Babu took his generous seat, while Amir stood and ordered three cups of tea and three sweet raisin breads. He did not know why his father had asked him to join them, but he did know that the woman seated in front of him was the mother of Ghulshan—girlfriend of his friend Ali, the swinging, stylish bachelor with the best cars and the best women.

Babu the baker introduces Noor to his standing son, making certain that Noor takes in his strong build, his good looks and courteous behaviour. The tea and sweet breads arrive and Babu gestures to his son to serve the lady. Babu then clears his throat and speaks. He cautions Noor, advising her that he is about to broach the subject of her surviving daughter, with all the best intentions. "It has come to my knowledge that she has been roaming around town with a certain Ali. A man who drinks, gambles, smuggles and hangs out with ruffians of every imaginable race. A man with whom I would not want my own son to share company, let alone a daughter." At this point Amir clears his throat with the knowledge that he had shared a bottle of Johnny Walker's Red Label whiskey last night with the said Ali, at their friend Nizar Diamond's—so named for his huge success in smuggling diamonds. Meanwhile Amir's father, Babu, was delicately hinting to Noor that, "Your daughter, beautiful as she may be, is not getting younger and this kind of behaviour will not be tolerated by any respectable family. I, however, the same Babu the baker who had helped you in your times of need, will overlook this unfortunate incident and allow my precious and only son to ask for her hand." But Amir Karmali would not dare impose upon Ali's woman. He was silently cursing his father and made up his mind to go see Ali that evening and tell him about the tea meeting.

The playboy's sister Kulsum was coming to Moshi from Nairobi. She would be at Darkhana, the central mosque, that evening. Ali wanted his beloved to meet her. But Ghulshan, after Noor's infuriated scolding, was forbidden even to pray. Around nine o'clock that Friday evening, after prayers, Amir Karmali came around to Noor's humble home and requested her permission to take her daughter out for a cup of tea and some bitings. Noor agreed, silently blessing the kindness of Babu the baker. Amir Karmali delivered Ghulshan to the doorstep of Nizar Diamond's house, where Ali and his sister Kulsum awaited her with tea and bitings.

Actually, he was Ali the twelfth son of Zahra, Noor's friend and confidant. Zahra, whose memory had continued for twenty-one years to soothe Noor.

After Razak returned from prison and buried his sons, he decided to stop working for Mr. T. Instead, he opened, with the minuscule sum Mr. T paid him for compensation, a small corner dukan from which to sell sundries. He would take trips to Congo, before it became Zaire, to return with fine Belgian perfume, powder, lipsticks and chocolates for the ladies.

Razak protects Ghulshan fiercely. She is one of his two remaining precious children and he will not allow social convention to cage her. Her cheeks have once again embraced the glow of roses. It is for this embrace that Razak lives, and so he allows her to meet the playboy. For the first time in their thirty years of marriage Razak crosses his wife Noor. He will not listen to her injunctions about the tainted virtue of their daughter. And so Ali continues to romance Ghulshan.

Two days later, Ali comes into the dukan. Razak, recognising him as Zahra's son, asks him to sit, motioning to a stool behind the counter. He offers him a cup of tea. Ali accepts. In the back of the shop, where Razak keeps a small gasoline stove, Ali asks Razak for his daughter's hand. Razak approves the marriage, while pouring chai into glass cups. They move to wooden chairs on the street outside the shop and silently sip their tea. Razak turns his head to see the handsome stranger lounging on the cracked wooden chair, embraced by the sun, sipping tea. He has just handed him his daughter Ghulshan, the elder of his two surviving children.

Having settled their business, the men summon the women to settle theirs. Ali's elder sister Fatimah, whom he calls "Ma", in place of his mother, accompanied by her neighbour Jena Bai, makes the trip from Arusha to Moshi and arrives at Noor's modest home the following day. Noor is reluctantly expecting her. She does not know that the woman, almost her own age, is Zahra's daughter. However, she recognises her instantly. She is tall, still slender and carries Zahra's grace. Noor had intended to interrogate the woman with cold eyes. Instead, overwhelmed, she embraces her. Ali's sister also recognises Noor, remembering the rosy child she brought to the coffee farm more than twenty years ago.

"Is it the same Ghulshan?" Fatima asks.

Noor smiles and the women concede to the mysterious hand of Fate, acknowledging her with a gesture of impotence. Ali's family had believed that Ghulshan was a woman beneath their standards. They were wrong.

Razak travels across Africa to Congo to buy wholesale goods for the shop and gifts for Ghulshan. He is determined to send her to Ali's house with an appropriate trousseau. While bartering in the streets of Kinshasa, Razak experiences vertigo, a spell of dizziness. Under the fiery sun, his blood pressure rises higher and higher. Finally in the midst of the noontime trade zenith he collapses at a stall over a heap of women's silk lingerie. The merchant, oblivious to Razak, or perhaps habituated to such a dramatic response to his intimate apparel, ignores him and continues his sales. Another man in the bazaar raises the alarm and a generous Indian taxi driver takes Razak to a local hospital without charging him.

Noor and Ghulshan are sharing a pot of evening tea at their modest kitchen table, munching on almond halva, when the telegram arrives. Ghulshan is thrown into shock. As Omar Ali is away at hostel again, Noor has no option but to go to Jamaat Khana and telephone Ali, who is not at home. Tadqeer, his eldest brother, informs Noor that Ali has not yet returned from Arusha's Kilimanjaro Club. Taqdeer then telephones the Club. Ali is not there. Taqdeer, now in his role as patriarch, gives up on finding Ali and drives to Moshi himself. Noor and Ghulshan have agreed among themselves that Ghulshan will go to Kinshasa to attend to Razak in the hospital. Omar Ali will be kept in school, as surely that would be his father's wish.

Ali returns to the farm, rather late in the night, from an evening of philosophic scotch-drinking at the home of his Hindu friend Nervine. His sister-in-law Zeenat informs him that Taqdeer has sped off to Moshi to attend to an emergency at the household of Ali's fiancée. Ali rushes out in his inebriated state and climbs into his Ford Opal. Speeding along the dark road to Moshi, he crashes into an army truck. The windshield smashes into his face. The soldiers take him to Mawenzi government hospital in Moshi.

Ghulshan packs a bag as Taqdeer prepares to drive her the 2,500 miles to Kinshasa. He leaves to fill up on petrol, and to telephone Zeenat to let her know where he is going.

As Taqdeer sets out to do his errands, a soldier arrives to inform them of Ali's accident. Ghulshan races out to catch Taqdeer. Running into the street in her cotton nightie with her long hair flying, she flags down the car. Noor follows Ghulshan, waving a shawl. The soldier gets into his jeep and they all drive to the Mawenzi hospital.

Ali lies unconscious. Ghulshan spends a silent night, motionless in a chair next to Ali's bed. She watches the face of her beloved, mummified in white gauze bandages. His hand is warm but there are no other signs of life.

The following morning Ghulshan takes her first airplane flight. Taqdeer has managed to book her on a 6 a.m. military flight out of Kilimanjaro International Airport to Kinshasa. She had slept fitfully in the firm visitor's chair by Ali's bed. But she is young and she is beautiful, and like many such women, who, when their world falls apart, cling to their beauty, Ghulshan spends a half hour in the small hospital toilet to administer to her appearance. When she exits, she is rosy cheeked. From the hospital to the airport, she maintains her spirit. In heels and red lipstick, Ghulshan sashays up the steel steps into the doorway of the military plane. No less than four soldiers, one of them British, help her to her seat.

In Kinshasa, the British colonel drives Ghulshan to the hospital. He doesn't merely drop her at its door, but parks the car and escorts her to the room where her father lies in a stupor of medication. Ghulshan takes leave of the gentleman and softly turns the handle to Room 312.

A gentle septic smell fills the room. There are three beds. It takes her several moments to identify her father, who is asleep. Two large eyes, bulging out of a mask, watch her as she approaches. He lies like a scientific experiment with a tangle of plastic tubing protruding out of his nose and mouth. A thin needle juts out of his left wrist. It is attached to long green tubing that leads to a sack full of liquid suspended on a steel pole with wheels. Her father is wheezing. A foam of yellow droplets has formed around his mouth and drips from his eyes. Ghulshan finds a paper towelette and wets it in the sink next to his bed. She wipes Razak's face clean. Her fingers tremble but she is careful not to shift the mass of tubes. She moves away from the bed and turns to the wall. Covering her face, she erupts into a torrent of tears.

Razak is transferred to Malago Hospital in Kampala, Uganda. Here they have better facilities. Noor wishes to transfer him to Moshi, but the doctors will not agree. During the course of Razak's illness and Ali's recovery, Ghulshan continues to work at the dentist's office. She knows there will be high bills from the hospital. She also knows that she must pay for her own wedding. Ghulshan spends her weeks shuttling between her home, the dentist's office, the hospital in Moshi and on weekends, via military flights, the hospital in Kampala.

Ali's face has been disfigured. His vision is impaired but will improve. He confronts himself, sees the broken face, and tells Ghulshan she can leave him if she so pleases. But Ghulshan is committed. She has decided to marry him or no one. Taqdeer admires her strength. She prays for more of it.

After a month Ali is released from Mawenzi Hospital. He wears large dark glasses to hide the cuts and scars around his eyes. On weekends he drives Noor, Ghulshan and Omar Ali to Kampala to visit Razak. Razak has regained a fleeting consciousness. He tells his daughter he wants her to marry.

"I may never be fully well again. At least marry while I am alive."

Ghulshan and Ali decide to marry unceremoniously. The hospital in Kampala does not allow Razak to travel to Moshi. Her relatives cannot all afford to travel to Kampala. So they have decided to marry in Moshi and drive the next day to Kampala for her father's blessing. The bride does not even henna her hands and feet.

Ghulshan and Ali are married at the Moshi Jamaat Khana on December 21, 1963. At the wedding supper in the social hall of the

Jamaat Khana, the telephone rings in the midst of the din of celebration. Ghulshan rushes to answer, expecting her father's good wishes. Dr. Patel from Malago Hospital, unaware that it is her wedding day, informs Ghulshan of Razak's unexpected brain haemorrhage.

Ghulshan, wed in her twenty-fifth year, leaves her wedding supper with her husband, her mother and her eldest brother-in-law. They drive overnight to Kampala, claim Razak's corpse, and return it to Moshi. The following afternoon, he is buried in the community's cemetery, beside his two sons and daughter.

The moon is full. The moon is full and I am delirious, remembering the moon on Kilimanjaro. My mother's face is like the moon. All women of pure blood are moonfaced. They are beauties with capes of midnight sky. My face, unlike the moon, has rippled branches. Like the baobab tree: surreptitious. As children we were told not to pass under the baobab tree after dark. Long, thin poisonous snakes lived on the thick, wide branches and would nip you in the neck with a forked tongue.

When Ghulshan shines, Ali cannot distinguish between her and the moon.

GHULSHAN

Ghulshan's first son was "dark". Ali named him Sultan. Her first daughter, named Yasmine after Ghulshan's deceased sister, was fair, as was her second son. Ahmed was named after his mother's lost brother. The last daughter was premature. She arrived three months early and repented one year for her impatience. Named after Zahra, paternal grandmother, her Maji, no curse could cure her of her scarlet infection.

Ghulshan suffered from fear and loneliness. She was isolated on the farm, and she had before her the serious business of proving her worth. To this task Ali, for all his love, was oblivious. Ghulshan is brave and her heart is warm and crackling. It heats the cold, and the fire never stops. Soon Ali's brothers and sisters warmed to her. They hovered around her chatter. Nourished by her lunches and dinners. All wished Bapaji, the thunderous Vilayat Khan who had died only two years before, could have been alive to see how well their wild Ali had fared. All but sister-in-law Zeenat.

Sadly for Ghulshan, although Ali fared well, he was still wild. He still loved to gamble—not with women but with cards, and later politics. Ali was in his mid-thirties now: successful, charming, handsome and rich. Every pleasure and luxury were his for the taking. After work, he was often invited for a drink at the club with the sahibs while Ghulshan waited patiently at home with his favourite meal hot on the table. On weekends he had to choose between hunting game on the Serengeti and playing snakes and ladders with the children. Ali could not resist the seduction of adventure and power. His life led him away to far-off lands and all-night casinos. Ghulshan would wake up in her cotton nightie in the middle of the night and with bare feet tread across the long hall to the children's rooms. She would gather her children together, even waking them from sleep, to join her in the large teak bed from which her husband was absent. She cradled her children, their presence helping her to sleep. Let him live his life and I shall live mine, she thought.

Ali cuts quite a figure. People take notice. The various faces of Ali evolve into businessman-entrepreneur, then philanthropist. Finally, all-around-bigwig. One foreign car follows another. Sons attend international schools. Bickering victims of poisonous quarrels arrive at Ali's home seeking the firm hand of justice. The needy seek food, perhaps even employment. The community stretches out a hand for donations, reminding him of his Muslim duty to charity. Ali becomes a big man, a patron. Ghulshan's fire grows, her cheeks bloom, her house is never empty of charity. She becomes Mrs. Ali and everyone in town knows her children's names and the taste of her pilaff.

ZAHRA

Sunrise. Wake up. We are in another country. It is called Kenya. I am about to be wrenched from my mother's stomach. The seed plucked out of the fruit with a hundred incisions. The fruit must live. We must preserve the fruit. A perennial lack of patience brought me into this world with yellow blood, three months early. Ghulshan and Ali's negative-positive blood forces finally collide during the sixth month of my gestation, so I am wrenched in Caesar's way from my mother's womb. The doctor at the Aga Khan Hospital in Nairobi thinks that my short life has already ended. He is now concerned primarily with preserving Ghulshan. Imagine his shock as I emerge with heart beating thunderously. There is rhythm in my jaundiced, haemoglobin-deficient blood. It is not scarlet, but it has rhythm. Ghulshan is efficiently stitched up, while a forty-year-old Englishman—left over from the Raj, or adventurous safari man, I will never know—is diluted of red blood so I can have a transfusion. All three pounds of me are placed in an incubator. The rest is left to the will of Allah. Ali telephones Noor to give the news. Noor gathers her scattered spirit and prays to Allah for twenty-seven hours. Until the telephone rings again. Ali tells her the child will live. He has decided to name me after his mother, Zahra.

I spent the first year of my life in an incubator. Jaundiced, I sucked my father's scarlet blood. My mother fed me red roses, plucked straight from her bosom. I embraced a rosy pink. Slowly it became red. One day I woke up to realise that my blood had become scarlet. I never knew when it happened. But my mother knew and my father knew. Ghulshan and Ali knew.

ALI

When Ali was twelve years old, selling coffee at the suqoni in Moshi without his father, his friend Amir acquired a new bicycle. All the boys from the neighbourhood gathered at the marketplace to witness the amazing new vehicle. Amir allowed his favourite friends a turn to mount, an attempt to ride. Two boys pushed from behind while a third balanced over the bicycle.

It is Ali's turn to ride. Skinny limbs climb onto the bicycle, hands on bars, Ali begins his ride. Grinning from burning ear to burning ear, eyes ablaze, teeth glittering in golden sunlight, he rides faster and faster. The two boys stop pushing, Ali pedals in circles around them. The flapping sole of his torn right shoe slips. His foot slides forward, the shoe swallows the bicycle's pedal and chokes. Ali crashes. Knees and elbows scrape into the gravel on the ground and bleed. Head falls hard and nose erupts. Blood flows, sparkling under the sun. Marketplace is flooding with scarlet. What colour, Burmese rubies now seem dull. Laale Ali. Look! This is the Red of Ali. The song of ecstasy.

Ali returns home with torn shoe and bloody face. His father beats him, severely. Hammering the lesson home as it were. Learn from your mistakes, scarlet one. Sister Kulsum stitches his shoes. Cleans and bandages wounds. But blood will not subside. Wounds will not heal. Mother Zahra is not there to heal, to steal from household funds and buy new shoes.

ZAHRA

I became addicted to the sea at an early age. We took holidays in Mombasa. We also went to Kunduchi Beach on the outskirts of Dar es Salaam. I met the sea at the age of two. The sea was blue, green and clear. The light pierced her, exposing her curves. At night the sea was calm. Sombre. Sleeping now with the moon. She watched us. We cradled her shining children. In the morning she rose with rolling energy. Her tresses cascading, and raising us from our sleep. We embraced and washed. She returned at midday, seeking refuge from the sun, to be calmed and fed. She whispered her secrets to the shore and we could only hear the melody. But it soothed us. Sea and sky and sleep. Until she woke again. Gently, this time. Luring us to a new horizon. Violet and rippled. Leaving us free in the vastness of night.

I waded along the shores of the Indian Ocean glazed in a synthetic yellow swimming suit with fluorescent pink rubber floaters in place around my arms and waist. I wandered further and further until Ghulshan's voice grew hoarse from calling me. My ayah, Betty, came and wrestled me from the sea. My screeching wails, as she lifted me out of the water, halted the sun at the edge of the horizon.

I remember the first time I tasted chillies. It was the middle of the night, we had guests for dinner who had stayed on and on.

Yasmine and I sneaked into the kitchen to find a cauldron of pilaff still warm, with a plate of chillies and salt waiting beside it. We decided to take a big mouthful of rice and a small bite of the chilli. I did not feel anything, no rush of blazing fever, just a little prickliness right before I swallowed my mound of rice. I took another mouthful of rice and this time a big bite from the smooth, green curved chilli in my hand. I had bitten a witch's finger. My mouth erupted with a prickly heat. Soon it was steaming. My mouth under a jug, while Yasmine poured water between fits of laughter. I too was laughing. I enjoyed the bittersweet taste of chillies.

During the season of mangoes, we buy them by the dozen in large wicker baskets lined with banana leaves. Yasmine loved eating mangoes. She inherited her love from our mother who also loves eating mangoes. Beads of sweat on the glistening skin, which Yasmine and my mother peel, undressing the flesh, moist, sweet and succulent. She tastes it gently with her tongue, and the sense overwhelms her, her fingers become tense and she bites deep into the flesh, its filmy juice leaving her lips to trace sinews down her chin and neck, sliding upwards from her fingers until she has devoured the whole thing. She is left with a shiny seed, its veins still swimming, her fingers sweet and sticky, her face dressed in its sauce. Yasmine and my mother love to eat mangoes.

When I was six I fought with my mother. She evicted me from her kitchen. I packed a small bag with oranges, two chapattis, my nightie, a jar of water, and colouring pencils. My courage took me to the end of the lane that led to our house. I sat on the grass and dropped my chin into my palms, soaking in self pity. The workers from the coffee fields came and went, each stopping to ask why I was there—they knew I was the Sahib's daughter. I announced that my mother had expelled me from her house. They smiled with jeering pity and advised me to return to be forgiven. For some reason they seemed sure that she would forgive me. And would I forgive her? Pride licking the dust on the ground. I feigned interest in those who gave me company. Nor was I interested in my oranges, chapattis and colours. I was interested instead in the injustice my mother had done me. This same woman who had lived in the hospital with me during the first year of my life actually had the nerve to kick me out of her kitchen. What a strange woman. Women are so much stranger than men.

My father drove into the lane. He gave me a lift on his lap. When we arrived at the house, he scoldingly pleaded for my amnesty. My mother conceded, without choice. But I wasn't allowed chocolate for one week. And so my skin became dull. Like drowned cocoa diluted with milk.

My mother used to make chips of potato and cassava. Yummy roots of the earth. They were cut into tiny squares, with toothpicks jutting out and standing at attention, like pagan prayers to Ishtar. I used to lift each toothpick and let the chip fall into my mouth.

When my father was away I had fevers that would subside as soon as his car entered the driveway. When I am ill my mother makes me chicken soup from chicken legs, necks and gizzards. She chops onions, ginger, garlic and sizzles them together. She cracks cardamom, cloves and cinnamon sticks into the pot. She crushes a tomato. Grinds whole black peppercorns and turmeric. Finally she pours in two cups of water and covers the pot to let it cook. When I have a cough she boils milk with saffron and turmeric. When my bones hurt she makes a paste of heated turmeric and salt. She covers me with it, sealing in the heat with thin cotton towels. She washes my face with lemon and honey, mixes henna with coffee and eggs to smooth over my hair. She cleanses my body of its hair, oils me with coconut. When I am with my mother, I glow. Espouse beauty, only to return to disease.

My mother has no money she can call her own, but she buys me trinkets of gold and silver. She finds saris, shawls, shalwars, pyjamas, kurtas, and qamises, in whatever colour I happen to be celebrating at that moment. In winter she gets warm socks and flannel nighties. For summer she gets flowery panties with matching brassieres, and she buys me dupattas and pachedis in which to drape my honour. Her favourite colour is pink.

When my mother smiles, her face lights up. It glows. This fire stays with me.

Ours was a gendered household. The boys and men functioned in the outer world. The women remained within the sanctity of home.

Every morning, my father left the house for business trips to Moshi, Arusha, Kisumu, wherever. He takes Sultan and Ahmed, my brothers, to be dropped off at school. Yasmine and I linger at the breakfast table with my mother and our ayah. All of us still in our nighties. The arrival of Mrs. Romeo, the tweed-wearing governess who comes to the house to instruct Yasmine and me in the English language, mathematics, and the virtues of European civilisation, is imminent. Betty bullies us into the bathroom to clean, groom and dress before her fastidious arrival.

I spent every waking and sleeping moment of my childhood with my sister Yasmine. We truly were one. There was no solid or dotted line where one ended and the other began. Her joy was mine and my pain hers. We combined earth, fire, water, air and ether to build our own universe. Together, we lived on this plane of consciousness, exploring it at our will. Half of me still lives there. My brothers I saw only socially. We never played or talked together. We talked about each other. Greeted and teased each other, but lived essentially as different creatures, in different worlds. During my childhood, I knew my brothers Sultan and Ahmed only from a distance.

Sabah, Sabah. It is Tanzanian Independence Day. We are winning the war against Idi Amin, the fanatical African nationalist, fascist, racist, genocide-inducing dictator of Uganda. Our soldiers have come home for the celebrations in Dar es Salaam. Ali has driven us to Moshi to celebrate at the community fettae carnival held outside the grounds of the Dar khana. Yasmine and I, Sultan and Ahmed, and their friends from the International School are running through the streets with ribbons and flags. I am five years old and Yasmine is seven. Ali joins, raising me unto one arm, and linking Yasmine's hand with the other. Vendors are selling roasted corn, cassava, plantain and peanuts on the street, with the optional salt, ground red chilli and lemon chutney seasonings. Barbecues are smoking with skewers of mishkaki kebabs. Ali buys Yasmine and me some plantain, and a mishkaki skewer each. His hobnobbing political and business friends from the community hover around us. We play games at the carnival. Sultan, with the aim of a marksman, wins a huge stuffed pink mouse at the darts booth. Yasmine and I name him Nickey, a variation of the Disney mouse, and split him between us as we saunter, each holding a paw. Ahmed has won a relay race, but scrapes his knee, giving Ghulshan an excuse to break into a tantrum directed at the boys for their roughness. A nurse from the Aga Khan Health Board treats both Ghulshan and Ahmed's knee. Ghulshan is pressured to play one of the games for adults. Men sit on straight-backed wooden chairs with hands tied behind their backs. Women who are not their respective wives, feed them from elegant and slim yet curvacious, red and white Coca- Cola bottles. The first couple to finish their bottle wins the game.

Yasmine and I play musical chairs, holding hands, causing me to be disqualified in the second round. I am upset, but open to solace. Ali takes me away and buys me some ice-cream so that Yasmine can finish her game. The ice-cream comes in half-cup sized plastic containers with a cardboard peel-off lid and makeshift wooden spoon. Yasmine comes second in musical chairs.

At seven o'clock, Ali drives us quickly back to the farm. We arrive within half an hour. We are not fed as no one could conceivably be hungry after the day's orgy of rich foods. Betty bathes Yasmine and me. She warms cocoa and milk for us. My mother comes, refreshed and elegant, ready to entertain the arriving company of friends and acquaintances following from Moshi whom Ali has invited. She stuffs us into our fresh cotton nighties and rubs our heads vigorously with a towel. She oils, combs and braids our hair. She sits with our heads in her lap for ten minutes, synthesising the lessons and quirks of the day, then commands us to sleep. Yasmine and I sleep with Nickey between us. I ask her why people must fly to London, and cannot simply drive.

"Because London is a cloud in the sky," she says.

When I was eight years old, Uncle Taqdeer died of a heart attack. It was December and the summer was at its zenith. But our evenings were cooled by Kilimanjaro breezes that descended from the mountain peaks, swished through the coffee plantations and fanned our courtyard. Uncle Taqdeer was sitting on the swing in the courtyard of the farmhouse chatting with his family, taking tea outside, in place of the evening meal. Although we farmed coffee, we were very much, in loyalty to Indian heritage, a tea-drinking family. My father could sip coffee and pontificate for hours but preferred milky, pot-brewed and delicately spiced tea at breakfast, lunch and dinner. Some of his sisters, especially Kulsum-Fui, drank coffee in the morning and after dinner but even they didn't give up four o'clock tea and bitings. Tea has always played a central role in the theatre of our family's conversations, gossip and memory.

Having sent Yasmine and me, the youngest children, off to bed, the family was sitting around in the courtyard. Uncle Taqdeer reclined with curly-haired Ahmed and his new jigsaw puzzle at his side, on the soft voluminous daybed that was also a swing. It faced Kilimanjaro in all its majesty and was a favourite spot among the family. There was usually a tussle to occupy it. However, Uncle Taqdeer was the oldest member of the family and everyone deferred to him. Ghulshan and Zeenat sat happily catching up on the day's gossip, on a long divan. Ali, cushioned in a rattan armchair with legs stretched and resting on a wide stool, sipped his sweet tea and munched on butter pound cake. Sultan lay on a wicker mat on the grass, biting on freshly sliced mangoes that he shared with his mother. A variety of deep fried masala treats and precious Cadbury's milk chocolate, smuggled in from Kenya, lay set out on a low glass table. Ghulshan was just reaching for some chevro when Uncle Taqdeer rolled off the swing and collapsed to the ground. Ali was the first to spring to his feet. He sprinted across the grass. Zeenat screamed and ran towards Ali. Ghulshan phoned the doctor. Ali and his elder brother Mustahfah, who also lived on the farm with his wife and three sons, carried Uncle Taqdeer inside and lay him down on the divan in the sitting room. Doctor Kumar arrived from Arusha within half an hour. But he was too late. Uncle Taqdeer had died within fifteen minutes.

By morning the house was full of people and Yasmine and I woke to the scent of myrrh burnt to fumigate the body, mingled with brewing tea and spicy aromas from the kitchen—the distinct smells of mourning. The house was like a zoo but sombre under the cloud of death. The furniture had already been removed from the sitting and dining rooms. The floors had been lined with mats, carpets and cushions and then covered with white sheets. What seemed like hundreds of men gathered in these rooms. They sat crossed-legged on the mats and cushions, sipped tea, ate goat-meat pilaff and consoled our family. The women had gathered in the kitchen and spilled out into the back yard, facing the plantations. They busily brewed tea, prepared pilaff, sliced chillies and wailed. No one paid attention to Yasmine and me. Still in my nightie, I ventured out of the kitchen into the sitting room to find my father sitting on the floor, under the window, his lips thin, his eyes red and drooping. I ran to him, making a place for myself in his wide lap. As I reached up towards his face I felt the wetness. It was the first time I saw my father cry.

WAR

Dr. Jitendra Kumar, our Hindu family doctor, was quite perplexed. Uncle Taqdeer was a healthy man, although already in his sixties. Dr. Kumar decided to conduct an autopsy. He won Ali's approval by repeatedly exclaiming his astonishment at the event. Dr. Kumar conducted the autopsy and kept his mouth shut until after the funeral and subsequent forty days of mourning. In the meantime he ensured that one of the servants, hired just last month, was relieved of his duties and sent to Arusha Police Station. At the end of forty days he telephoned the farmhouse and asked Ghulshan to send Ali to the clinic as he wanted to check his heart condition. Ghulshan spent fifteen days convincing Ali to pay a visit to the doctor. In the end it took Ali's sister Kulsum screaming hysterically into the telephone from Aga Khan Hospital in Nairobi to get Ali to the clinic. When Ali got there, he found that the doctor awaited him not with stethoscope and heart monitor but with news.

"Hello Khan Sahib. How are you? It is good of you to come. May I offer you a cup of tea?"

"Not unless it is necessary for the heart examination."

"Ha, ha. Come now. Take a seat. Have some tea. I want rather to talk to you than to examine your heart. Although I may examine your heart after we have finished."

Ali's curiosity is captured. Lighting a cigarette, he raises his eyebrows.

"Khanji, I have some unfortunate news. Your brother Taqdeer's death was extremely suspicious. It is very rare that a man in excellent health should have a heart attack and simply roll over and die. The autopsy confirmed my doubts. Your brother did not die of a heart attack. He was poisoned! What is more, the poison was intended for you." Ali bechara, bewildered poor thing, Allah have mercy upon him, not for the first time in his life, is utterly dumbfounded. Silence. An inch of ash dangles from his cigarette. His teacup remains suspended in midair. "I realise this must be a shock for you. It must even be difficult for you to believe, but I assure you it is true. I have even found the servant who was responsible for the poisoning. It seems some official from the military tipped him for the job. Khan Sahib, are you understanding me?" Ali who has been gazing listlessly at the tips of his shoes, lips parted in a stunned stupor, raises his head and meets the doctor's gaze. "Khanji, surely you are aware, the political climate in East Africa today is not favourable towards us Indians, particularly ones who own African land. But surely you know, after the fiasco of Idi Amin. Surely you know, the world is spinning. East Africa is falling apart. She is having a crisis of identity, one that far surpasses schizophrenia. She is hollering. Idi Amin is her voice. He resonates, imbuing Uganda and infiltrating her siblings. East Africa is black only. Non-blacks must be expelled. But where will we go? We have melted into the soil, sown our own seeds here and harvested the fruits, for decades now. Especially us Indians, we have become victims of the English and victimisers of the Africans. Many of us hoard amongst ourselves the prize fruits of East Africa.

"After 1972, when the Indians of Uganda were exiled, for almost a decade now one coup d'état after another has been exploding across East Africa. Tanzanian soldiers who went to fight Ugandan fascism were indoctrinated. They were literally infected by the disease of Idi Amin. They returned to threaten their rulers, whose power is drawn from sheer force of threat. What could they do without that threat? The soldiers want money and power, a retribution. Money rules the world, doesn't it? Land is money. Money is power. Seize it. Get it anyway you can. Nationalise. Redeem your humiliation. When you have it, do not share with your people, be they black, brown or white.

Keep it for yourself. Hoard, be avaricious. Greed is good. Deny your people. Rule and handcuff them. Keep them at sea. Protect your daggered luxury. Exploit authority. Do not ever let them see: you are human and just like them. Let them covet and die. Lock them in. And freedom. Freedom must be denied, to all of us alike. Oh and yes, the workers must be rewarded. Yes, the labourers must be fed, and housed, and pampered. What to do with the employers? Kill them. Destroy. Destruct. Purge, so that we can build again, new jobs for those same workers. But where will we go, we Indo-Africans? No longer Indian yet not African. Stranded between here and there, orphans of the sea, where will we go?

"The African people, they have never ruled themselves in this modern nation-state way. But we are living in a modern world. Newspapers, universities, schools, clubs, rallies, they are necessary, although accessible to only a handful. We are not Europeans. We were not raised to live like this. In carpeted homes, wearing socks and shoes, sitting in the air, perched on high seats. We, we are comfortable on the floor, in the earth, barefoot, legs crossed, Buddha-style. This is how we sit. Why then, try to fit a European mould of politics? Government and society. Create your own, do not follow.

"And now borders are shut, the doors closed between Tanzania, Kenya, Uganda and Zaire. We are locked in a violent embrace. Sooner or later, in the midst of this bitterness, war will rise. From this anger, violence will maim and destruct. Where is compassion, that old-fashioned word?

"Yes, some of us Indians are prosperous. We have our own news-paper, *The Samachar*, printed in both the Anglo vernacular and Gujarati. Our men wear James Bond-style safari suits and smoke Matinée and 555 filter-tipped cigarettes. They drive Ford Anglias and Peugeot 504s, even Mercedes Benzes. They gamble in the casinos of Nairobi and Dar es Salaam. The ladies dress up in the latest saris and sunglasses, modelling themselves after Bollywood starlets. We are always informed of news about the homeland. Our political discussions concern Ghandi and Nehru more than Nyerere and Kenyatta. Many daughters are sent to hostels, not in England, but in Pakistan and India, with high expectations to return engaged. But the homeland has changed. All the good families shunned our girls.

They have become East African, not Indian, nor Pakistani. They return to marry our own bachelors, boys they have known since five-year-old fluttering infancy. Yes, we Indians are racist. Which community is not? Bound by tradition, we have handcuffed ourselves to our own kind. Indian families, particularly wealthy, land-owning or otherwise visible in the greater communities have become targets of the Black Africa movement. The British, lords, returning still to ride through the Serengeti on white horses, are above repudiation, floating on the lofty glory of their deeds. And so the Indians bear the brunt of their colonial sins.

"Khan Sahib, you must leave. Do you understand? You must flee from this land. A fervour of soldiers has returned from General Idi Amin's Uganda. They are infecting the people. They are raiding homes and murdering men. Very few can ignore the sweeping momentum and oppose the soldiers or remain loyal to colleagues, employers, friends, lovers. It is dangerous for you here now.

"Especially for your family. Your family will be persecuted severely. A revenge for your successes. You have positions of power in your own communities, and also outside. You have inaugurated classrooms on the farm for the children of your workers and you pay for doctor's visits with your private capitalist money. All this they find suspect. There are rumours that you and your brothers smuggle monies of your community in and out of the country. You have entertained senior army and government officials. You and Taqdeer Sahib have bribed these officials to serve your own interests and those of your community. Do you remember the colonel who could not get his son out of prison for smuggling cocaine and diamonds out of Cape Town? He rang you, Khan Sahib, and pleaded for your help. The very next morning he found his son waiting for him on the veranda. These stories are being circulated. People are talking. Even your people from your own community. They are jealous. Your own people have betrayed you. You must leave, Khan Sahib. You must leave at once otherwise they will never let you go. They will come after you, they want to kill you."

Ali sat in Dr. Kumar's clinic until midnight, then he sped back to the farm. Dr. Kumar finished their open bottle of whisky and then shot himself in the head. Ali would later arrange for the safe journey of the doctor's wife and two daughters to London. He also sent Zeenat and her unmarried daughter Zarina off the farm into a high-security residence in Arusha. Mustafah left with his wife, his son Alnoor and two daughters Ayesha and Amina for London. They travelled with Mrs. Kumar and her daughters. But Ali would not leave, not yet.

Zeenat was furious. She had invited her neighbour, the portly, elderly Shirin Bai to tea and was spewing bitterly between sips. "That idiotic woman who was raised in a hut has taken over my farmhouse! How could it be? Allah how could you be so unkind, to rob me of my husband and my home? Just look at Zera and me! Living in a two-bedroom apartment like some working-class widow and orphan. How the hell am I going to find a suitable husband for Zarina, while living in a block of flats! How can one invite anyone decent for tea? When will I see Ali, my only living protector? That uncouth third-class chit of a girl who eats using four fingers has thrown the entire family off the farm and taken it over for herself. Watch her mother move into the house at any time now. Oh, I can't bear it to have been robbed of my home." Zeenat cried to Shirin Bai regularly. Shirin Bai's husband, an aged Nurmuhammad Bhai, told Zeenat a thing or two about the political climate of the time, in an effort to comfort her by explaining her expulsion from the farm as a practical precaution.

SOLDIERS

The first time the soldiers of the Tanzanian army came to the farmhouse everyone was at home. It was Sunday afternoon, a day designated by Nyerere to be a nation-wide petrol fast. Except for the military. The military and the government could run their vehicles at any time in any place. We were playing cards, and basking in sunlight, when Ghulshan swept the four of us inside our rooms, with strict orders not to budge.

The soldiers had come to search for banned foreign capitalist goods: bottles of scotch and caches of European or American currency. Everyone knew my father drank a bottle of Johnny Walker's every day. Every colonel in the military had imbibed this drink in our living room. So why had they come, these soldiers? My father, civilised still, invited them to search the house while Betty brewed pots of tea and my mother prepared bitings. Jerradi, the cook, took his holiday on Sundays.

The five soldiers wander around the house and into every room, looking, but not searching. They want us to feel their presence, that is all. One of them stops in front of Yasmine's and my room. He pauses and opens the door. We are sprawled on the bed with our drawing books, not speaking. My father comes up behind the soldier and stands very close to him. Ali shuts the door in the soldier's face and together they retreat into the sitting room. My father and the five men are seated. The one in charge sits next to father. Complimenting him on the house and land, he explains that it is just a routine search. Ghulshan serves them tea and bitings.

Several months later, my father disappeared for a month. Our mother nervously told us he was away on business. Yasmine didn't believe her. I was young and naive, believing Ali was godlike, and therefore invulnerable and infallible. I believed he was away on business as usual. Many years later, in Canada, I learned that my father used to smuggle the tithes of our Muslim community out of Tanzania to Europe. On the occasion of this month-long disappearance, he had been caught and detained. Every respectable man in East Africa knew that Ali took these funds through the closed borders. He also knew that Tanzanian socialist nationalism forbade the export of any monies out of the country, requiring that it be poured back into the soil from which it came.

"Someone from the community must have tipped off the border guards at Kisumu as to exactly when he would be where. You remember that white Mercedes Benz 220 from 1977 that he used when on safari? He used that car because it had a secret compartment in which he hid the money, a very large sum if I remember correctly. Anyway, they caught him and jailed him. For a month, they searched every nook of the car, without finding the money. Finally after various bribed government officials interfered, they released him, but not the car. For six months, they kept the car. When they returned it to

Ali, he found the secret chamber untouched, and delivered the monies in cash, back to the community, to be flown by plane, by that son of Mr. T, to Geneva. Neither the police, nor the Border Patrol, nor the military found your father's hiding place. You should be proud of him."

"But if everyone knew he was doing it, then why was Ali caught?"

A year later, when I was ten, they came again, the soldiers. It was Friday evening. Ghulshan and Ali had gone to Jamaat Khana in Moshi. Sultan and Ahmed were away on a weekend expedition with the mountain climbing club of the International School. They were climbing Kilimanjaro. Yasmine and I were at home with Betty. She heard the growling engine of a military lorry. Peeking out a window, she saw it snarl to a stop outside the house. She came screaming, "Run! Run! Zahra! Yasmine! Run!"

She chased us into the upstairs bathroom and locked us in. Yasmine and I, disorientated, shared the closed toilet seat, and listened in silence. First we heard a thundering knock on the front door. Then we heard it open and shut, four times. We heard hoarse loud voices, but not the words. This was followed by stamping footsteps, clamouring, banging, shouting and a then amidst all of the gurgling commotion a high-pitched shout pierced through the house into our hearts. Finally there were two or three loud, resounding gunshots, and then silence. Yasmine and I sat motionless. We heard the front door shut. The lorry started, and pulled away. Neither of us rose to try and unlock the door.

About two hours later Ghulshan and Ali came home to find a rampaged house and Betty lying naked in a pool of her own blood. We, their daughters called to them with wavering voices from behind a locked door, in the bathroom.

Months later, after several Indian businessmen and their families had been robbed, tortured and murdered, Ali received a threat. Leave East Africa. Leave now: alive. He fled. He left his wife and children on the farm, and he disappeared. Ali was gone.

I was sleeping on the sofa in the morning room, Yasmine and I had just finished our lessons with Mrs. Romeo. I had just failed English for the fourth time. Sultan and Ahmed were on holiday from school. Sultan had gone to Arusha to see Zeenat and her daughter in my father's capacity. Cheerful Yasmine, having passed English, was outside playing marbles with Ahmed. Our mother was preparing lunch in the kitchen with Jerradi.

I was jarred awake by a loud burst, and the room began to tremble. Chairs and tables, the sofa, and the jingling chandelier were shaking. I awoke as in a dream, and walked to the kitchen. Mummy was hollering with terror. Her eyes like ice. Twitching, she pulled me towards her, changed her mind and pushed me towards Jerradi. Behind her through the kitchen window, the farm was ablaze. A scattering of workers from the farm were running, screaming, in every direction calling "Mama! Mama!" They clutched themselves and their children. Ghulshan commanded Jerradi to get into the Land Rover and drive me to Zeenat's home in Arusha. Jerradi did not argue, nor object. He swiftly pulled me off my feet, threw me into the back of the jeep, simultaneously opening the front door and starting the car. We took off at the speed of thunder, with clouds of enraged, dry sand spinning in front and behind the car. I began to scream for him to wait, for Yasmine, Ahmed and my mother. Please, at least for Yasmine. But he behaved as if deaf and mute. Ignoring me completely.

Sultan was standing outside the compound with Zeenat, both of them perplexed, anxious, waiting. I was ripped from the car, Sultan got in and Jerradi drove back to the farm. Zeenat's youngest daughter Zarina took me into the flat and straight to the bedroom. I tried to tell her a million things. But she didn't listen. For my own good she held my head back and popped a Valium into my mouth, handing me a glass of water and commanding me to swallow. She knew already. Ghulshan had telephoned.

I awoke with a desire to see Yasmine. Dazed, I stumbled into the kitchen expecting to find a family scene: my mother, Sultan, Ahmed, Yasmine, Zeenat and Zarina. Zubaida, Zabeen and Mustahfah's family missing because they were in London. And Ali missing. But the kitchen was empty. So was the entire apartment. Isa, Zeenat's houseboy, emerged from the back room with his wife Mariam. She prepared some food for me, bathed me and tucked me back to sleep, in silence. The next morning, I found Ghulshan, Sultan,

Zeenat and Zera in the kitchen. Where were Yasmine and Ahmed? Yasmine? I missed her, and I missed Betty too, and Ali my father. I didn't ask. No one told me. I interpreted their silence. Yasmine had left, and taken Ahmed for company. My blood, throbbing in my veins, told me. My mother's dim, swollen, senseless eyes, her ragged hair, and proud Sultan's meek movements told me. I thought perhaps Ali, too, was dead.

Three days later, we returned to fragments of the farm. Amidst the debris, we prepared lunch, set the table and left East Africa out the imaginary back door.

KILIMANJARO

Get out! Who asked you in here? Get out! Out of my sight. I do not want to see you. This is my life, not yours. And you are not welcome. You cannot possess me. I am an illusion. History's bastard. I am East Africa.

I left Africa, at twelve years of age. My father left Africa without his spirit. It is buried on the foothills of Kilimanjaro, at the border of Kenya and Tanzania. My father's spirit tasted like cocoa-coffee: soft, strong, round, warm, bittersweet and with an unmistakable aroma. It is the colour of the earth. My father was in love with Kilimanjaro, and I know she misses his affections.

> *Killie man jau rahou*
> where are you?
> In Black Africa
> White Peaks
> And Brown Murders
> I still love you
> *Oh killie man jau rahou*

My skin is the colour of red earth: scarlet and brown. In England they only see the brown. So I prick my thumbs to show my scarlet. We see their red in the pinkness of white. No need to prick.

In Africa, among the foothills of Mount Kilimanjaro, teary-eyed elephants glide across the grassy plains of the Serengeti. Hips swaying, billowing ears flow with sensuous trunk in unison. Families migrate, led by mother matriarch. They follow the bond of blood. Calves suckling, learning their own pace but always following. Mother, goddess, queen leading the way. Bringing life, nourishing it and then sheltering until the males leave to battle strength and explore bravado. Only to return. To mate. Regenerate. And the females. They shelter the young who graze amidst them. Obeying their mistress.

A herd of elephants cascading across the Serengeti. Horizon shifts from clear-eyed sapphire to rolling emerald hills and scorched parchment in summer when the rains are absent. A herd of elephants seeking fertility: livelihood. The young feeding at mother's breast, devouring her dung while she seeks nourishment. Amber blaze at dusk, a dynastic trail shifting across the plains, tassels on a tapestry governed by Kilimanjaro and her soldiers, the baobab tree which stands erect, piercing the crimson jewel. A sun from which Burmese rubies turn in shame.

We left Africa amidst torrents of rain. The earth was weeping with us. Opening her wounds so that we could bury ours inside them. Cities, towns, villages, camps and farms, all were drowning. Kilimanjaro shedding her ice to cool the earth's passion.

I remember sitting in the car, watching the river of rain splashing against the window. I didn't understand why we were leaving Africa with our skirts drenched in her tears.

I cannot remember my mother at this time. I know she was totally distracted. Nor do I remember my brother. He was overwhelmed. I remember my dress. It fell to the floor coloured yellow and black. The bodice was yellow with a black string that laced up across my budding chest and the skirt was full, long and black with a border of yellow lotuses. I wore black sandals with a silver buckle. My cardigan was yellow, patterned with black flowers. I still had my tavit then. Around my neck, hanging on a red and green string. Red for passion and green for peace just like our veins.

I had not seen my father for sixteen months. I thought he had died. But I was wrong, he hadn't been killed only exiled. He was in London. Imagine my surprise at Heathrow when I encountered a man with a waning spirit and my father's features. I embraced him all the same.

We spent an eternity behind the immigration counter. My mother spoke and Sultan helped her. We were asked to take a seat behind the counter. We were shuffled to the refugee office. Then we were returned to the waiting room and told to board the next plane to Dar es Salaam. At that moment my mother burst into tears and someone took pity. Someone else allowed my cousin Alnoor to come through the gates and see us. Ali was waiting behind him. We were granted a three-day visa to London, our dying imperial capital. After an interval of five hundred and fifty-four days, Ghulshan embraced Ali.

YASMINE AND AHMED

Sometimes I dream. I dream of the footsteps of angels who have hovered around me since my traumatic entrance into the world. Sometimes they leave and I miss their chatter, our secrets. I miss their white light. But they always return and I embrace their figureless forms. I am always afraid that one day they will leave me forever. When I dream, they bring me the sound of the sea, enraging the wind and then kissing her cheeks. The wind whistles, winding, mourning, and I brood with her. Yasmine comes alive in these dreams. She is the colour of the sky when damasked by the sun. Her pupils glittering like the moon. Sister moon, come and lay upon us your soft kiss, we have not forgotten. When I dream, I dream of iridescent laughter discoing across my face. I laugh on the streets becoming that madness for which the music plays, forgetting my own name, Zahra. When I dream, the colour is silver, violet and blue, all together. When Yasmine smiles it becomes pink and when she dies I see her scarlet.

Yasmine, are you dreaming with me? I asked the angels to bring you.

Whenever Fate has beckoned me with her forefinger I have followed. Every time I turn around, fall asleep or become numb with hunger, when madness settles in and I sleep, she comes and she wakes me. Sometimes she is gentle. She caresses my face, draws a line from the nose out towards the eyebrows, around my temples and down. She brings me water to drink and it tastes of roses, she kisses and holds me. I take her hand and we dance now and again. At other times, she slaps my face with her cold hard hands. I weep, hating her, wishing I were never born. Crawling on my hands and knees, in tethered rags, my face bleeding with disease I follow her, becoming accustomed to my own ugliness and hers. Eventually the sun shines among our morose catacombs and we awake like mummies to partake of the rituals from which we find life. And we resurrect ourselves from a million deaths. Only to die again. When she beckons I always follow.

Yasmine and Ahmed were killed on the coffee farm with ammunition left behind by the military during the Tanzanian civil war. The war was a coup staged by soldiers who had returned from Uganda enflamed by Idi Amin, the very man they went to fight. Newspaper clippings, when divulging reports of this "civil revolt", speak of the "fervour" of nationalism and the "brutality" of war. What they forget to mention is that war lives forever. Its violence once executed, is indelible. It raises you from the deep recesses of sleep and delirium with terror. It interrupts you in the midst of lovemaking. It leaves you speechless at the altar. It tattoos your memory. My four paternal uncles were killed, one by one. Mustafah eventually died in London, of grief. My father was exiled. The farm was consumed by fire. Our lands were nationalised. My mother was raped of her senses. My brother was slapped into adulthood. I was left numb, drugged and ignored. Ignore | ig 'na : | v.t. refuse to take notice of. How loud can you scream? Can you scream loud enough that these walls built by cowardice in front of your eyes shall crumble?

Ghulshan and Ali never recovered from the deaths of their children. Death is resurrection and immortality. Sultan and I, we are the survivors. How will we survive? Yasmine would have lived graciously, elegant as the khatak dancer, enshrined, protected from the world. Delicate creature, resisting the lures of conformity, with her grace. Ahmed would have photographed: documenting the world with his contorted eye. But Sultan and I, what will we to do?

LONDON

I became reacquainted with my brother during those early grey days in London. We had no choice but to wander together, through narrow streets, drowning in tears and rain. Sometimes we laughed, even. Giggling with apprehension, I would convulse with hiccups. We survived separately, locked within the unity of our blood. During those years Sultan was my lifeline. My brother was the strength that pushed me out of my cocoon, into the world. His voice resounded in my ear as I faced death, slum, denunciation, rage, poverty. His eyes shone like Ghulshan's as I walked proud, my head held high as the moon, surviving, succeeding, striving and always returning home, to our tragedy. Sultan survived privately. I would trip with excitement as I telephoned him at university, describing my adventures. Filling books with my drawings, writing and photographs to send to him. Did he read them? I wonder. A distraction. Eldest son, prince of the family, carrier of Ali's name, he would live up to his burden, restoring the fortune that Ali had lost in East Africa.

Our mother never grew accustomed to the escalators in London. How often at the end of a staircase, we would glance around and find her at the top of the stairs, leaning on the railing in terrified confusion but still smiling at us.

When I was a child, I was afraid of two things. Geckos—the pale yellowish-pink salamanders that live in moisture and crawl on the walls. If you cut them in half, the halves run in opposite directions. And the rain. Now I live in London.

In London, there was the community. Immigrants gathered from India, Pakistan, Uganda, Kenya, Zaire and Tanzania. I could have found refuge among their daughters, but I wanted to be alone with my dreams. Ghulshan and Ali, sometimes reluctantly, socialised with them. They were never appropriately frivolous. We did not fit, tainted by Zahra's blood. They lived in oblivion. I chose to find my own way. While my parents watched films from Bollywood to forget both Africa and this new land, I found my inspiration in the 1980s zeitgeist of new-wave pop. *I made a break, I ran out yesterday, tried to find my mountain hideaway, maybe next year, maybe no-go.* I stumbled across music, and found myself intrigued by the sound of cameras clicking. It helped to drown the sounds of gurgling machine guns and screeching pain. *My face in the mirror shows a break in time, a crack in the ocean which does not align.* It helped me to accept my own weirdness in this new world. It became my transition from Africa to England. One with full visual detail of what was culturally appropriate. I watched music videos and learned how to dress, speak, behave, smoke a cigarette. Clearly the rest of the world was just as weird as I was. Maybe I took this music too seriously. Music has always been serious for me. I never wanted to marry the rock band, I wanted to spread their message. I was fourteen, this was my new religion.

Much to my mother's humorous horror, she sat with me in the evenings, by the record player, in front of the television screen, while I translated lyrics for her. She thought some of them were handsome, these Angrezi men. Such a shame they were kafirs. It came as a shock to me, that women and colour were a minority in my burgeoning record collection. These moments with my mother, while we fought to become citizens instead of refugees, are among my happiest memories of those times.

My father, of course, was tolerant. He knew that all women, especially my mother and I, began to rave in difficult times. His tabla, santur and sitar accompanied ghazals, and qawalis took their natural precedence. All was well until one day I found the gall to suggest that the voice of David Bowie was as painfully sweet, as wide in its range as that of Mahedi Hassan. We were driving to Wembley on a Sunday to buy rashan from a grocery shop owned by an East African Swahili-speaking Gujarati Hindu. Yes, we were driving to him, so that my mother could cook her pilaffs, biryanis and saks. My father stopped the car, my heart stopped beating, scarlet blood was rock-still. He stopped the cassette through which Mahedi was plucking our heart strings. He turned around to face me. How does one translate my father's poetic elegance when he quotes Muhammad Iqbal to me? His swimming pupils, the gestures with which he puts ballerinas to shame?

I learned to live alone. Ghulshan and Ali were entrenched in their own catharsis; Sultan was at university. I hid the past under lock and key. I was ashamed. I felt betrayed by God. I could not face the truth. Again and again, I lied. By lying, I could be sane, normal. I dreaded questions about my family—where we came from, how, when, why? I answered with lies, building an edifice between me and the world, a castle to shelter my tragedy. I knew I was sinning but I preferred repenting for my sins to revealing a truth that lurked between dishonesty and tragedy.

We eat cereals for breakfast. My mother eats toast with butter and jam. When I go home she makes yellow "Uganda" toast in the oven. She buys sweet bread from the Portuguese bakery and adds fennel seeds. I love to spread butter over yellow toast and dip it in my sweet tea. We used to eat fried eggs, with the yolk yellow and runny, Heinz baked beans in tomato sauce, lamb sausages, toast and cups of hot tea. For a while we tried English muffins with honey and cheese, we called them crumpets. Sometimes my mother bakes yellow pound cake with orange and lemon rind, and my father eats this for breakfast every day until it is finished. On Sundays we rise late. I stumble into the kitchen to find my mother already there. I pretend to help her to roll and fry her parathas or make omelets with onion, tomatoes, coriander, green chillies and cumin. Actually, I just make the tea. The tea must have cinnamon, clove and cardamom. It must be piping hot with a teaspoon of sugar in the pot for colour. Ali appears after his one-hour shower and shave, wrapped in his perennial brown silk robe with loud red roses splashed in the style of 70s disco heyday. My brother, still half asleep after Saturday night's exhaustion, joins us for a hearty breakfast.

In Africa we used to wake up to the smell of coffee and the cocoa harvest. The sun would slide around Kilimanjaro and slip into my bedroom, inviting me to partake of his golden day. A new-born day. We were lovers, the sun and I. Kilimanjaro watched over us, protecting me from his burning passion. Little did she know I wanted to burn.

We ate fresh hot chapattis straight from the griddle, dipped in mango and papaya pulp. With murba, a jam. Sometimes we also ate eggs or pound cake with orange and lemon rind. In the later years we had corn flakes covered with sugar and hot milk. I never liked corn flakes. The smell of boiling milk makes my stomach churn.

In Africa, my mother used to boil potatoes and dress them with lemon, salt and red chilli pepper. She used to pack these for my brothers' lunch at the International School. My mother used to eat the heads of barbecued fish, covered in aubergine and tomato masala, with millet rotlas. Leftovers from last night's dinner. Actually we never ate dinner. We ate lunch. We slept. Then we had tea. At night, we had late bitings. Samosas, crispy bhajias. Dumplings made of chickpea flour batter, coriander, potatoes, cauliflower and corn seeds. Dhalvadas: pigeon-pea dumplings in yoghurt raitha. Pakoras: more dumplings. Chevro: a homemade version of the Bombay mix with dried lentils and beans. Cassava and plantain crisps. Chanabateta: chickpea, potato and tomato warm soupy-salad. Unde-vale toast: bread dipped in seasoned and spiced egg mix, then pan-fried. Toasted kheema sandwiches. Potatoes fried in cumin. And we drank spicy, stove-top-brewed masala tea.

Sunday mornings we sit with our cups of tea and watch the "Sounds of Asia" on the multicultural channel, while our father smokes his cigarettes. Sometimes, after eating, my mother, my brother and I linger at the table. Our mother cajoles us with her jokes and we cry with laughter. Our father announces that he has had the fortune to live in a madhouse. Once in a while he enters the kitchen, rummages in the fridge to find some of his Lindt Swiss chocolate. Uttering some witticism, he leaves the room, chocolate in hand. We erupt in laughter once again. Teasing him. He returns to his smoking chair, pretending not to care. I have a peak, to see him grinning from ear to ear, sucking on a piece of his beloved chocolate. I pretend not to notice. But I can't help smiling.

I remember learning how to cook in my mother's kitchen in East Africa. Yasmine and I were shuffled into the large room overlooking the courtyard that faced Kilimanjaro. When the screens over the wide windows had been left open, long, thin, poisonous green snakes might come flying into the kitchen. The snakes slithered down the foothills through pregnant masses of chocolate earth and minty cocoa plants and up into the branches of the baobab tree that hung low outside our kitchen window. When this happened our mother would experience a momentary lapse of control, and begin to shriek. Jerradi and Juma the gardener would come running in and sweep the snake outdoors. Juma would then magically clothe the snake in a gunny sack and deposit it back in the foothills. I have always wondered if the same snake came back. Yasmine and I used to call him Sir-Up.

One day Sir-Up came on Sunday when Juma and Jerradi were on leave and Ali was out of town. He flew onto the wooden counter via the kitchen window. Our brother cut him in half with a hatchet. When Juma returned he buried him in the garden under the baobab tree. A few days later another long, thin, poisonous green snake came and hung off the branches of the baobab tree. Juma said that she was the dead snake's wife. We called her Lady-Up. When Ahmed and Yasmine's corpses were found in the foothills, amid scorched cocoa plants, Lady-Up was coiled around their ankles, dead.

By ten o'clock on the morning of Navroz of my seventh year, the kitchen is already populated with half a dozen women. Three of my father's six sisters, Ghulshan and Kulsum and Fatimah, the kitchen help, are bustling. The heart and stomach of our household has always been its kitchen. We are preparing a feast for Navroz, to be served to the family after we return from evening prayers. We begin by peeling and chopping onions. Yasmine cuts a rim off the dome and crown of the onion, slices half way into the centre and passes it to me to peel. I peel and pass to Fatimah-Fui who cups the naked onion in her left hand. With her right hand she strikes horizontal and vertical gashes while rotating so that the flesh becomes a juicy cubic grid of onion flesh. Then she slices rings that disintegrate into shredded onion. Yasmine and I separate cloves of garlic from their flowers and peel them. Jerradi grinds them with pestle and mortar. We soak the coriander and mint in water and pick each leaf from its stem. I am given the coriander and Yasmine the mint. We soak almonds, cashews and pistachios in bowls of water. When they are softened, we caress them, allowing the skins to slip through our fingers. Ghulshan spreads them on a mat in the courtyard. Under the sun, they dry and become crisp. At this point, I decide I need to rest. Fatimah-Fui rolls out a straw mat. She sits on it and allows me to put my head in her lap as she sifts through a large, round, stainless-steel bowl of long-grain rice, picking out the stones.

Everyone is chatting. Laughter and apprehension abide. Spices pop. Onions sizzle. Garlic is crushed. The pestle grinds. Meats are grilled. Chicken oozes. Sauces boil and bubble. Knives thunder falling into a rhythm. Hands slap together. Vegetables burst with crispness. Sev slides around. Water runs, cleans, soaks and cooks. Mummy shouts periodically. Yasmine crashes into some pots and gets told off. Amidst this symphony, I fall asleep.

Betty wakes me. Time to bathe and dress for evening prayers. I am excited because I have a new garara to wear.

The first time our mother cooked was in my father's house. The spoon got stuck in the khadhi and Ali threw the whole lot out the window.

Now her food is mouth-watering. Her children dream of her flavours. I have learned to cook from years of apprenticeship in her kitchens. She has no order and no recipes. No discipline. No routine, but she has total control of her kitchen. She cooks with love sizzling in the flames. Sometimes my food tastes like hers. Sometimes it doesn't.

Thai
Africa

Finally, the people of the Swahili Coast raged. They screamed and stormed for Independence. This time, they screamed in the language of the European. A language that he understood. But, they, the people of the Swahili Coast, had changed forever. Foreignness had infiltrated them. It had become one of them. The Swahilis were diluted, no longer just African, but also Arab, Indian and European. Europe was weak. Still recovering from the ravages of the Second World War. Like aging parents, they could no longer sustain the colonies of their children. The children were clamouring to be free. Thus, freedom was granted.

India was dissected to create Pakistan. A land for the Muslims of the subcontinent. But more Muslims live in India than in Pakistan. Tanganyika set the East African example in 1961. The Gregorian calendar had become universal. Uganda followed in 1962, and lastly, Kenya, the Queen's favourite, was released in 1964.

But who, what were these nations? How would they rule the diverse branches of their people? From where did their power come? Who legitimised it? What was Africa? Whose? Who were the Africans? Who were not?

KUNDUCHI BEACH

I am losing my mind, sitting in the kitchen with my mother and Mrs. Karmali, planning a day trip to Kunduchi Beach tomorrow. Haven of childhood holidays, at Kunduchi my father took me out to sea in a dingy dhow, threw me into the water, and made a bed of his arms for me to lie on. I learnt to float in this way, amidst sibling taunts—a whirlwind of teasing menace whipped up by Sultan, Ahmed and Yasmine. My siblings, already mobile by virtue of expert lessons at the Kenya Safari Health Club, surrounded me while I propelled my limbs into a swimming motion, assisted by my father. I am the youngest child. My father missed three childhoods, and became committed to mine. But then came persecution, exile and migration, and my childhood too was lost. I did not take swimming lessons at the Kenya Safari Health Club. My father taught me how to swim.

From his seat on the veranda, he is emitting a running commentary.

I am amazed at my mother's patience. I would have erupted into a tantrum by now, but Ghulshan remains calm to the unknowing eye. We have changed the menu three times and the car seating-plan remains unresolved. It is half-past six, at the juncture between afternoon and evening. The sun has changed his colour: ripened from lemony oranges to saffroned pomegranates. How delicious, flirting seeds with promise of crimson juice. There are fourteen people to accommodate, including three elderlies. Breakfast will be here, at our rented cottage, at six in the morning, mother's responsibility: white flour puria, vitumbas, masala fried eggs and omelets stained green with leely chutney, papayas, bananas and mangoes, homemade yoghurt, tea and coffee. Lunch at one in the afternoon is scheduled to take place on the mainland. We are not going on excursion to Arusha, no. Return home but not to the scene of the crime. Everyone has serendipitously decided to steer clear of

Arusha and Moshi. Instead, our cautious foray into Tanzania will
be limited to the coast. We shall spend a day on the shores of Dar es
Salaam and return at night to sleep safely in Zanzibar. But what to
eat for lunch? What to serve the elderlies: chanabetata and chevro
or chat, sandwiches or salads, crisps or chips, juices or sodas, teas or
coffee, fruit or pound cake? One of each, of course.

The lawyer, his wife and her parents are joining Ghulshan, Ali,
Mr. and Mrs. Khan, her parents and spinster sister and me for the
outing.

Six a.m. I am frying white puria in the kitchen. My face is covered
in a thin layer of shiny grease. Mrs. Zamakhshari arrives dressed
from head to toe in skin-tight denim and gold. Her husband, unfortunately, will not be joining us. The others have joined Ali on the
veranda. Breakfast table is waiting for hot, moist puria. Ghulshan is
watching my face. Look me in the shining eye, mother dear. Then
you will know what I know. And how will you hold your rage? You
know already don't you? I have to run and wash my face in time to
join Ghulshan and Ali and their friends for breakfast.

The sun has risen. I am about to confront. The sun is going to
burn us.

I am walking along the shores of Kunduchi Beach with my father. I
have hooked my arm into his elbow. We walk slowly, my head resting
on his shoulder. He is looking to the sea. I remind him of the time
he taught me to swim. He smiles, his eyes shining as he remembers
with me. The sea is whispering to us. I want to tell him about last
night. I want to confront him with his mother. But I cannot. I cannot
pluck the scabs from those ageing wounds. So we walk in silence.
Listening to the sea.

Some children play with a ball in the water. The ball escapes
and Ali catches it. He teases the children with the ball. Ali is laughing.
Really laughing. The children whirl in circles around him, spraying
him with water. I have not seen him laugh like this for fifteen years,
his face golden under the sun. My heart bleeds. Ali throws the ball
to me. I catch it and run into the sea, a trail of children behind me.
I turn around and throw it back to Ali on the shore. He catches it
and gives it to the tiniest girl among them who cannot yet run, as I

could not run when I was tiny like her. We wave goodbye and leave the shore, walking to join the others. They sit drinking tea on a cotton rug under a tree. Ghulshan, who is sharing a joke with Mrs. Karmali's mother, looks up at us. Her eyes caress Ali's face. They have returned from a stroll amidst the stalls and shops that now populate the beach. He is still laughing. Mrs. Karmali teases Ali about his youthful outburst, how much energy it must have consumed. "Come, sit, have a glass of tea." We have decided to stay here and have barbecued kingfish and ugali for lunch. Long one of my father's favourite meals, Ghulshan prepares it still, even in Canada.

I cannot face his wife, Mrs. Zamakhshari. I cannot meet her gaze. She is flirting with Amir Uncle, much to the dismay of Mrs. Karmali. I sit at Ghulshan's side, fully aware that eventually I will place my head in her lap, as a grown child should not do. After lunch, I leave the others and take refuge in a lonely stroll.

Three little girls are sitting on the grass. They smile. Told about the girl in the tower, they are happy. Can I be happy? I *am* the girl in the tower. For now it is okay.

When we return to Zanzibar, I telephone him. His wife is with Ghulshan and Ali in Mr. and Mrs. Khan's courtyard. I tell him I want to see the papers concerning the house.

At midnight I slip out of the cottage into his car. Ghulshan and Ali will leave Zanzibar day after tomorrow. I wear a cotton sundress with straps that slip over the shoulders and across the back. He gives me his jacket to wear and takes me to a bar that is smoky and full of men. We sit in a corner, at the back. I want to ask him why he didn't come to Kunduchi but I don't. Instead, I ask about the papers. The barman comes to the table. Hussein orders two drinks and tells him we do not want to be interrupted. "If you still want the house, you have to get an assessment of the market value and buy it from her. The government's evaluation is 125 million shillings or $200,000 U.S. The house is valuable because Stone Town has been declared a historic site. Can you get a loan from your bank in London?"

"Yes. Maybe. I don't have much credit." First, I have to confront Ghulshan and Ali. Then I have to telephone Auntie Zeenat at her daughter Zubaida's house in London, and convince her to sell a house I'm not sure she knows is hers.

Hussein pulls out a manila envelope. I open it and sift through the documents. The last one is dated November 10, 1982. It is written in English and Swahili. The said house is transferred to the name of Mrs. Zeenat Khan. At the bottom of the page is her signature, under it, my father's name signed in his sprawling script. My stupid hands are shaking. He is looking at my stunned face. I want to melt into nothingness. Instead, I gulp my drink and rage. Weakness impairs my fingers.

HUSSEIN

The retired Abdel-Aziz Zamakhshari had been alarmed upon learning from his former secretary, who is now his son Hussein's secretary, that his son was digging his handsome nose into the case of Ali Khan's house, on the once-upon-a-time imperial estates of the Busaidi Sultanate. The case had become notorious in Zanzibari real estate circles. How do you explain an Indian from Arusha inheriting property on the imperial lands of an Omani Sultanate, and that from an elderly Egyptian woman? A property that would remain untouched for over two decades, only to be signed over to an even more mysterious Mrs. Khan, apparently not the wife of said Mr. Khan, and then let to the Ministry of Interior. Abdel-Aziz Zamakshari had been the one to supervise the hush-hush transfer of property from one Khan to another in a closed waiting room at the international airport. It had taken years for the malicious flames of gossip to die. And now, over a decade later, why was Hussein disturbing sleeping graves? He decided to question his son at dinner that evening. But, alas, Hussein came to his father first.

"Father, I wanted to ask you about an old case of yours. It was one of your last ones, just before you retired."

Abdel-Aziz decided to feign ignorance. "Which one, son? You know my memory is not what it used to be."

"That rather famous one, you know, about Indian land on Arab property."

"Oh yes. That one is hard to forget. What about it?"

"Well I was just wondering, did you ever find out exactly what was behind the whole affair?"

"There was nothing to find out really. Lutfia Sultan, whose father Ahmed Sultan I had known in my youth, and who is my cousin, wrote to me from Alexandria just before she died. She asked me to transfer the family property into the name of a Mr. Ali Khan from Tanzania, and I did so. It took ages to actually find Mr. Khan but after a year, we managed to locate him. I wrote to him personally, informing him of his inheritance as it were."

"What do mean, inheritance?"

"Oh, it's a long story son, most of it speculation. Why do you ask?"

"I suppose I'm curious, that's all."

"From where this sudden curiosity?"

Hussein looks at his father for a rather long minute, shuts the door behind him, sits down and prepares to confess. "Well you see, this Mr. Ali Khan, it seems that he is in town and he has with him a daughter who is curious about the house. I don't know why she just doesn't ask her father straight out, but she won't. Maybe he hasn't got any answers to give her. Anyway, she came to see me. I recognised the case immediately. I thought you might know something. Like who this Mrs. Z. Khan is for example?"

The expression on Abdel-Aziz's face is changing. He had no idea Mr. Ali Khan was in Zanzibar. What the hell is he doing in Tanzania?

"How did she find you?"

"What?"

"How did she find you? This daughter, what is her name?"

"Zahra. I don't know."

"Zahra, yeah Allah, Zahra. That was Lutfia's sister name! I knew Ali Khan was her son! It's the only logical explanation. Of course."

"Papa, what are you talking about?"

"It's quite a story, my son. Let me tell you."

ZEENAT

Zeenat was born into a somewhat comfortable Indian family living in Tanganyika. The family had acquired wealth and perhaps some honour. However, the honour was tainted by the blood of the caste of their forefathers, who were remembered as harijans.

Zeenat was a social climber, raised for the sole purpose of catching a good husband. Her daughters grew up to be clones of their mother. They were brought up with the utmost emphasis upon public behaviour and superficial grace: figure, length, width and proportions. Seasonal clothing requirements, both eastern and western. Jewellery: cut, weight and worth. Shoes, handbags, cosmetics and the art of their most flattering as well as seductive application. Nail and hair length, shape, colour and upkeep. Removal of excess body hair, upkeep of skin texture, tautness and flexibility.

The eldest daughter, Zoraine, born Zubaida, married a wealthy unaristocratic and therefore honourless Englishman. They spent fifteen years trying to establish a reputation in all the right circles until tragically separated after vicious rumours of his spicy love affairs with the same sex. They have not yet divorced. The second daughter, Zureya, born Zabeen, married a pauper who then became wealthy via his brother's underground smuggling operation and unfortunately turned to women and wine. After ten years of marriage, his mistresses began to live with them, and Zureya's children prefer them to her. They also have not yet divorced. The third daughter, Zera, born Zarina, shocked everyone by marrying an African—a beautiful, noble, intelligent, Kikuyu man with whom she lives in Kenya. Her mother disowned her, but she lives happily with her husband and children at a holiday resort that they manage in Mombasa.

Zeenat's husband Taqdeer as a boy was once at death's door. During moments of feverish lucid consciousness, he heard his mother speak her heart in a foreign tongue. He rallied, at his mother's behest, to seize life again. Tadqeer was an extremely rigid man who believed in ascetic discipline, but he had also inherited some of Zahra's scarlet passion. He often sought comfort away from his wife. He was preoccupied with terribly noteworthy business or community matters, consequently when Zeenat had a problem she had to turn to Ali. This was particularly true of the early years before Ali married, when he lived at the farm with them. So it was that when Zeenat had a problem with her finances, the milkman, the butcher, the gardener, her in-laws, or the wagging tongues of the town's women, she would call upon Ali. Her daughters learned from her, and also turned to him when distressed. This was even more of a habit after Ali's marriage as it brought an excuse to visit Ghulshan's private home on the farm grounds, and meddle in her affairs. Zeenat would pop up unannounced in Ghulshan's rooms during one of Ali's absences, and feign surprise that he was away. She would proceed to repeat the horrible gossip she had heard in Jamaat Khana last night. The women were saying that Ali doesn't spend time at home with his family anymore, must be seeking his rest elsewhere, no? Tch tch. "I only just came to see how you are, but now that he is not here, I must say I am a little bit worried. But don't you fret, I will find out everything for you. Aren't you going to offer me some tea? And fry up some of your delicious bhajias in the kitchen?"

Zeenat hated Ghulshan, the new lakshmi of the household. When Ghulshan was cooking, Zeenat would sneak extra handfuls of salt and chilli into the food. She hated the fact that Ghulshan's husband loved her. It reminded her that her husband did not love her. She told lies to Ali about Ghulshan. And she took every occasion to remind Ghulshan of her humble origins, and of her extreme good fortune in finding herself now a member of a land-owning and notable family. For Vilayat Khan had become prominent, partially due to his wife's fame. While Zeenat hated Ghulshan, she envied her sons. She resented that the heir to her husband's name had been born of Ghulshan's womb and Ali's love. And Zeenat hated Ghulshan because Zeenat loved Ali.

So it was that every Eid, Navroz and Kushali, gifts of clothing, sweets, garlands, money and toys would arrive for Ali and his sons, but not for Ghulshan and their daughters. They were regularly tormented by eyes, tongues and curses for the crime of usurping the attentions of Ali, father and husband.

Taqdeer was lost in his own lofty world and managed to be oblivious to the snakery between the two sisters-in-law. Rosy, sweet Ghulshan did not have the venom to match Zeenat's. However, she had allies who formed a golden pillar of support. Zeenat spun her cobwebs all around her. Her victims before Ghulshan were the beautiful daughters of Zahra, loving sisters to Ali and Taqdeer. Threatened by their strength she transformed them into monsters, telling Taqdeer wild tales that he foolishly believed. Ghulshan, having already tasted her venom, saw through the masquerade. She joined forces with Ali's sisters, and formed an alliance with one in particular, Kulsum-Fui. Kulsum-Fui was the first "native", that is, not "African" but also not white-skinned, female nurse at Aga Khan Hospital in Nairobi. On trips to Nairobi where Ali was wheeling and dealing in the clubs and casinos, Ghulshan and her children stayed with Kulsum-Fui. Ghulshan and Kulsum firmly believed that they would manage to overpower Zeenat. But reality would shatter that faith.

Indeed it was Zeenat who sent the soldiers and the bombs to Ali's farm, just as it is Zeenat who owns Zahra's house. These were the tactics of her paranoia. Having been sent to a flat in Arusha after Taqdeer's death, she could not swallow the bitter pill of simultaneous exile and widowhood. Widowhood in our community is a treacherous state. A husband is to a woman like an umbrella for the rain of the world. Imagine then a haughty, venomous woman in the thundering storm of Idi Amin and Nyerere's East Africa without an umbrella. She learned from gossip and speculation at Jamaat Khana and rumours in the suqoni that the poison that killed her husband had been intended for Ali. She had been widowed instead of Ghulshan. Oh the rage! She vowed her revenge. In her spare time, between cups of tea, Zeenat plotted Ghulshan's demise. She could have widowed her too! But no. Alas if Ghulshan became a widow, Zeenat would not be any better for it. Two women in the storm without an umbrella. What she needed was an umbrella. Yes, but from where in this autumn of life to catch a man? But of course, kill the other woman and snatch hers.

Zeenat looks for the servant who had been caught by Dr. Kumar. He has joined the militia. She finds his hut and visits him. In the presence of his wife and children, she pleads with him, and he confesses that a general in the Tanzanian army had sent him to the farm to poison Ali and then after two days, to shoot Taqdeer. But Zeenat hears only the first part of his sentence after which her ears are ablaze with a deafening rage. Zeenat looks the soldier in his shining eye and tells him that she will help him get Ali. He is startled but not unbelieving. He has seen in this brief encounter Zeenat's green venom, the power of her desire, her hate, her fear, the lexicon of her cruelty. The soldier's ego balloons as he imagines the bravado of killing the enemy. So he promises to follow Zeenat's instructions.

So it was that Zeenat tipped off the soldier as to where and when Ali was crossing the closed East African borders. It was with her help that the militia found Ali at Kisumu and detained him for a month and his car for six. Zeenat had given instructions not to harm Ali, and then after a month to allow him to return home. Throughout the elaboration and planning of Ali's destruction, Zeenat dealt only with the servant-soldier, who now both feared and revered her. Through him, Zeenat managed to manipulate the militia, and decoys from the community, and made sure rumours were spread regarding Ali Khan's impending murder, to ensure Ali's prompt exile. It was Zeenat who sent the soldiers who raped and killed Ali's children's ayah Betty. Zeenat sent the soldiers with the bombs. She convinced them that killing his family and destroying his land was an infallible strategy for returning Ali to Tanzania. She was wrong.

Zeenat was sitting at her kitchen table in Arusha, sipping tea and nibbling whole-wheat theplas with her daughter Zera. There was a knock at the door. Zera opened it. It was Sultan, who was not expected. Zera welcomed him with an embrace and set about preparing tea for him. Zeenat was astonished to see Sultan. She rose from her chair and smiled. It was all right, she said to herself. Now she would have not only Ali but also his son. Zera prepared eggs with cilantro and cumin for Sultan to have with his tea. They chatted about the good old days on the farm.

Sultan and Zera were playing rummy and Zeenat was crocheting a white doily when the telephone emitted its shrill cry. At the other end was a hysterical Ghulshan praying for the sanity and support of her eldest son. Zera answered the telephone to hear Ghulshan screaming her son's name into the receiver. She hands the telephone to Sultan. Brave Sultan is choking at the sound of his mother's voice. He has not understood her words but her anxiety speaks clearly. Zeenat is now definitely worried. Zahra arrives, driven by Jerradi. The others are waiting at the entrance to the compound of flats. Zera takes her cousin inside. Sultan climbs into the Land Rover and he and Jerradi rush off to the farm. Zeenat goes to call Ali's brother Mustafah in London, where Ali was staying.

It was then that she negotiated for the house in Zanzibar. But it was not out of pity that Ali surrendered to her. Oh no, Ali surrendered out of trembling fear for the lives of his wife and surviving children. Having realised that she had lost—that the beckoning finger of Fate had intruded upon her future—Zeenat decided to throw in her cards and salvage what she could.

Zeenat reached Ali at his nephew's home in London. Lamenting the family curse, she wondered aloud why Fate had spared him out of all the brothers. She was weeping senselessly, asking Ali how the family would survive. Ali inquires about Ghulshan and his two surviving children. Zeenat announces that the weak woman, not fit to be a mother, having lost her mind is hiding in her own mother Noor's pathetic home. The children are with Zeenat, as it is entirely inappropriate for them to live in a hut with a mother gone mad. Zahra, who has become shamefully obstinate, is demanding to go to her mother—and Zeenat has no idea what to do with the shameless girl. Thankfully, her sensible brother seems to be handling her. Ali orders Zeenat to send the girl and her brother to their mother, at once. At this point, noting hysteria in Ali's voice, Zeenat decides to address him as the new patriarch of the family. He is the man now responsible for all their well being, including Zeenat and her children. How are they going to survive? She mentions that Taqdeer at his last breath had whispered to her, "Don't worry, my brother Ali will take care of you and your children." Now here was Ali, far away in London when hell was consuming them. Surely Ali, resourceful Ali can help his own brother's widow. Mother of the children who share his blood; mistress of the home that fed and nurtured him before marriage.

Ali must help Zeenat, wife of his elder brother, mother of his diabolic nieces. He has known for fifteen years that Lutfia Sultan bequeathed the house which was left for her sister Zahra, to him, but he has not been to Zanzibar in that time. He has kept the house. He pays a monthly fee for its maintenance, but Ali has not set foot in his mother's home. Zeenat has learned of the monthly payments in Zanzibar and consequently of the house. "You have a nice little villa hidden away in Zanzibar, I hear. So lovely, overlooking the sea and nestled inside an orchard from what I hear. So romantic. The women must love it there. So sly you are. Well at least you keep your girlfriends out of Ghulshan's face. Listen, darling brother-in-law. I have grown up a little since you moved me off the farm. I have learnt a thing or two here and there. I am in a position to do a lot of harm. Not only to you but also to your precious wife and children, but I am going to be kind since I have such a soft spot for you. All I will ask of you is to live up to your brother Taqdeer's promise. I think Zera and I could set up a nice little life for ourselves in Zanzibar and by the sea, oh how lovely!"

"The house is not yours to have."

"Oh really? Is that so? Well what did you have in mind then? Are you going to divorce Ghulshan, disown your children and marry me? Oh splendid! Dreams do come true!"

"I have no intention of divorcing Ghulshan—"

"Well you don't think I am going to be a second wife, do you? Oh Ali, all these years and you still don't know me?"

"You are mad, Zeenat!"

"That may be so, but listen carefully. I want the house. If I don't get it and you are not willing to divorce Ghulshan, why then you'll just have to be widowed won't you? Just like me. And then we can get married."

Ali cannot believe his ears. She is hysterical. She must be.

Ali makes use of his connections to make a few enquiries. He telephones a colonel in the Tanzanian army, whose son he wrangled out of prison five years ago. Ali asks the colonel to enquire about his sister-in-law. The colonel has no need to enquire. He spills Zeenat's secrets in Ali's burning ears. Poor Ali. The third time in his tragic life, reality leaves him speechless, shattering the looking glass. Ali books a flight to Zanzibar. The colonel, as dutiful as Ali, joins him in a gesture of honour and arranges for the transportation of Zeenat from Arusha to Zanzibar. He also arranges for a solicitor to be present, a certain Abdel-Aziz Zamakhshari.

The unnameable colonel, Mr. Zamakshari, and Zeenat come to Zanzibar airport to meet Ali. They bring with them some papers and a pen. Ali, despite the colonel's influence, is refused entrance into Zanzibar. He will not set foot in Zahra's house. He will not even see it. He will only sign it over to Zeenat. They meet for two hours inside a square room with large rectangular windows, white walls and dusty tables and chairs made of wood and black leather. Ali smokes a pack of 555 cigarettes and with the stroke of a pen donates Zahra's house, in an act of charity, to his widowed sister-in-law. He also agrees with Zeenat to a vow of secrecy.

After two hours in Zanzibar airport, his lips sealed, Ali boards the British Airways flight to London where instead of going back to his nephew's home, he hires a room at a hotel.

ALI AND GHULSHAN

Ghulshan landed in London an exact month after Ali's return from Zanzibar. She arrived with two children. After hours of waiting at the arrivals gate in Terminal 4, Heathrow, following several cups of tea, Ali's wife and children emerge from the clutches of the immigration office. When he sees only two children, one grown and the other just emerging from childhood, he collapses. He should have cried. He should have wept his heart out. But he did not. He offers a weak embrace to his surviving son and daughter. Later that night, at the home of Zulficar Bha, after the children have gone to bed, in the dark silence of their room, Ghulshan and Ali attempt a difficult conversation.

Ghulshan is beyond tears. "Don't blame me! It is your fault! You ran off to your safety, your luxury, in London! While we were dying. And that too is your fault! You and your politics, and your pride, living your life as if you were a bachelor. Never, never did you think of us, your wife and your children! If you wanted to live like this you should not have married, never have sired a child! Shame on you!" Ghulshan speaks violently with great rapidity. Her words burn in his brain.

He is overcome—that red red blood which flows in his veins rises and whirls into a storm. She saw him rise, but the strike came unexpectedly. He beats her wildly, almost without consciousness, just letting it all go. Releasing, finally. Ali has beaten Ghulshan black and blue. Her tears have found her again. She screams Zulficar's name. Zulficar comes running. Ghulshan wants to be taken away. She wants to leave the house at once. Ali, after all these years has proven to be his father's son, has shown his father's blood. Ali is weeping now. Finally he is weeping. He bows to her in repentance.

ZAHRA

Questions swarming in my mind like bees. A deafening buzz. Listen. Can you hear? Betrayal. A fall from grace. The earth is shattered. My own father, god-hero, I no longer know. What else is not real? How can I possibly still believe? From where to find the faith? From where the strength? I can feel delirium settling in. My grandmother's sister put five teaspoons of sugar in her tea. So did my sister Yasmine.

And I am waiting to die. Sleep. Lightly, lightly. Slowly, slowly. During daylight's rhythm of sanity, my desire under the sun. Unspeakable moon. Dancing without rhyme to kisses of the flesh. Dawn. Fear. Awake. An imperfect rhythm. Day into night. An opera, sung in perfect harmony. Polyphonic desire, listen.

I had a dream that told me that I wanted to remove Ghulshan and Ali from their chilly Arctic climate and install them in a house between sea and sand, upon the warmer terrain of Zanzibar. In a world where they could stop being aliens. But my dream was flawed. Ghulshan and Ali are no longer so. They are now Ali and Ghulshan. I must accept their new identity. They live with the expatriate community in Canada. Ghulshan will not live in a house Ali has given to Zeenat. Ali and Ghulshan have grown old. Their legend, linen-stained, belongs to a different age, Zamana, this is the new age where standard of living overrides quality of life. They now live with their new faces, as elderlies, with full health insurance, in a community that sees their brown skin without scarlet blood, and accepts them as immigrants. Foreigners with weird food, even weirder language and intolerable customs. They must become clones. Assimilate. Ali and Ghulshan, an elderly immigrant couple living around the corner in a flat, lonely without their children. I must come to terms with my histories. What happens to my desire, the need for resolution? For whom do I resolve, for me or for the world? So that I may have a concise answer to that dreaded question, Who are you?

I wanted to telephone Auntie Zeenat. I wanted to confront her. To demand what I do not know. How did she coerce my father? Why has she never lived in the house? Does she have a dirty tale for me? Probably. The problem is, she will not utter a word of it. Auntie, we would love you so much more if you just shared your pain and joy. Speak, speak, silent tongue, that venomous poison shall turn to honey, if you only speak.

I telephone Auntie Zeenat at her daughter's home in London where she now lives. I identify myself and feel England's morose chill infiltrating the telephone. I announce to her that I would like to buy her house in Zanzibar. "I know," she tells me. "The price is two hundred and fifty thousand US dollars. Can you afford that?"

"I want a contract."

"You will have a contract when I have proof that you can pay."

"Who told you I wanted to buy the house?"

"Why else would you take your precious mother and father to Zanzibar? Remember darling I have always been smarter than you. I want a full payment, two hundred and fifty thousand dollars. No negotiation."

"I think you are a thief."

"So you may."

HUSSEIN

I don't love him now as I did then.

I have telephoned Auntie Zeenat from his third-floor office. Hussein has left me alone. He waits for me at the reception, sitting in Miss This-Is-Not-A-Drop-In's chair, fiddling with the gadgets on her desk. It is three o'clock in the morning. I must go home to Ghulshan and Ali. I can think of nothing to say to him. I am not sure I want to see his face again. But I will and I do. He takes my hand which is shamefully frigid. His hand envelopes mine, bringing me an illusory moment of warmth. We descend the staircase and walk along the street towards his car. Mercedes Benz convertible from the 1950s, the pale yellow colour of dawn. This is a man whose standard of living is perfect. I have been beguiled to think he has a quality of life. Rhythm is more ancient than metre. I sit silently in his car. He drives to the sea, not to Ghulshan and Ali's cottage. I break the silence.

"She wants two hundredand fifty thousand. She will not succumb to negotiation."

"Why can't you just let it go? I have something to tell you. If you can get a loan from your bank to buy the house, my wife and I will rent it from you for two thousand dollars a month. After about six or seven years, the house will have paid your loan and its interest. You can then evict us."

"Why will you rent the house?"

"My wife is pregnant. We need a larger house—cleaner air, a quiet place."

"Where do you live now?"

"With my father. In his house."

"Do you love her?"

"It's not about love."

"I didn't ask you what it was about."

Tomorrow is Navroz. March twenty-first. The New Year. Coming of Spring. New Life. Love. The death of Winter. Navroz. New day. Welcome. We will try again to love and to forget. Forgetful love. Will I forget the angels? I don't want to forget the angels.

NAVROZ

New day. I awake to find Ghulshan at my bedside. Her eyes hold my sleepy gaze. She is holding a cup of tea in her hands. I know it is for me, but I cannot take it. "Navroz Mubarak, Beti."

"Navroz Mubarak, Mummy."

My father is walking along the curves of the sea. We are alone in the cottage, Ghulshan and I. But I cannot speak. What is this fear that grips me, extending its long, shadowy fingers until it curtails my very existence? Hinders the utterance of that which I know is real? Mystics and knights waging battles in the silent darkness of the moon's domain. But we are under the sun. A blazing sky above us. We cannot look, do not dare. Mother, who are you? Where do I find a voice to tell you my tale? I cannot bear to speak. Silence unfolding the knowledge of cowards. Look into my eyes and you will not see your own face. This face is mine. Scars are beyond repair.

Ali returns from the sea and we breakfast. Ghulshan and Ali leave Zanzibar tomorrow. They will return after a fortnight in London to Canada, where they have moved to the foothills of the Rocky Mountains. Rocky Mountains replace Mount Kilimanjaro. He works as a customer relations representative and drives a car. Ali goes to bed at nine o'clock, wakes at four, but does not arrive at his work until six. He needs two hours to make peace with the day. Last year they were still living by the sea. But it robbed them of their last hopes. Gypsies, these parents of mine. Nomads. Orphans of the sea. He no longer lives, Ali. He only enacts the motions of life. Spirits are dead. Murdered by the earth. Ali destroying his own blood. Blind, blind king, when will you see? Ghulshan sparkles and crackles. Cooks and cleans. Breathes fire, nourishes and soothes, to help us, and help Ali, carry pride, withstand the combustion of spirit and blood, and face ourselves.

Ali has seen my face. I have a tacky habit of naming cowards: speaking my mind to their astonished faces which smirk and contort in response. They happen mostly to be men, these cowards. Ali is not one of my cowards, he knows this.

"Navroz Mubarak, Papa." I embrace him.

"Navroz Mubarak, Beti."

Breakfast is a sombre occasion until I begin winding my soliloquies, my mother tells her jokes, and my father's face at last melts into laughter as I fall into his lap enacting the joke of the two lallus, spilling his cup of tea. Ghulshan's face is beaming while she wonders aloud when I am going to learn to behave according to my age. What she really wants to know is when I will marry. I wonder myself if it is worth it. Picking the scabs of their wounds so that I can see their blood. This vampiric obsession of mine. I have scarlet blood. It may be wiser just to let things be. I might be happier if my blood was only red, but I wouldn't be me. I would never be able to look myself or anyone else in the eye.

Mr. and Mrs. Karmali have invited us to their home for Navroz lunch. He will be there, accompanied by his mannequin wife. The one whose life will end on the day he leaves her. My smooth-talking lawyer has not considered the possibility of her finding another Adam, whose rib will give her life.

In addition to Mr. Hussein Zamakhshari, Mrs. Karmali has invited his father, Mr. Abdel-Aziz Zamakshari, also known as Abou Hussein, the father of Hussein. Yeah Allah, his father. Why didn't I think of this before? Of course, good sense has come mumbling back to me. I wonder if his ageing father will manage to attend at the Karmali household. And Ali. Oh good Lord help us, Ali. Who would not recognise such a name? Oh cocoon spun of ignorant lust! Assuming my father's tension was born of his daughter's lust for a man named Zamakhshari. Perhaps he did not see lust at all?

We embark towards the house of Amir Karmali to celebrate the new year with a lunch. Ali, who will drive, has put on a khaki safari suit, Ghulshan, in the back seat, is refreshing in a mint-green shalwar qamise. They are waiting for me as I come running out the front door to take my place, beside my father, on the front seat. I have indulged in the optional scarlet: sleeveless sheer chiffon, fitted, with a plunging neckline. As I bend into the front seat, the neckline droops—it casts its net wide. Ghulshan is not pleased, especially as I have not tied my hair, and I have rimmed my eyes with kohl and painted my lips a glossy red. Her face scowls. "What are you doing Zahra, look at you, scarlet, like a whore! And such a revealing qamise, I can see your breasts from here! Where did you get these clothes? Look at your hair! Loose, like a vagabond's!"

I, Zahra, burdened by my name, confused by history, aching to carve an indelible cry into the world, cannot rely on the man-and-home equation to find her peace with a world with which she is so bitterly angry. And nobody else allows themselves to feel. So Zahra feels for everybody. Too much emotion, till it crawls up from my liver, through my heart and upon arriving at the lungs threatens to choke me. I know that I must find my own peace, but Allah it is so difficult, so unsure, so fragile, risky, a gamble. In a world of instant gratification and lifetime guarantees how does one obey an impulse, the non-linear logic of the liver, doubts of gloom and doom so ominous they knock you down. And you! The rest of you, liars, cheaters, inhuman, unfeeling, gluttonous beasts, how do you sleep at night?

"Mother, in this century, it is not a crime for a woman to leave her hair loose."

"And that qamise, clear as crystal, in broad daylight, sleeveless, why bother to put on clothes then—"

"Mother!"

"Don't call me 'Mother'! Shame on you, in front of your father, and Amir Uncle. Have you no shame! And that lusty gigolo of a lawyer, where will he look? Certainly not at his wife whom he sees every night? How dare you dishonour—"

What to do? Confusion. Oh my God, what am I going to do? The question comes pounding through, shattering like a giant the walls of shelter that protect me from the world. King Kong metamorphosized into a question, paws wringing my neck. How very daunting it is. And so I decide like Noor to consult cards, stars, sun, moon, everything. But there is no sun. It has already retired behind the earth, even its embers, now dying, do not light my path. Then I consult the cards, then put on spectacles, find torch and peer at the lines on the palms of my hands. What is the truth? Who is lying? Does he love me? Should I believe or abdicate? Is this regression, escapism or madness? Circle the correct response.

"Stop it, just shut up! Ten times a day you tell me I am plain and will never find a husband—"

"Don't tell me to shut up, I'm your Ma. I tell you to make yourself pretty, not to flaunt yourself like a shameless harlot. Look at you! Tie your hair at once, and cover yourself with your dupatta, you have no idea where men's eyes wander to, even I can't look at you.

You are my daughter!"

"Mummy when are you going to arrive in the twenty-first century?"

"Never!"

Sister Fate. Some pure, heavenly, magic that inspires the blind to dance through a labyrinth guided us towards the sins of the flesh. Rapture awoke, then smiled. Someone sang, and the stars applauded. This birth, still premature but kicking wildly. The pains of labour have just begun. I have holy curses for that sweet magic. Music of the flute caresses the waves of the sea. Which do you drink, the water, or the wave? Undulating sapphire. Fire. Fire of the loins, it heats and burns in the same breath. Take heed, dear one. The blind do not see their labyrinth, but we do.

Silent up to now, Ali speaks. "Listen to your mother and tie your hair. Mother and daughter, why can't you get along? You've been taunting each other since you were five years old. Haven't you grown up yet? Just respect your mother."

Silently fuming, but lacking the energy and the gusto for further disruption, especially since Ali is now involved, I decide to lose. I tie my hair, and wrap my bodice with the dupatta. *I have no idea where men's eyes wander.* What about touch, mother? What about where men's hands touch? And their lips? *That gigolo of yours, his lips, yes.* So many secrets. Hiding behind these diaphanous veils. How do you know what I wear in London? Who I roam with? Do you even know why I have come to Zanzibar? Secrets these clothes could never reveal, lurking just behind my dupatta. Mother, I am not just your daughter. No longer a child, I am Zahra, and I have scarlet blood. What will you do when I tell you?

We arrive at the comfortable home of Mr. and Mrs. Karmali. Amir Uncle greets us at the door and informs my mother that his wife is to be found supervising the kitchen. I decide to join Ghulshan and Mrs. Karmali in the kitchen. On my way there I meet his wife. She takes my arm and pulls me aside. "Hussein has told me that you have a house for us to rent. Khuddah, I can't tell you how pleased I am. I can't stand living with that old geezer anymore. Well you know, no privacy, and such old-fashioned values. I mean I have to take my drink in a teacup and pretend I'm indulging in chai. Hussein said he was very impressed by you. He said you were businesslike. I do admire independent women, but you know, I prefer to have a man around. I don't suppose you know what I mean, but well, one day when you find your man, you will. Anyway, tell me about the house. Hussein has described it to me, but you know how men are—no attention to the details that can make it or break it for us. Oh, you must come home, visit us sometime, and we can have a ladies' get-together. You know, girl talk! By the way, this colour red does suit you. I don't think I've seen you in makeup before. You look so nice. I always say, 'Just a little colour makes all the difference.'"

"Navroz Mubarak, Zahra." At the entrance to Mrs. Karmali's kitchen, with his wife's arm linked to my elbow, I encounter him gazing at my breasts. "I hear your parents are leaving Zanzibar tomorrow. I hope you will be staying with us a little longer."

"Yes, I will be staying until the weekend."

"Wonderful."

"Yes, yes, I have told her she must come for lunch and meet Abou Hussein your father—"

I loathe this. It makes me loathe you. Do you understand? I only pretend to. Masquerade, masquerade. Will I ever see your face?

Three days later. Six a.m. Wake-up. I have a plane to catch. I crawl out of bed with no sense of rest. Ghulshan packed my things for me two days ago before she left for London. She and Ali are staying in my flat for one week. I have given him keys, address and mini-cab number. I will meet them there tomorrow. But, now, I am concerned with the array of belongings scattered about my room. How will they fit into my already bulging canvas bag? Allowing the question to linger, I pull on my rubbery swimming suit and run into the sea for one last encounter.

Morning glory. I am half wishing the sea will take me with it, so that I can dissolve. Fanafillah. I am searching for nothingness. No shadows, no echoes. No indefinable moodiness rocking to a rhythm of angst that pleads for satisfaction. No circle of unmitigated justice. The wheel will stop. Full circle interrupted. I cannot finish what I started so I let it falter, hoping it will dissolve in the sea.

Reluctantly I emerge from the sea. I am still Zahra. The sky is blue, heated yellow by the sun. Gargoyles are swimming in my stomach. He is waiting for me at the shore. Pressed khakis and starched shirt at attention. Face gleamingly clean. "Are you ready?" He laughs, mocking what he thinks is my fragility. This defines me in his mind as a woman and an "artist": temperamental. My inability to persist via the mechanics of a sound, task-oriented regimen. The world is shocked that I haven't taken a Palm Pilot with me into the sea.

"Yes." I shout to him. "I am ready."

"Who irons your clothes?" I ask him inside my room, while I roll and tumble my belongings into an exhausted bag, finally resigning them to the green plastic Marks and Spencer's bag in which I brought Ghulshan her underwear and Rich Tea Fingers.

"The servant," he replies, sulking because I have refused to remove my rubbery latex obstacle to his attention. "I thought you might want a lift to the airport."

"How thoughtful."

On the way I ask to stop at the suqoni to buy lemons. I love lemons. They are yellow like the sun. When you squeeze them and add water it makes you feel cool. I also like to add sugar. We squeeze lemons to remove bitterness and envy from love. You can keep your love. You will leave anyway. Angels never leave. They are immortal and I am selfish. I am leaving now. Please won't you stay? Frosty Winter. Look. All your flowers have died. You must bury them and buy new ones. Magnolias, orchids and queens of the night. All white.

LONDON, A YEAR AND A HALF LATER

According to the waning sun, it is afternoon. My eyelids have just fluttered open. I am lying on a bed that has been dressed in white cotton, in a room I do not recognise. It smells like Zanzibar but the dull sky and cloudless rain tell me it is London. Then, why am I in this hotel room? I turn my head over, my eyes shut again, refusing to acknowledge the world around me. And in it, my presence.

A dull English afternoon. At four o'clock the door opens. He enters the room. Walks towards the bed and sits at the side. I open my eyes and face him. He is dressed in a grey suit and dull tie. Colours to suit the mood of London's morose winter. He is still smiling at my temperament.

"Where did you go?"

"To my meetings."

"Businessman at large."

He undresses, sliding out of his grey suit and dull tie and joins me in bed. We watch television and order coffee and the newspaper. He opens the newspaper and typically passes me the "Arts & Entertainment" section. I choose a film for us to see at a cinema in Soho, across Chinatown on Shaftesbury Avenue. As we walk a chilling wind sweeps through the fog, bringing with it the smells of fish, ginger and fried spring onion. He is wearing jeans and I wear his grey suit trousers. I am smiling because I feel happy. In the darkness of the cinema, just after the previews have ended, he tells me he has not been to a cinema in five years. I run out to the lobby and buy him some popcorn.

ZANZIBAR, THREE DAYS AFTER NAVROZ

At the airport, we part. He will return to his wife but I'm not going to think about that. Two days ago, I parted from Ghulshan and Ali. This time, it was I who stood behind the metal detectors and waved goodbye. An eternity seems to have passed since then. Each time we part and meet again something changes. A momentary shift in mood. Like tomatoes of the same vine which you eat everyday and each one tastes different. The taste blending into the larger platter of what you have already eaten and how you ate it. But lingering still, that distinct sweet and acidic taste which allows you to name it a tomato.

I always cry at airports. Usually in the lady's toilet, locked inside the cubicle. The airport has become an icon for my emotions. I often visit them when on the brink of neurosis, sometimes just before I bleed. Salty seas dripping across my cheeks. A prelude to the ocean I am about to cross.

NAVROZ

Navroz. New day. New year. New life. Mrs. Karmali's Navroz lunch is served in her courtyard. A long table has been covered with a patterned cloth of white linen, set with pale blue dishes and a bowl of pomegranates. My mother sitting across from me notices the lawyer's attentions while I humour the conversation of his wife. Mr. Zamakhshari converses with Ali. I can see no sign of recognition. No remembrance of that lonely day fifteen years ago. My father still looks the same, only his hair has silvered. Why is his crime so terrible it cannot be recognised? Ali has betrayed himself. He has lost his own flesh and blood. He left them to burn on a farm. He is his own silent judge. His justice is without a trail, so harsh it sits within him silently drinking his red, red blood, and leaving to us a mortality without its breadth. He passes days without the sun, banished to darkness. Nothing could be so terrible. Ali is the sternest judge of all. He has imprisoned himself by his own sentence. But we love you, father. We, who have survived. Come and live with us. We want to free him, but we can only watch.

Ali, in silence, drives us back to the cottage. Ghulshan, unrelenting, confronts me. How dare you dance clandestine with that married man? Have you no shame? Ali's red temper erupts. So does mine. I want to accuse him of a much greater crime. One towards which the Qur'an only hints. Those fateful elephants killed by a shower of stones from the beaks of floating birds. The sorry herd, a complacent tool beguiled by some evil lord. Such a lord could only be evil, is that not so? Scarlet betrayal that matches my clothes. Why else would he give her the house of his beloved mother?

I want to tell Ali. I want to tell him everything from beginning to end. I want to tell Ali about Zahra, Noor and Ghulshan—those peripheries that he could not see. I want to tell him about the mangoes of which I still dream. I want to tell him about my anger, this bitterness. All those wild tears: his and mine, and Ghulshan's. Plucking heartstrings to a rhythm that even Ghalib could not match. And Yasmine, her smile forever erased. Ahmed's laughter silenced. Sultan's private grief, sweetness in torrents of rain. I cannot face it. My lips will not move. Forever shut.

I want to free Ali, my father, and this is my only voice. The only utterance which will not gag, only choke. So I pile mask upon mask. In these pages the truth lies. My disguise, this invented identity. False histories born from the desire to speak. Uttered to reveal and conceal and reveal again. Language like a veil. In the desert that jewelled blue oasis which floats and sinks to rise again. With each movement, harmony like the wind. These intervals, I cannot bear. Anarchy swimming in darkness during your intervals. Please do not shut me into my lonely world of fiction. My sister came today and brought me her love. She cooked lunch, massaged my feet and listened to my stories.

The day after Navroz. Ghulshan and Ali rise early. They pack their things and I run to the market to fetch those vitumbuas that have become a favourite. I return and brew a pot of tea. We have breakfast and I explain to Ali, once again, where I live in London. I give him the telephone number for mini-cab and my keys. Ghulshan takes a bag of my things with her so that my baggage is lightened. She has not been to London since she arrived for the first time over a decade ago.

Amir Uncle arrives. Ghulshan and I force him to sample a vitumbua and have a cup of tea. We pile into the car. I sit in the back with Ghulshan. We hold hands. She looks very smart in a crisp ivory trouser suit. The airport scene does not change, except I am the one waving goodbye from behind the gates.

Ghulshan's eyes are watery and Ali's face is soft.

I have allowed my parents to leave without fulfilling my lofty purpose. I have failed in my self-assigned duty to my creed. I have not reclaimed Zahra's house. Oh Fatima-Fui, what will you say? Amir Uncle drives me home. I request an international phone call and wait for it to be approved. I call Sultan in New York. Sultan the Successful. To the hum of brokers shouting on a trading floor, I tell him our story. He is silent.

"Do you think the loan will be approved?"

"Why do you need a loan? I will buy that damned house. I can't believe this. One more fucked-up family tale is just what I need. How am I supposed to face the world with this constantly gnawing at my back?"

"I don't want you to buy the house. I want to buy it."

"We will buy it in your name."

"No!"

"Zahra, will you listen to me? How are you going to get a loan from Lloyds in London approved while in Zanzibar? I do not want that woman to have the satisfaction of humiliating you, or the family. Think about it. She will tell the whole world you planned this escapade and failed. How do you think Mum and Dad will feel?"

What about Ghulshan and Ali?

"I haven't even told them!"

"What? Zahra! I can't believe this? ARE YOU OUT OF YOUR MIND?"

Of course I'm out of my mind! Why else would I be combatting history. Confronting the world, instead of quietly occupying the space that has been allocated for me. "I thought maybe it could be a surprise."

"Mum and Dad hate surprises, they're not exactly the surprise type you know?"

"What exactly is a surprise type?"

"You know what? Stop. Let's just solve one problem at a time, okay? As I was saying, you have no credit history. No one is going to give you a loan based on the rent collected from some Zanzibari lawyer. Do you understand?"

"You give me the loan, then. He will pay the rent directly to you."

"I want it to be a family house. I don't want some stranger and his wife living there. Don't you think this has been complicated enough as it is?"

"Yeah Allah!"

"I don't understand. Why do you want this guy to live there when I'm telling you I'm willing to pay Zeenat and have a family house in East Africa? It will be good. You can hang out there and paint, read, write, dance or whatever it is that you do, and Supria can visit with the kids. This way they get a break from New York— some non-American Third-World exposure. Who knows, I might even come."

"I already told him he could rent the house!"

"Tell him you changed your mind! Bloody hell, who is this guy? Look, it's peak trading hours, I have to go. Give me your number. I'll call you tonight. We can talk about this tonight."

"Okay. Do you have a pen?"

"Yes, yes. Shoot."

"The country code is the same as Tanzania, 255, then, 5884."

"2 5 5, 5 8 8 4"

"Yes."

"Okay, now, Zahra?"

"Hmm."

"Calm down. Don't freak out. It's not the end of the world. We're going to get the house. Okay?"

"Okay."

"Who loves you, baby?"

"You do."

"We all do."

"Thanks."

"Tell this lawyer guy to go to hell. I'll talk to you tonight."

"Okay, bye."

I replace the receiver with a sigh. Then I pick it up again and call the lawyer. The phone rings.

"Hello." Miss This-Is-Not-A-Drop-In answers.

"Hello, can I speak with Mr. Zamakshari please."

"Who is calling?"

"Zahra."

"Just a moment." She puts me on hold for a good five minutes. I light a cigarette that I have stolen from my father.

"Hello, hi." Hussein answers.

"I wanted to speak to you."

"Here I am."

"Are you free for lunch tomorrow?"

"Not exactly. How about tea? The Intercontinental Hotel. Do you know where it is?"

"I'll find it."

"It's just west of the harbour. I will see you in the lobby at four o'clock."

I replace the receiver with another sigh. I spend the rest of the day by the sea. In the evening I buy some fish and rice from the harbour and share it with my friend the woman who weaves and sells wicker baskets on the shore. With her I practice my waning Swahili. After we have finished eating, she gathers her things and prepares to return home. She invites me for tea, apologising that she lives in in a small, second-floor room in an alleyway just by the train station. It is a long walk, but the tea will be sweet. I refuse, explaining that my brother is going to call me from America. I promise to take tea with her on another occasion. "From America?" She is impressed.

"Okay, you must come when you are free. I want you to meet my family," she adds, looking me up and down this time. I am now wondering if she has noticed me loitering about with the lawyer at odd hours of the night. I watch her wrap a khanga around her head, place her tools and merchandise in a large basket shaped like an urn, and shut the hat-like lid. I help her hoist it onto her head and watch her figure melt into the night. She walks erect, chin tilted towards the stars, arms raised, hips sashaying. I return to the cottage and take sheets and a pillow onto the wooden bench swing on the veranda. The wind sings, seducing the sea and I lie facing her, falling asleep. My brother does not call.

In the morning I awake to the sea and swim for a while. A man comes along the shore selling madaaf. I buy one, quenching my thirst with its water. The man then cracks it for me and I eat the young, luscious coconut flesh. I try to lie on the beach and read but find that I am brimming with apprehension. I return to the cottage. Take a shower. Dress in those now not-so-white cigarette pants and a T-shirt. I walk to the harbour and go alone to the restaurant where he took me for lunch. Unfortunately, he is there, with two clients. One of which is Amir Uncle. I try to gracefully slip away but both he and Amir Uncle see me. Both stand up, greet me and insist that I join them. He introduces me to the other man. A European. German, actually. He happens to be Mr. Van Horne who was on the flight from London. Derek stretches out his hand.

"Hello Zahra, nice to see you again."

The lawyer's eyes shade, "Do you know each other?"

"Yes. In fact, funnily enough, we were on the same flight from

London. She was sitting next to me. What a surprise." Germans always succumb to the facts. We sit through a civilised lunch, full of comments about the unpredictability of coincidence. After lunch, while waiting for the coffee Amir Uncle asks me what I am going to do.

"Well, some of us do have to get back to the office. Where are you off to, lucky lady?"

"Oh, I think I'll just wander around the bazaars for a while."

"Yes. Enjoy your holiday. Please don't hesitate to call if you need anything at all. You are like my own daughter, you know."

"Yes, of course. Thank you. Please give my regards to your wife."

A tall, elegant, cinnamon-skinned man brings the coffee. He has a head of silver hair and moves with the grace of a prince. I try to smile at him but he avoids my gaze. He has been taught his place and knows how to keep it. As he leans into my right shoulder to pour the coffee I am accosted by its smell. The aroma is dark and rich, fresh, with the vitality of Kilimanjaro. This is *our* coffee. I am sure of it. The surprise of it stuns me. For a moment I feel as if the room might slip away. The waiter places a hand on my shoulder and stills me. No one else seems to have noticed. Amir Uncle is still talking to me.

"I will indeed. Feel free to go around and visit her. She would love some company. She is already missing your mother."

"All right. Thank you."

I excuse myself, hurrying towards the loo so that I can gather myself together again. When I return, the men are shaking hands. They agree to meet again at half past ten tomorrow morning. The lawyer calls his office to say he will be away for the afternoon and asks me where I want to wander. I suggest the Hotel Intercontinental, just to the west of the harbour.

LONDON, A YEAR AND A HALF LATER

After the film we walk around the streets of Soho looking for a place to have dinner. We pass a man lying on Shaftesbury Avenue. He smells of vulgar medicine. His eyes are red. His face is cracked. There is an open sore above his lip, infected by the hairs of his beard. He stretches his hand out. I take a pound from the lawyer's pocket and drop it into his palm. The man does not thank me. It seems he has not recognised the coin in his hand. We find the London rendition of a French brasserie and decide to eat there. Two hours later, when we leave the restaurant and again pass the same spot on Shaftesbury Avenue, the man is no longer there. I am so tired. Exhausted.

I awake to find him asleep beside me. Rare London sunlight filters through the windows behind the bed. I leave him asleep with a note telling him I have to go to work. This is a lie, told because I have a desire for loneliness. I roam around Kensington and sit in Patisserie Valerie where I drink two cups of diluted cocoa. I walk into the Victoria and Albert Museum and find myself in the Nehru wing. At the entrance, framed into a cabinet are fragments of Gujarati textiles found in the fifteenth century in Fustat, Egypt.

ZANZIBAR

It is nine o'clock in the evening. We have spent the afternoon at the Hotel Intercontinental. He has returned to the cottage with me. I am sitting on the veranda with the lawyer, wrapped in a bed sheet. He is asleep. His head nestled in my lap. I am attempting to read the Swahili paper. The telephone rings its shrill cry. I lift his head and place it on a cushion. Leaving him with the sheet, I walk naked into the cottage.

"Hello."

"It's your brother."

"I know."

"What are you doing?"

"Just sitting on the veranda reading."

"Sorry I couldn't call you last night. Did you talk to this lawyer?"

"Yes. I met him at the Hotel—"

"Zahra, I don't care where you met him, just tell me what happened."

"The house is not going to be let. We can buy it directly."

"Good. Now what about Zeenat?"

"She is in London."

I look out over the sea. It is calm now, flat and smooth. Deceptive. A deep turbulence lurks swimming beneath the surface, waiting to emerge, and when it does there will be a storm.

Sultan's voice is booming out of the telephone. "Okay, now listen. I'm going to transfer the money into your account. It should take one week to clear. I want you to call Zeenat and tell her you will see her next week."

"Okay. Who's going to tell Mum and Papa?"

"It can be a surprise. No need to tell them anything until we have secured the house."

"What happens after we buy it? It is being used as a warehouse, it will have to be cleaned, furnished-"

"Zahra, Zahra. Calm down. Don't get too excited. Let's get the house first?"

"Okay."

"Right, listen, I'm really busy, I've got to get on the trading floor. I'll call you in London."

At the Hotel, we meet several of his acquaintances in the lobby. I stand aside awkwardly as he greets and guffaws with them. He introduces me as Miss Zahra Khan from London. A few eyebrows rise but he does not pay any heed. We decide to sit outside, I head towards a table in the garden overlooking the pool. He excuses himself and I look around me at the huge pool, filled with the children of privileged Zanzibari families having an after-school swim, minded by their ayahs. Scattered around the pool are local and foreign scantily-clad prima donnas. And around the women, local and foreign businessmen, schmoozing.

Soaking in ambience, with sunrays beaming on my face, I remember other such occasions. Melodies of the scorching African sun, mingled with the smell of chlorine and the sound of screaming children. My own childhood: family holidays at Kunduchi beach with my brothers. Yasmine and me jumping in and out of the pool in our fluorescent floaters, occasionally gulping down the water, and then choking.

He returns with my favourite freshly-squeezed lemonade and a gin and tonic for himself. He seems to be in good spirits, jovial and bubbly like champagne. I am feeling a bit nervous. Unfortunately I do not have a flair for diabolical scheming. I decide to speak some of the truth. I tell him about my telephone conversation with my brother, that he wants to buy the house, which means that the lawyer cannot rent it. Effectively what I am saying is, thank you very much we will take it from here. I leave out the interrogation I had planned about why he didn't tell me about his father. Perhaps he also did not know until he saw those fateful papers. Why then did he show them to me? He could have simply left it with the house in Zeenat's name. The rest is my business, no? And from where this idea of him and his pathetically pregnant wife living in Zahra's house? What weirdness.

When I stop speaking, he places his drink on the table. He lights a cigarette, leans back into his chair and gazes at me, looking into my eyes straight through me into a very private place. Expelling smoke, he grins and says, "A shame." I am thinking that he seems disappointed but not terribly. He looks at me again, reaching over to my face and turning it twenty degrees so that I look him straight in the eye. Then, he says something interesting, "But it won't be yours."

"What?"

"The house."

"What do you mean?"

"Your brother buys the house, it will belong to your sister-in-law. It will be her territory, you and your parents will merely be guests."

"That is not true. He is buying it for the whole family."

"Zahra, you are naive."

"No. I am not."

ANGUISH

This is the new age—zamana. Here stones bleed scarlet. Transformation. Unsanctioned. This is the way of the Amir. The gaze of the angels, throne of the Shah. This is the tenth avatar. Sadru Ali told us that we will know him in his presence. When an age has passed, then you will find, if you sit in darkness, the light. The transformation is awakening, and the moon turns to her disciples; that is, you. These days, the tenth friend will come. You are your truth. Ali is in my blood. This is my darshan.

When you listen, something escapes, and it becomes worthwhile. I speak soliloquies and you hear melodies. Such is its rhythm.

Some people recite their prayers, others sing, still others scream. Some whisper, others expound, I dance and you are too shy. When will we dance, fluttering in ecstasy? Twirling with the angels. Like the moth courting candlelight. When the music dies and the moth burns, I will be left with nothing but you.

LONDON, FOUR DAYS RETURNED FROM ZANZIBAR

Sultan has sent a cheque instead of transferring the money into my account. I have telephoned Zeenat Auntie and arranged to see her at Zubaida's house. I am due for dinner at eight o'clock. I have asked her not to mention the business of the house to Ghulshan and Ali as my brother and I are hoping to surprise them. She, in turn, has asked me not to raise the subject in the presence of her daughter.

My cousin Zubaida lives in the northwest of London and I live in the southwest. I take an expensive taxi to her home as I cannot face any other means of transport and neither can my clothes. I am decked out in a sky-blue short-skirted suit, sheer stockings, high heels, and sapphire ring and earrings. I have spent the afternoon with large curlers setting my hair. I have plucked my brow and brightened my nails the colour of a sunset. The intent is to kick Zeenat where it hurts. I also contemplated a tale about my engagement to the son of a Pakistani Mir but realised that names, relations and other details would be demanded, and I would not be able to pull it off.

Zubaida answers the door and gives me an embrace which seems genuine. Zeenat Auntie, wrapped in a sari, glittering with diamonds, is seated by the fire. I approach respectfully and kiss her hand. But Zubaida, who is usually brimming with warmth and affection, is cold. She doesn't really speak to me. I wonder why. We dine on a practical garden salad, chicken pilaff, carrot achar and fruit salad. Dinner conversation involves polite chatter about who married, who had what kind of baby, who died, who divorced, who made money, who went bankrupt and how difficult it is to distinguish cubic zirconia from real diamonds. Zeenat claims she can tell from a foot away. Under the sun, the brilliance of a diamond prism is unsurpassable, no cubic anything can imitate it.

We take tea in the sitting room. Zeenat asks Zubaida to leave us alone for a few minutes. My cousin politely obeys. Zeenat turns towards me but I decide to speak before she does.

"I have a certified cheque in American dollars here for you." As I reach for my smart eel-skin purse, she stops me.

"There will be no need for your cheque, Beti." I do not understand what she could possibly mean. I stare blankly at her, waiting for her to explain. "I suppose I should have telephoned to tell you, now you have gone through all this trouble of the cheque, but I really wanted to see you, and I must say you are looking rather well, I'm sure you will find a husband very soon. Anyway, yes, I wanted to see you, and knowing what a busy life you people have nowadays, I thought let her come and meet her cousin sister, her Auntie, we can have a meal together, after all we are family, and then I will tell her. Besides, of what importance is this house matter when we share the bond of blood, family, you know."

My mouth is dry. I cannot swallow or speak. My shoulders are tense. My stomach has formed a knot. My hands have pressed themselves together and are perspiring. My mind is creating and rejecting, at the speed of thunder, every possible scenario of what could have happened. Surely, I can still make a deal with her. Yes, surely. I am at this moment, so afraid: terrified and totally alone. Like I was when they were bombing the farm. I knew Yasmine and Ahmed were there and I could not bear to see Ghulshan's face. I can feel myself shivering and I am hoping that Zeenat cannot see. Indeed she cannot, she is too busy talking.

"You see Zahra beti, what I wanted to tell you was that your Maji's house has already been sold to a higher bidder, in fact, just two days ago."

I am staring at the milky tea that fills my cup. The colour matches my skin, and I want to drown in it. I have developed, over the years, the ability to lift my heart out of my body and into another state. I look away from my teacup into Zeenat's green eyes. They are still unflinching. I do not have the strength to match them. My lips begin to quiver. Sweaty teardrops begin to glisten at the corners of my kajaled, shadowed and mascaraed eyes. I cannot stop them. They begin the journey towards my chin, sweeping with them the blue and black colours of my eyes, smudging the rose of my cheeks, and infiltrating my scarlet lips with their acidic taste. My face stripped, blue, Picassoesque.

"Oh dear, you must be missing your mother. How many times I have said, young girls should not live alone, abandoned by their mothers." Zeenat offers me some tissues, "You will dirty the collars of your expensive suit."

I am not sure if I should take the tissues. I cannot think. I take the tissues. I do not use them to wipe my face. They remain clenched in my hand. I stand up and take my purse. As I begin to walk out of the room, she asks me if I will not wish my cousin sister Zubaida goodbye, and thank her for the delicious food. I ignore her words. This is not difficult as my ears are burning scarlet and I can hardly hear her. I find the front door and walk out, shutting it behind me. I walk three blocks before I see a taxi.

Back of the taxi, I decide I cannot go home. Good Lord, yeah Allah, if I sit alone tonight in that flat—recently cluttered with three pairs of shoes, three trouser suits, one skirt-suit, one coatdress, two handbags, all tried and rejected, and an assortment of cosmetics— I will freak the hell out. My best friend Anxiety will come to visit, and then I will be sure to destroy. Destroy that scarlet blood. Better to create.

I tap the taxi driver on the shoulder and ask him to take me to Bellini's, off Kensington High Street, just behind the Market. Bellini's is one of my hideouts. It is an Andalusian inspired, black-and-white tiled, ceramic-pillared haven with blue walls and plastic palm and olive trees. The décor allows me to imagine I am gazing at the Mediterranean Sea. I pull my powder compact and lipstick out of my purse and fix my face. The barman is a Spanish queen who mixes killer vodka martinis. I order three at once.

Perched on a barstool and sipping on the third, still waiting to die, I am being watched. My skirt fits like a blue suction-corset around my ample hips and thighs. My stockings became laddered in the taxi, and I have dutifully removed them. Yes, I am Ghulshan's daughter. All this designed to kick Zeenat where it hurts, hardly worth the trouble really. I could have gone to Harvey Nichols and spent a month's salary on a complete makeover and Zeenat would not have been hurt one bit, armoured as she is with her poison.

I am causing a stir among the crowd of Bellini's chic, *Vanity Fair*-reading and *Wallpaper*-following, stylish, super-hip but still typically polite in a London-kind-of-way clientele. Francisco the queeny barman, ex-lover of my friend the son of a Pakistani Mir, is carrying on a conversation with me from across the room. My language is fouler than his orange Lycra trousers as I describe for him my evening.

Just after the midnight rush, Francisco and I dance flamenco, whose footsteps and rhythm are the same as that of khatak. We dance between the tables, my heels stamp out the staccato rhythm. Heads turning once, twice, thrice. In the company of Francisco, I consume my martinis and spend several more hours at Bellini's until he finishes his shift and we take a taxi home. I tell him to remind me to call my brother in the morning.

There is no morning. Francisco and I sit on my couch until a grey dawn. We brew bitter pots of Kilimanjaran coffee, purchased at Marks & Spencer's, and I tell him about my wicked Auntie Zeenat. My rage: unbelievable. I could kick her in the face until she turns blue and scream obscenities at her until she turns red. But what good will it do? This rage, my capacity to hate, is surprising even to me.

Relieving himself between these bitter doses, Francisco parades around the flat in the shoes and accessories I rejected not so long ago. He also rejects them, lifts my pale-blue jacket off the coffee table, slips it on, slides half of his large feet into half of those heels and asks me to remove my skirt.

"Get out of that skirt and into your pyjamas darling. I am trying to empathise exactly. Brew some tea. I will do my makeup, and then tell me, darling," he says.

"The eyeshadow must be blue," I shout over the hissing kettle. I am staring at the milky tea again.

Francisco tidies up my flat and takes a marathon shower, while I panic about what I am going to tell my brother—how will I relay the sorry news. These scars charred into my face, drooling plasma, when will they heal? Do you remember, like I remember? Where is your pain, scarlet brother? What have you done with it? What sounds, whose scream, which gunshots echo in your head? Whose sweet forgotten laughter? Where are you running? We must go on. We cannot stand still, not even for Yasmine and Ahmed. Not for Ghulshan and Ali. This is your life. Make of it what you will. Seize the bloody day.

I run out to buy pain au chocolat and orange juice. At eleven o'clock, I telephone my brother on the other side of the ocean, and wake him up. I tell him straight to his face:

"Hi, sorry to wake you up, it's Zahra calling. I have torn up your cheque. Zeenat sold the house to a higher bidder. Too bad."

"What? What are you talking about?"

"Zeenat sold the house to someone else."

"Who?"

"How the hell am I supposed to know who?"

"Oh my God, Zahra, sometimes you can be so thick."

"What do you mean?"

"I mean think about it. She sold the house to your friend the lawyer. It doesn't take a rocket scientist to figure that out!"

"No!"

"What do you mean, no? You told him I was going to buy it, didn't you?"

"Yes."

"And for how much?"

"Yes. But he wouldn't do that."

"Why the hell not? Out of integrity? Get real Zahra. Things don't work like that. Who is this shit? How did you meet him?"

Nausea sets in. It seems last night's martinis are still kicking around in my stomach. This little piece of news is not helping out. My head begins to spin. I pull myself out of the cloud and focus on my brother.

"He is a lawyer, in Zanzibar. Amir Uncle's friend."

"Zahra, what is his goddamn name?"

"Hussein Zamakhshari. Yeah Allah."

"Spell that!"

"h, u— "

"The last name, Zahra."

"z, a, m, a, k, h, s, h, a, r, i."

"Hussein Zamakhshari?"

"Yes."

"What is Amir Uncle's phone number? Now Zahra, listen to me. How many times have I told you, you need to learn how to deal with people. You trust too easily, and tell the whole world what's on your mind. You will not survive. The world is full of bastards. Do you understand?"

"Yes." I am reduced to tears now.

"How are things otherwise?"

"Fine."

"How is London?"

"Fine."

"Tell me what happened at Zubaida's house."

Five days later Sultan left a message confirming that it is indeed Mr. Zamakhshari who bought Zahra's house in Zanzibar. Thank goodness we have said nothing to Ghulshan and Ali.

I thought that I would never see him again. I would never forgive him. For a while I even forgot him. I believed I could release my fantasy and live the scattered reality that was mine.

I changed my home, relocating to an idyllic cottage in Barnes, facing the woods where yuppies were now living. The cottage has a rose garden at the back and a crackling fireplaces in each room. It is a short walk above the river, across from the village pond. It turned out that the family from whom I was renting the cottage was Egyptian.

I came home early one autumn afternoon having fought the rainy, bustling, already cold streets of London. I passed through Barnes village with its quaint family-operated shops. I bought lamb, mint and apricot sausages from a small butcher who specialises in homemade oh-so-gourmet sausages. The elderly woman who runs the dry goods shop founded by her grandfather indulged in some gossip about the pending divorce of a wealthy banker living in a Tudor mansion by the pond. She also persuaded me to buy marmalade and shortbread. Lastly, I got a Cadbury's milk bar from the chic supermarket operated by none other than a Gujarati family. Having fulfilled my quota of British delicacies, I returned to the cottage between the pond and the river. I laid my bags on the kitchen table, and the telephone rang. The office wanted me back in London for a meeting. The little red light on my answer-phone was flashing. I pressed the button and heard his voice. He informed me that he was in London and would call again. I could have collapsed. Instead I ran upstairs, struggled into a pair of jeans and threw myself into the bus-and-train labyrinth that would eventually deliver me to the office.

That evening, when I had retraced my way back home and was enclosed by the warmth of a fire, collapsed on the sofa watching nothing on television, the telephone rang again. Our conversation was odd. I felt tense. It occurred to me to ask him to come to my cottage, and to cook for him. Feed him those British delicacies. But I agreed to meet him at his hotel. I put on a scarlet cashmere sweater, released my hair from its braid, and misted my wrists and neck with the scent of sandalwood and eucalyptus. I jumped for the third time that day onto the 9A bus into London and got off at Queensgate. He was staying at the Gore Hotel. I was late. As I entered the lobby, he was standing in a corner by the bar. A spectator in anticipation. I saw him. How different he looked in woollens and dark colours. Black and grey. The colours of English winter. I walked towards him unsure if he recognised me. He had. Moonlight spread across his face. Standing close, I offered my hand and a smile that was real. He took my hand, embraced me. He held me for a minute and a half and then kissed my lips. I was anxious, confused and a bit shocked at the intimacy of this greeting. Sometimes politeness and conversation offer refuge when the thought of silence is unbearable.

"I wasn't sure you would recognise me."

"Of course I recognised you." His accent, in England, seemed heavy. Tainted with foreignness, my memories of exile.

"Have you eaten?" Why do I always think of food when I have nothing else to do or say?

"No. I'm not hungry. Are you hungry?"

"A little. I haven't eaten since lunch."

"Why don't we sit by the window and have some wine. And you can eat."

He settled my hand into the crevice of his elbow. We walked into the restaurant and asked for a table by the window. He ordered a bottle of wine: Frescobaldi Chianti, and I had steak frites with a salad. I could not eat. It was so totally confounding to be sitting in London, at a table across from him. He had lived as angel and demon inside me. I had tried to exorcise him with bitterness and scrutiny, sharp doses of realism and ethics, and other men.

I study his face while he tells me about his divorce. I am trying to revive my bitterness, my anger, but I am losing the battle. I want to forget and remember, remember and forget, throw away the yardstick with which I have been taught to measure others and myself. I want to be free of the instruments I have used to record and catalogue his every move. I want to let him exist without judgement. And yet, somewhere in the dungeons of my mind, sirens are screaming Caution. I try to avoid them as one avoids the sounds of city streets in urban bedrooms.

I spent the night in his hotel room. The wine had worked its magic. I couldn't face a rainy ride back to Barnes. I lay nestled inside the bed while he sat hesitantly on the sofa smoking cigarettes and recounting his thoughts of the last year. Four hundred and forty-five days. He ordered pots of tea from the bellboy. I had erected a chilling barrier around me, one that kept him from touching me. This, ostensibly, was my intent, but I was longing for those caresses that arouse all the forgotten nooks and niches of my body, bringing me to an edge where fear and joy collide. As I questioned his face, remembering my fingers as they had traced the lines around his eyes, forehead, lips, he met my gaze with moist eyes.

"I have always loved you, Zahra."

Just as I was about to reach for him, surrender to his mouth my heaving breasts, melt, something stopped me. I refused to fall for the same man twice. "I will sleep now," I told him, and curled into my bosom, hiding inside the sheets.

At four o'clock, just before dawn, I lay in a chasm somewhere between sleep and delirium. He came to the bed and sat on its edge. Taking my hand he stroked the fingers, moving the ring I wore on my third finger up towards the knuckle and back down to rest at the web between hand and finger. He stopped. Gazed at my hand, traced its sinews, and lifted it into the cup of his palm turning it around to look at the lines of my palm. He pressed the palm against his left cheek. A crescent to hold the moon. "Your beauty shames budding roses."

"Shame comes to those who are ashamed. But roses are shameless. Shame is ashamed of them."

Please stay. I will come and pray to the Hand that will allow these roses to bloom. And they will no longer feel shameful. You must believe. Kiss the thin air. How will I resist?

These are the thoughts swarming in my head as I walk through the rooms of the Victoria and Albert Museum. I am not looking at artefacts but their spirit imbues me all the same. I spend half an hour sitting on the bench in front of a white tapestry with red threads woven into a herd of elephants crossing the bottom of its width. Their trunks form tassels. It is the shawl of a Kashmiri nawab. For three-quarters of an hour I stand in front of the wooden minbar taken from the Fatimid shrine of Al-Azhar. I have the vague sensation of being in the house of a thief. But what a thief. Had he not stolen, I would not have the luxury now to escape into this metonymic sanctuary. But selfishly, now, here, living my life, I am concerned more with Hussein and his theft of Zahra's house.

I need to know why. A reason, so that I can forgive. Stop hating the world and questioning its Creator. I want to end this beautiful nightmare. The twisting tale of sacred loves. Passionate religiosity.

I still dream of living in the rooms of Zahra's house in Zanzibar.

Thai
Egypt

It lies under the Sahara, kissing the tongues of the Nile. The majestic Kilimanjaro juts from its breast flanked to the west by sweet, moist lakes and plush tropics. To the east a series of descending valleys end in dry plateaux whose beaches hover over the ocean, spitting islands into her curved mouth. East Africa, where scientists, historians and archaeologists place the metamorphosis of ancient ape into modern human, lived eventfully but harmoniously with the civilisations of the Bantu, the Kikuyu and the Masai.

The Swahili traded somewhat symbiotically with their cousin across the Indian Ocean, India herself. Their alliance was interrupted during the ninth century by Arabs; initially they came from Oman and Yemen, but later from as far away as Egypt, our own countrymen. They were introduced by the Indian Ocean, a diversion from the southwestern route along the coast of India. The Omanis came and were intrigued. Over centuries, they built a port in Zanzibar. The Sultan attempted to hire local men, few of whom lived along the coast, many of whom were nomadic, for labour. But these men knew nothing of commerce or the exchange of labour. Their economics were indigenous, limited to the functional requirements of survival. Upon refusing payment of the useless gold, silver and bronze coins, they were taken hostage and exported. Hence began the stench of the slave trade. It followed the example of the Romans and drifted from East Africa around Arabia, to North Africa and across the Mediterranean, and roamed westward into the Americas.

ZAHRA

Zahra arrived at the port of Zanzibar with her family aboard a ship entrusted to her father's care by the Sultan Sayyid Barghash. Just before dawn the voice of the muezzin sounded, waking the ship and calling it to shore—a coda followed by an aria of roosters, howling dogs, the shuffling feet of men and women and the stamping hooves of horses and donkeys, to culminate in a crescendo of the ship's engine hooting its answer to the adhan. Zahra and her family were welcomed to Zanzibar by an unforgettable symphony, its orchestra an enigma for the unknowing eye.

Zahra had come from Alexandria. She was twelve years old, transported from one tip of Africa to another. Combustive in spirit, her heart exploded when she came to Zanzibar. The sea air slipped through her lungs and ignited her veins.

Her father, Ahmed Sultan, the merchant son of an Egyptian Pasha who had inherited neither title nor leisure but earned instead the favours of the Omani Sultans who ruled Zanzibar, attended to the off-loading of large gunnysacks. They were filled with yards of softly spun cotton, peppercorns, cardamom seeds, crisp dried red chillies, tea leaves, fat grains of rice, and odd bits of iron metalwork. These would be bartered with greedy sweat and spicy cunning at the harbour's suqoni. They would be traded with other merchants who had crossed the Indian Ocean from Gujarat and Sindh, Madras and Guyana, and descended from Yemen, Arabia and its Gulfs. Most importantly, they would be sold for currency to the British, German and Portuguese navies which sailed around Cape Town and ascended to Zanzibar.

Zahra and her sisters chase each other upon the docks of

Zanzibar harbour, around the toiling figures of a hundred Kamals, Ahmeds and Saeds. Actually the sisters Lutfia and Mouna chase Zahra. She is outwardly timid, built of a quiet, unshakeable strength. This makes her body heavy. It sticks to the ground. Zahra cannot run. She cannot fly like the wind. Instead she follows in the footsteps of elephants, slow and languid, gazing here and there at serpentine ropes, obstinate blocks of wooden boxes, straying crunchy spices, everything. Zahra becomes absorbed in detail, unlike her sisters who simply fly over all insignificance. Zahra takes notice of the sack of spilling cloves or the quietly curled ropes. Details scream for her attention. How do the cloves spill, in what pattern? Look where the rope has frayed, it opens like the thin petals of a spidery flower in spring bloom. Zahra cannot resist the seduction of detail, she sinks into it. By the time she emerges from her obsessions, so much has happened. Lutfia has caught her, tapped on her chest with two fingers and turned her into the jinn who must run with arms outstretched like a mummy to catch her sisters. Zahra must locate herself again, so as not to be lost completely. In the midst of such profundity, her sisters' games seem so childish. She runs after them blindly, her eyes savouring the aroma of Zanzibar. Imagine what unknown prospects linger here?

Zahra is the youngest of the three sisters. At last, all three expended, each by her own world, they fall into the comforting arms of their loving ayah, Fattheyah, to join their mother in the carriage which will take them to their new living quarters.

The family had not been blessed by the birth of a son.

Zanzibar is a city of winding streets, cobbled squares and palm trees, framed by sumptuous Mediterranean arches with haughty Arab domes and a necklace of lotuses borrowed from the house of Lakshmi herself. And the sea, it invades the city bringing not only ships, dhows, merchants and their foreign wares but also stories— histories and legends that have hatched in another land to be transported here, to Africa where destiny's hand will finish the tale. People are everywhere, they have brought with them their pungent smells and resplendent fashions. Their races, features of beauty, striking physicality, poise, manner, saturate the mood. The smoky scent of barbecued fish looms above the harbour. The chattering of dialects, Bantu, Hindi-Urdu, Gujarati, Arabic and Portuguese culminates finally in Swahili.

The sun was shining gloriously, spinning a web of sycamore shadows across the courtyard of the newly built villa, when Zahra arrived at her home at the edge of the Sultan's imperial estates. It had a view from the southern balcony of the notorious, newly built House of Wonders. The family settled predictably into their new life with one shining exception. Zahra's spirit was soaring in anticipation.

Indeed their life was not new at all. Zahra's mother with the help of her numerous servants had packed up the family's life in Alexandria and brought lock, stock and barrel with them to Zanzibar. Zahra slept in the same wooden bed, with its short flat mattress, white sheets and mosquito netting as she had in her room in Alexandria. She even had the same view of the sea, albeit no longer of the Mediterranean. This, well, this was not even a sea was it? It was an ocean. The sea is warmer, cosier, stewed with salt. And the ocean, it is larger, more monumental—monstrous waves joining sequestered continents. But the Mediterranean Sea is vast like an ocean, and the Indian Ocean congenial as the sea. One faces west and the other east. Both were nuclei in an expansive mesh of trade routes where civilisations met and sometimes clashed.

Zahra had high hopes for adventure, even transformation, upon arriving in Zanzibar. She desperately imagined freedom from the life prescribed for her since the moment of her first breath, perhaps even before. She was not a subscriber. She longed to take Fate into her own two hands. To live, actually be alive, a custodian of the earth, rather than mime the motions of living, a mere puppet of society and history. But, as was often the case, Zahra was disappointed. Everything was the same. They ate the same food. Flat bread, boiled eggs, cheese, murabah and fruit for breakfast. True, some of the fruits were new—coconut, papaya, jackfruit and green prickly flowerfruits whose flesh was soft, white as snow and speckled with small black seeds (the Indians called them sitafur). Chicken or shish kebabs, rice and salads were served for lunch, or else lamb stew with courgettes or peppers stuffed with rice and minced meat. She was sure her birthday or any other such festive occasion would produce roasted stuffed pigeons, although she did not know where the pigeons would come from as she had not seen any in Zanzibar just yet. Presumably her mother had imprisoned some and brought them to Zanzibar in cages.

Zahra's mother Amira, the high-born Alexandrian, blonde-haired wife of the darker son of a Cairen Pasha, mother of three daughters and no son, had not wanted to come to Zanzibar, a land of black-skinned Negroes. She had not wanted to leave her precocious family, her intimate childhood friends, that good society which she knew so well. And Alexandria. She had not wanted to leave Alexandria, a prize among the charms of the Mediterranean—even the Europeans came to its shores, not to conquer but to frolic. The Alexandrines themselves, they could perhaps be called Europeans, certainly they had more affinities with their Mediterranean cousins than with the Arabs of the south or heaven forbid the Africans! Unfortunately her husband thought differently. To this day she cannot imagine what had overcome her father when he agreed to marry her to this dark man. Ahmed loved Africa. He had spent a year on the Swahili coast, venturing inland on the plains of the Serengeti before offering his merchant services to the Sultan who had welcomed him. Thus he had returned to Alexandria with long tales for which respected gentlemen visited their courtyard. Whilst managing a kitchen bewildered beyond its capacity of tea, sweets and sometimes even lunch, Amira would catch snippets of his voice. His voice was strong and commanded authority yet simultaneously it was reassuring and inviting, almost seductive. It flowed in a slow, thick, mellifluous wave. He sat on a divan, in the courtyard of their house at the edge of the sea.

The Mediterranean sang her lullabies while he spoke with crisp consonants and gentle vowels. It was the Arabic of the tradition of adab. Powerful and respected men came to listen to him. Those who came early found empty divans for their comfort, and were privileged with a shisha pipe from which to draw the occasional breath of apple-scented tobacco. The late arrivals scattered among stools and cushions, often uncomfortable under the afternoon sun, but they stayed all the same. Many stayed the whole day, taking their meals at the house and catching Ahmed aside for a moment or two to indulge in some kind of personal enquiry. Amira was flattered but also exasperated.

In the sixteenth century, Portuguese ships floating in the Indian Ocean discovered the Cape of Good Hope, unveiling and christening her simultaneously. The Portuguese joined the trade of spices, textiles and slaves in the enterprise of the Indian Ocean trade routes. The silk route began to dip southwards. Soon, Portuguese ships dominated these routes; founding entire towns along the Madras coast, and developing Zanzibar. Thus Europe joined India, Arabia and Africa in the masala of the Indian Ocean. The power of the Portuguese would decline during the sixteenth and seventeenth centuries.

The British arrived looking for the sun. They discovered the interior plains of East Africa. Their fleets firmly planted in the Indian Ocean, they dominated the northern and western provinces of India, inaugurating the British Raj. How quickly the proud British navy took over the control of the Indian Ocean trade routes, seeking to develop the civilisations of its victim and victimising merchants and middlemen, and slaves. Their demise will come one day but perhaps not soon. But Zanzibar remains an Omani Sultanate, under the Busaidi Sultans.

Her daughters helped Amira to organise the staff and kitchen to accommodate the guests. Except Zahra, that is. Zahra sat hidden from the men's view, behind her father's divan, listening and dreaming.

Ahmed decided to move his family to Zanzibar, reassuring Amira that Africa would spoil neither the breeding nor the marriageability of their three young daughters. Thus six months were spent getting ready for the journey on a ship entrusted to Ahmed's care by the Sultan Sayyid Barghash. It will travel from Alexandria through the Suez Canal and the Red Sea into the Indian Ocean in time to catch the southern monsoon.

On the day of their departure, Zahra wakes excitedly to a flutter of butterflies soaring in her gut. The sky is grey and dull. Rain. How will they journey with the rain? But they do. Ahmed Sultan will not be swayed by the skies. Amira sends Lutfia into the sisters' room to wake and dress them, and send them to breakfast. The family gather for their last breakfast in Alexandria, at their home among the prestigious houses of the corniche along the Mediterranean. Seven trunks wait at the doorway, one for each of the daughters and two for each parent. The rest of the house has been packed, boxed, trunked and already loaded onto the ship that awaits them at the harbour. Amira's mood over breakfast shifts from sullen gloom to anxiety as she gathers and organises her daughters, the elder two of whom have already entered womanhood and at fourteen and sixteen been introduced to Alexandria society as eligible women. She bitterly regrets what this move to dark Africa could do to their chances of a good marriage but has learnt already that arguing with her husband once he has made a decision is futile. Lutfia and Mouna carefully mimick her footsteps as she swings from dull gloom to hyper anxiety. Zahra however does not take after their mother, but rather their father, who is in a thundering mood of excitement and high spirits. He arrives at breakfast freshly scrubbed and glowing like the sun that today has neglected its skies. He speaks of adventure and new horizons and life and the world and good character but above all of hope for the future. As they near the end of their breakfast, relatives and friends begin to drop by for a last Goodbye. Some of the men—Amira's father and brother and one of Ahmed's maternal uncles—will assist with the embarking and then wave goodbye and recite a quick prayer for their safe journey.

The sisters have their own compartments next to their mother's on the second deck. Lutfia and Mouna settle in and proceed to organise their belongings. Zahra leaves her things where they are and runs out to explore the ship before her mother can stop her. The men, including their father, reside below, on the first deck. Zahra knows better than to stray past the second deck. She explores every nook and cranny of her domain and thus possessing it, reigns over it. She also knows that her mother and sisters will not venture beyond their compartments unless absolutely necessary. She is happily queen of her queendom.

They arrive at the port of Zanzibar just before dawn. The voice of the muezzin called them to shore.

Two or three times a week Arab women, most are from Oman, come to the new house on the southeastern shore of Zanzibar. They arrive in time for coffee, just after the siesta. They are the type of women who used to come to the house in Alexandria: fair-skinned cunning beauties with wagging tongues. They come adorned in their twinkling jewels. Always fussing about everything insignificant and resigned to their own place in the world of their men. When Zahra or one of her sisters serves coffee and sweet pastries, oh how they look, ogling each new curve and twist as the testament to a transition from girlness to womanhood. Perhaps they remember their own transitions, the youth of their flesh. More likely they have become voyeurs, twice displaced, looking with the lust of their men, which has transmigrated, like a spirit, into their forms. Zahra's blood boils with rage at these scenes. She loathes them. Has watched her cousin Salima metamorphise from an intelligent spirited woman into a limp, gibbering wife-cum-servant who speaks coquettishly in riddles. Surely men are more respectable than to want this in their wives. Surely women are not the same all around Africa? Zahra mutters a prayer under her tongue, "Allah, save me from this monotony." Uneasiness fills her. She knows she will break the cycle. Her spirit soars in anticipation.

A sheikh comes to the house twice a week to instruct her and her sisters in the virtues associated with the emblem of Islam. They begin not with the first verse of the Qur'an, but with the first verse revealed to the Prophet Muhammad by the archangel Gabriel, the Surah of the Ovum Cell:

$$\text{بِسْمِ اللهِ الرَّحْمَانِ الرَّحِيمِ}$$

$$\text{اقْرَأْ بِاسْمِ رَبِّكَ الَّذِي خَلَقَ}$$
$$\text{خَلَقَ الْاِنْسَانَ مِنْ عَلَقٍ}$$
$$\text{اقْرَأْ وَرَبُّكَ الْاَكْرَمُ}$$
$$\text{الَّذِي عَلَّمَ بِالْقَلَمِ}$$

In the name of Allah, the Most Beneficent, the Most Merciful,
Read in the name of your Lord who Created,
He Created humankind from an ovum cell,
Read and your Lord is the Most Noble
He Who Taught by the pen
Taught humankind that which it did not know.

Zahra forgets the words she is reciting and becomes lost in their curves, following each twist until delirious. So the sheikh's wife comes to teach her to embroider. She buries her face in the life of the threads around her, unravelling them, the poignant colours screaming at her. She pricks her thumbs to prove that her red is scarlet and the threads' only red. Two weeks after she pricked her thumbs, she bleeds. Becomes a woman. Now her mother fusses in anticipation of blood-stained honour every time Zahra goes running through the streets, wanders in the markets, goes to the sea to collect shells and eat barbe-cued fish drenched in salt and lemon juice with chillies.

One evening the women of Zanzibar's Yemeni, Omani, Lebanese and Egyptian élite are due to gather at Zahra's house. Her mother has prepared halawat: sweets of every imaginable nature. That morning, Zahra wanders around the kitchen and eats stray pistachios, chunks of cocoa and lumps of sugar. She lingers over ripened apricots and flirting seeds of pomegranate. Green luscious figs seduce her. She loses her grip, falling into a bowl of blushing berries.

In the afternoon, before bathing, Zahra is filled with excitement. She detects a pain in her stomach, it comes from somewhere deeper than her insides, like the sound of a conch. While she is bathing, Fattheyah comes with a loofah to scrub her body. Then Fattheyah dries her, and sprinkles a fine, soft talcum on her body. All over her body, how new this is. Fattheyah wraps her in a cloth and takes her to her mother's room.

Six women have gathered here. Her two sisters Lutfia and Mouna. Her aunt who is visiting, her father's widowed sister Johara, with her daughter, Zahra's cousin Jihan, her mother Amira, and finally a tall dark-skinned Somali woman with strong, well formed arms. Perplexed and somewhat shy, Zahra sits with them until her mother calls to her.

"Come," she says. "This is Auntie Sahar," pointing to the Somali woman. "She is going to clean you. Muslim women must be clean. She will remove all the dirty hair from your body and make it clean with this halava of cooked sugar and lemon. It is bitter and sweet. When you feel pain, close your eyes, hold my hand and squeeze."

Sahar takes her to a corner of the room. Beside a thin straw mat covered with a cotton cloth, is an earthenware bowl. Amira follows her daughter to the mat. She lifts the cloth from Zahra's legs and gathers it at her pubis to tuck under her bottom. Sahar kneels with bent haunches opposite Zahra, and pulls one leg towards her. She takes the golden dough in her hands and, moulding it, breaks off a piece. She rolls the piece between her fingers, pulling and stretching until it loses some of its golden sheen and eventually takes on the tones of muted amber. At last, she sticks a rounded ball of dough to Zahra's knee and then stretches it down towards her ankle. She massages the dough onto her leg until she is sure it has stuck, then with one swift movement she pulls it off and Zahra feels a burning sensation as her hair and an invisible layer of her skin, affixed to the paste, fly off. Amira is expecting tears but Zahra looks at her with dry red eyes. It was painful, but from the pain came release: bitter and sweet. She held her mother's hand but did not squeeze for fear of breaking her frail fingers. Auntie Sahar finishes both her legs and thighs, then she continues, now with her arms. She stretches her arm far behind her back and cleans Zahra's armpits of their sweet, sticky fine hairs. Sahar even cleans her face, buffing her upper lip and eyebrows. Then Sahar looks at Amira and Zahra's mother nods. Amira tugs the cloth from Zahra's bottom and lifts it above her genitals. Zahra is overcome with embarrassment and indignation. She looks questioningly at her mother who avoids her gaze. Sahar pulls Zahra towards her and lifts each leg to rest upon her shoulder. She takes a clean patch of dough and gently rolls it onto Zahra's pubis. When she rips it off Zahra screams. She bruises her mother's hands and Amira sees her tears.

Zahra's skin was now a different colour, like honey mixed with attar, shining and tender: soft as silk. Fattheyah washed her again. This time gently. When she finished, her mother came with coconut oil heated in amber, then cooled with mint, and rubbed it into her body and the undulating coarseness of the hair remaining on her head. That evening when Zahra met all the women from the neighbourhood, she wore a new mint-coloured ghalibeyeh, jasmine flowers were woven into her hair, and kohl circled her eyes. She entered amidst cadences of the Egyptian-flavoured taarab concert performed by none other than the Sultan's musicians.

The women were the same ones who came for coffee: the mothers, aunts and sisters of eligible boys from honourable families. They had come to inspect the newest offering at the altar of a tradition-bound marriage. The truth, unknown to Zahra, was that tales of her fabled beauty had reached the Sultan's court and penetrated into the harem. The Sultana is looking to marry her young son who will soon fill his father's shoes and become Sultan himself. He must be married before he becomes Sultan, but alas he is such a difficult young man and will not even look at the women his mother parades before him. The Sultana has high hopes that the Egyptian's beauty will melt him. Appropriately then, having first sent an emissary with a declaration of interest in Zahra to Ahmed Sultan, the girl's father, who luckily enough is employed by the Sultan—she has sent her most trustworthy maid to inspect the girl. Ahmed has spoken to Amira and asked her to prepare the girl. Thus Zahra's halava has been done, but Amira has not actually spoken to Zahra or to the elder girls. Although Lutfia and Mouna have probably guessed she is quite sure that Zahra hasn't a clue. Amira thinks it bad form for her youngest daughter to be married first but alas it is the Sultan's son and if the Sultan and more importantly the Sultana approved the match, then she cannot contest it. Ahmed wanted his daughters to marry Arabs, of the Omani nobility preferably, thus sealing the favourable relations between him and the Sultan. How could he object to the Sultan's son himself, even if he had chosen his youngest and beloved Zahra. After all, Amira had confirmed that since their arrival in Zanzibar, Zahra had become a woman, as ready to be married as any of her fair race. Perhaps it was providence, Allah's will that the family should come to Zanzibar so that Zahra could marry the Sultan's son. And perhaps Zahra, with her tempestuous

temper was best married off at an early age. Indeed, she would be a
Sultana, perhaps even with free reign to indulge her spirited fancies.

VILAYAT KHAN

Vilayat Khan was a poor, double-exiled Gujarati merchant-labourer.
He was more labourer than merchant but he preferred to think of
himself as a merchant. He had arrived in Zanzibar as a worker on a
ship. He was lodged at the coolies' living quarters ten minutes from
the harbour. They were instructed never to wander further than a
half-hour radius from the shore as ships, filled with cargo to be
unloaded, arrived without notice at all hours of the day and night.
But the monsoon had been held back. The rains were stuck in low
billowing clouds which would not break. No ships had arrived for
days. The workers lazed about the harbour swimming, chatting,
smoking their bedis and sampling some of this new Arab drink called
araq.

Vilayat Khan sat slightly apart from the rest of the coolies,
ostensibly not to be disturbed by them. He hated the fact that he,
Vilayat Khan, had been reduced to a coolie. Fate, how unpredictable
is your hand! So he would lie, as if born a nobleman instead of a
bastard, slightly aside, and remember the good old days in the
motherland. He thought of his deccased wife, how they had met at
the nawab's court. She had been a courtesan, ah what a woman! She
read philo-sophy and astronomy, composed poetry, knew the secrets
of alchemy, plucked moist ragas on the sitar, and oh when she danced
those thundering khatak beats. He could see her still, close his eyes
and hear her junjuru. She had loved him but refused to leave the
court. So he had joined it. After the marriage she stopped
entertaining male guests and instead taught the new girls what she
had learned from her predecessors. She and Vilayat were happy with
their rooms inside the staff quarters and their two cheerful sons.
Then the British came. They raged and plundered, raped and killed,
destroyed and rebuilt. The nawab's court had fallen to siege, ashen
under cannon smoke. Vilayat's wife died and he was left penniless,
with two boys and without skill. The British were followed by

sweeping droughts that came from the crackling plains of the Kalahari desert. So he left his sons with his sister and came to East Africa. He came to quench his thirst. Vilayat Khan sought fortune in Zanzibar.

It is on such an afternoon, before dusk, when the sun had launched a blazing fire of orange, red and saffron into the sky that Vilayat, wading along the shore, lost in a cloud of araq, spots Zahra. Her hair, dipped in sunlight and glowing, shines stubbornly through her pale headscarf. The soft round contour of her breasts with nipples proud and piercing salute the heavens in defiance of the cotton bodice of her ghalibeyeh. The sea air creeping through the crackling skirt to cling at her waist allows the hips to thrust through. And oblivious Zahra licking her lips and fingers for last traces of cumined fish. She raises, after an infinity, her affectionate head to receive the sun's last embrace before retreat, and turns to face the swooning Indian. He is neither humble nor servile, but graciously proud, for here is his promised Lakshmi, two in one lifetime. He has found her in the land where even the English sahibs have ventured in search of jewels. Africa, how unpredictable your secrets.

Zahra watches him emerge from the shore. He is long-limbed and lithe, powerful as that taut column which carries a dome. His skin has the colour of molasses, his nose is like the hook of a hawk. An Indian Adonis, plucked directly from the sculptures of the Vedas. But not Hindu, no. Observe Zahra's luck, the angels have been kind. He is Muslim. His people have been convinced by mystic pirs who came from Persia two centuries before the British, to pledge allegiance to Allah, the one and only Deity, and Muhammad, His Messenger, and Ali, His Imam. Later, when the Central Asian Turks arrived from the mountains of Caucus, they coerced those who had not been convinced by the mystics and their moon. Vilayat Khan, impoverished child of a fallen, disfavoured nawab and his Hindu consort, followed not only in his father's footsteps, but also an Islam that is heretic—one that recast the tenets of Muhammad and the Qur'an into the metaphors and legends of Vedic gods and goddesses. One God, one blinding light and many manifestations.

White shalwars rolled to the knee, shirtless, his brown skin glistening, muscles taut, head held high, high. Sullen beauty. He blinks. She sees with vampiric vision for the first time, a scarlet blood that rises to meet her own. How bizarre, this fateful concoction, to find that it is shared. Scarlet and scarlet strike a fire, it is indiminishable. A match made in heaven but with the heavy hand of tradition running contrary.

He walks towards her. She knows she must turn her head away and give him her back, but she cannot. Instead she smiles. He does not return the smile, only stares. His eyes shine. She must turn away. So she turns slowly, but towards him.

"Assalaam Wa Ailekum," he says.

"Wa Aileykum as-Salaam," she murmurs.

What will be their language? She speaks Arabic, Alexandrian Amiya. He speaks Gujarati and can recite the Urdu verses of Iqbal. Both know a little English.

"How do you do, lady?"

"Very fine, with thanks?"

"I see you speaking some English."

"Little bit," she gestures with her thumb and forefinger.

Finally he smiles. She laughs and looks satisfactorily at her feet. He wants desperately to touch her hands. In the distance, Fattehyah calls, "ZZZaahrrrah".

She turns and runs. This time like thunder. The heaviness is gone. And he knows her name. Zahra.

The next morning Zahra is lying in her bed with mosquito netting open, bathing in the first rays of the sun mingled with the sea's morning breeze. Zahra feels poetic, that is, she understands that these are the moments of which poetry is composed. Her spirit lulls her mind. Her mind swims amidst words and sounds, in a rhythm whose repetition is sensuous, infiltrated with desire-reminiscent, a caressing lightness: the sound of resplendent laughter in memory. Sweet, timid happiness and wondrous fate.

Ten thousand names but none as resonant as his.

Africa. Kilimanjaro, enigmatic and mystical. Calm under the burning sun. Surreptitious branches of the baobab tree, satanic in its implications. Birds that wail. Sad, brooding elephants. Zahra already knows, has a premonition that this day will be momentous.

Gargoyles are swimming in her stomach. She will go to the harbour for barbecued fish and for the Indian. She sits through lunch with her mother and sisters with a mounting anxiety cooked with desire. Her appetite has faltered. She cannot eat. Instead she picks at the plate of chicken and rice. She answers her mother and sisters, even Fattehyah, with murmurs and monosyllabic euphemisms. In turn, they happily attribute her sullenness to feminine angst. Amira makes a note: if all goes well, the marriage should take place sooner rather than later. After lunch has ended, during the hour of siesta, Zahra snatches some coins from a bowl above the shelves of flour and lentils that serves as the cook's kitchen bank and escapes to the harbour, without Fattehyah.

She walks towards the sea, heading down, straight, then right, right and left. She is walking now along a boulevard parallel to the shoreline. She strolls past the Royal Tombs, the People's Palace, the Royal Baths. Past the magnificent House of Wonders, the harbour unfolds before the Old Fort. Upon arriving at the seashore, she looks for him. She walks slowly away from the mass of activity at the harbour, through spicy market stalls, spilling baskets of fruit and vegetables, overflowing buckets of fish, aromatic vats of Zanzibari curry and rice, between stray children, donkeys and the odd horse, towards the labourers and the boats, the world of men. She approaches with trepidation a world from which she is banned—as close as she dares. She becomes acutely aware that she is a young girl, wandering alone without male protection, chaperone or even a group of peers. She feels the discomfort of male eyes on her. She searches for him. Not seeing him, she is crestfallen. Mouth dropping, head down, she withdraws with dragging feet, retracing her footsteps.

He is looking for her. Escaping at half-hour intervals from the dhows at the shore to hurry to the centre of the harbour, he peers among the faces of the women buying fish, selling their wares, strolling with husband and children or sisters and cousins, praying that he might gaze upon her.

Zahra, who has not eaten a morsel of her lunch, finally succumbs to the barbecued aroma. Coin in hand, she walks towards an old man squatting by a large bucket of burning coal above which rests a metal grill. Succulent fish lie oozing on the grill. Zahra silently hands him her coin. He removes four large fish from his grill, wraps them in a huge coconut leaf and hands them to her. The package is hot. She can hardly hold it. She hugs the fish close and lifts the sides of her ample ghalibeya to form a mitt to protect her hands from the heat.

Zahra walks past the noisy harbour towards the sea. She finds a quiet beach strewn with large angular rocks. Balancing, she climbs onto a rock and sits with her feet in the shallow water. She removes her sandals and places them beside her. Then she bends and reaches into the water to wash her hands. She mutters a Bismillah and unfolds the fish from its leaf. The fragrance fills her. The skin is flaky, charbroiled reddish brown and still hot. She lifts it off to find shining soft creamy flesh beneath. Zahra pries the fish open with her fingers, removes the skeleton and sucks the pieces of flesh off its bones. She finds a juicy morsel and drops it into her mouth, closing her eyes to savour the taste.

Vilayat is watching her. Having found her at the grill, he has followed her. Softly, he approaches behind her. She hears his footsteps and turns with fear, mouth full. She sees him, she swallows and her face softens. He joins her on a nearby rock, at a respectable distance. She offers him a fish and he takes it, they eat in silence, watching the sea.

Zahra, in one swift breath, bids adieu to her family, her home, and the nagging weakness of her mother who needed to conform and the sisters who could not but please the mother. And her father. Who was he? His mistress knew him better than anyone. Zahra, who was close to him, glimpsed emotion on his face only on the occasion of tragedy or religious duty. Never had she seen his face react in love or sorrow. Her mother was weak and her father was strong, this is how Zahra at twelve years of age, about to be wed, understood marriage.

Vilayat Khan arranged with his friend Jamil, a short, stocky, reliable man, to row by night from Zanzibar to Dar es Salaam in the dhow used by coolies to meet incoming ships. Zahra left Zanzibar from the harbour, just after dusk, the adhan ringing in her ears. She would never return.

Upon arriving in Dar es Salaam, Jamil takes them to the Jamaat

Khana, the Imami Muslims' prayer house. Here, tired, wet and hungry, they wait for the Mukhi Sahib, the Jamaat leader who represents the Imam. The Imam is the spiritual and material guide to lead Muslims towards the will of Allah, or the Right Path. Vilayat Khan explained it to Zahra on the boat, with the accompaniment of wild gestures. "We, you see, we, you and me. We are only like tears of water. Imam is like river. We join and follow him. He is leading to sea. Sea is Allah. Everything water, you understand?" Zahra had stared at him in confusion. It was dark, he mistook the shaking of her head to and fro for the Indian affirmative acknowledgement of truth. Resistance, he could not see it. Perhaps he was momentarily blind.

At 3:15 a.m. the Mukhi Sahib arrives at the Dar es Salaam Jamaat Khana and finds three strangers waiting for him. The two men rise to their feet.

"Ya Ali Madaad."

"Mowla Ali Madaad."

The woman remains quiet. Jamil pulls the Mukhi aside and in hushed tones explains that the couple want to be married. The Mukhi turns to catch a glimpse of the girl. He is astonished by her beauty. Surely she is not Indian, and if Indian then definitely not Gujarati.

"And her parents?"

"Bechari. She is an orphan. My friend is doing a great service. No dowry, nothing."

The Mukhi Sahib agrees to marry the two, against his better instincts. This is East Africa after all, not Junagadh, not Kutch, not even India. Not home. Strange things happen here. The man is saving an orphan, the Prophet himself, peace be upon him, himself taught to treat widows and orphans as your own. "We can hurry before the paro diya Jamaat arrives. She is Imami?" he asks.

"No," Jamil replies. "Only Muslim."

"Good enough."

And so, tired and hungry, in a red, fish-stained ghalibeyah, without henna, Zahra is married to Vilayat Khan.

After the dawn prayers the Mukhi Sahib takes them to his home. His wife, the Mukhiani, bathes and feeds Zahra. She dresses her in new clothes: a long fitted dress with bodice and skirt, frock, and a sheer piece of cloth bordered with twisting arabesques and silver moons. Thus frocked, with pachedi-veil over her head and kohl, except now it is called aanjar, around her eyes, she joins her husband on their wedding day. He is tired and eager to sleep. They retreat to an alcove behind the house. Zahra lies on a straw mat covered with a cotton sheet, no mosquito netting. She lies very still while he approaches her. Brushing aside the pachedi he smells and unties her hair. His fingers stroke her neck and he places his lips at the cleft where neck meets shoulder. Fumbling with the hooks at the side of her frock, he undresses her. She is stunned, cannot think what this might be and so lies silently still. His hand cups her young breast. His lips take hold of her ascending nipple. Deftly, he drops his shalwars and she finds herself horrified but still reaching for him. His hands move to her belly. Kneading her thighs he spreads them. His fingers open her where she is already moist. Swiftly, with the rhythm of a tabla, he enters her. His hand reaches to cover her mouth, silencing her cry.

Vilayat labours under the sweltering sun, harvesting cloves, cocoa and copra on colonial farms, and carting iron, steel and coal to the sites of new European railroads. Zahra soaks her golden hands in dust, grime and acidic vinegar, dips the ingots of her knees in filth, to clean the floors of mosques, temples, churches and government buildings. In the late heavy afternoons they return to their alcove in the Mukhi Sahib's house. Vilayat takes a seat on a cushion covered in kitange cloth, sitting on a thin mattress in the anterior room where they sleep, eat, wash and dress. Zahra washes her feet up to the shins, her hands up to the elbows, and face and neck at the kitchen sink. She collects water from the pump in a small pot and places it on a fire of coals. She adds long stringy dried tea leaves, a sprinkling of sugar and a couple of cardamoms to the pot. She fetches a glass of milk from the Mukhiani's kitchen, pours it into the tea and lets it boil and brew. This is how Vilayat has taught her to prepare his tea. When it is ready, she pours it into two glass tumblers and sets them down beside him. She fetches dry scraps of bread left over from breakfast and settles down beside him. They drink their tea and snack on the bread. She lays her head on his shoulder, desperate for comfort. He absently strokes her hair while pondering what irrational destiny he has brought to her, and to himself. They rise and he rinses his brow of the day's sweat. She changes into the Mukhiani's old clothes. They accompany the Mukhi and Mukhiani to evening prayers at Jamaat Khana.

Zahra finds gracious solitude here. She sits alone, by the walls at the back of the prayer hall. She understands none of the prayers or invocations chanted in various Indian dialects. The entire congregation prays in unison, with one person at the pulpit, leading. They stand for a quarter of an hour on their feet and recite the names of Allah and Ali, sending invocations for the blessing of the family of the prophet, appealing for forgiveness of their sins, understanding of Truth, strength of faith, barakat abundance in their daily bread. The Jamaat's resident missionary, a sort of muslim wise man whom the Jamaat approached with questions of the faith and help in meditation has translated for her the almost Vedic efflorescence of the Khoja ginans and tasbihs into the rigid austerity of classical Arabic grammar. She closes her eyes and releases her imagination from the day's prison. The melodies of the mysterious hymns swim around her. The incense and the seeds of the tasbih which she calls sibah moving between thumb and forefinger, calm her. She sits crossed-legged in the same corner until the ceremony ends and people scatter with their chit-chat and private prayers.

She helps the Mukhiani and her volunteers to clean and prepare the prayer hall for morning prayers. In the evenings Vilayat and Zahra share a meal of mishkaki, curried cassava, lentil bhajias and cool, salty lassi with the Mukhi and Mukhiani and their six children.

Zahra joined the heretic faith. She accepted Ali as Imam, river-guide, to Allah the sea. Zahra wore frock-pachedis and plaited her hair down the middle of her head. Vilayat Khan bought her glass bangles that jingled on both her wrists. How stupid she had been not to take even a little of her gold from home. Zahra met other young wives in the community. An introduction and reference from the Mukhiani of Dar es Salaam carried its own weight. Language was a problem but these women nourished her all the same. They helped her to find work. When neither she nor Vilayat had any work, the elder women of the Jamaat fed them. Having set a precedent in

Dar es Salaam, they slept with the authority of the capital's Mukhi at the house of every Mukhi at every town along their route. And so, Zahra was reborn. She adopted a new identity. It brought her a community. Acceptance: you are one of us, we are one. Helping hands, work, food, shelter. It nourished her, offered new venues for her spirit: love, beauty and loyalty.

Viliyat Khan, anxious that people will see that Zahra is not an Indian but Arab, and jealous of the affection his young wife receives from the community, restrains her. He forbids her to speak. He explains to those who inquire that she is dumb and mute, unable to speak or understand. This was true, but only with the Gujarati tongue. It was with this tongue that he confined her, with his culture that he restrained her. Zahra would hear her own language in the marketplace and long to chat with whoever was speaking it.

Once she met a Zanzibari trader at the suqoni. He was trading cloves. Zahra approached shyly. Inspecting his cloves, she made small talk. The trader offered her a cup of tea. Delighted at the prospect of a conversation and something to quench her thirst, she immediately accepted. That evening, at Jamaat Khana, Vilayat was informed that his wife took tea in the market with an Arab. At night, when they returned home, he forbade Zahra to set foot in the market. From now on he would do the shopping.

Fear drove Vilayat Khan. Surely the Arab Sultan of Zanzibar would take personally the insult to Zahra's family and indeed to the entire Arab community of East Africa. If they knew who he was, what he had done, and where to find him, he would not live to think these thoughts. Vilayat Khan did not lack the impulse for grandiose thoughts: We are one, they are one, must be, no? Fair-skinned, long-limbed, doe-eyed goddess stolen by mud-coloured filth? How could it be? And defiled, humiliated, rotting honour—Zahra's honour, her mother's, her sister's, but above all her father's. And his audacity to steal a second wife...

He must hide her. So Vilayat Khan, bitter and brooding, shocked at his luck, unsure if he was worthy of the goddess, silenced her. He did it fiercely and with pride. Never, not once, was the Egyptian allowed to scream.

Eventually they left the nest of the Mukhi Sahib's home, moving northwest. They settled first in Mwanza, then returned east to Arusha and, finally, Moshi. Vilayat Khan found a job working on a colonial farm near Moshi in the valley between Mount Kilimanjaro and Mount Mehru. The land grew coffee and cocoa. The pay was good and living quarters were included. So he and Zahra moved to a field nestled among the foothills of Mount Kilimanjaro. They settled there. She was expecting their first child.

All this time Zahra has been trying not to think of her mother, her sisters and her father. She misses them. She remembers how they used to frustrate her, but she loves them all the same. Tangled threads of red, red blood that can be neither cut nor burned. They preserve. Running away solves nothing. It only changes the perspective: Zahra learns this too late. Will she see them again? At times she cannot believe what has happened. What has she done? No one forced her to run away with him. What did she do? How did it happen so quickly? Sister Fate, I see you, here, now before my eyes. She must not think of these things.

In the mornings when Zahra prepares tea and millet rotlas for Vilayat Khan, she imagines her mother watching her with those disdainful eyes. Squatting on the cracked balls of her feet, her face sweating over the open fire, she sees her mother in the kitchen. Queen bee supervising her servants. Zahra bathes shamefully at the well, using water that is laced with the silt of Kilimanjaro. She is no longer fair but bronzed by the sun. Princess has become pauper. Her mother would have been happy with Zahra's neatness and organisation. O Mother! She laments. How you must have wept. I did not come home from the sea. It drank me. I hope and pray you think me dead. Washed away. In your world, it is a much better fate.

The first time Vilayat Khan beat her was in Moshi, just before they moved to the farm. She had burned the only rice they had to eat. He was furious. She was five months pregnant and had been as hungry as he. He screamed at her and she screamed back. "It's not my fault. I also have been working all day. Why do you come home and lie there? Expecting that I should always prepare your meal even when I cannot bear to stand. I was not born to live this way. I am not your slave and servant!" The inside of his palm caught her left cheek and swung her head towards her right shoulder. The pot of burned rice falls from her hands. It hits her shins, causing her to buckle under. She falls. She lands on her back. He lifts his right leg to kick her and she folds her arms and head over her belly to shield the child. His foot stops in midair. He turns and walks out into the night. Zahra drops her shoulders to the ground. She weeps with writhing convulsions. Then she faints.

When Zahra wakes it is the middle of the night. She finds beside her a wooden bowl filled with boiled cassava and stewed meat. He has covered her with a blanket. She cannot see him. He is out still. She is grateful for this.

Zahra gave birth for the first time inside their hut. She had been on her haunches by the coal fire preparing lunch when her water broke. She rocked herself up into a standing position and called for her husband. But he was not in a place where her voice could reach him. She became momentarily frantic, and then calmness came to her. She knew that she would be alone. She went inside and lay down on their mattress, being careful first to cover their bed sheet with an old dark-coloured kitange cloth. She removed her underwear and spread her legs wide before her, bending her knees. When she began to scream hysterically the African women who worked on the farm heard her agony and a group came to the hut. The women boiled water and found a cloth to tear into towels. They opened Zahra's legs wider and finally held her up to squat while her child pushed through into the world. They cut the cord which binds mother to child. They washed both mother and child, fed Zahra and taught her how to feed her child.

When Vilayat Khan came home from the Moshi markets that evening, he found his wife asleep beside his son. Her first child and his third son. Zahra was fourteen years old and her husband twenty-six. Vilayat names his son Taqdeer, after that Hand which none can betray. Destiny.

The child brings a new joy to Zahra's days. She keeps him at her breast as she would all her children.

Zahra is not allowed to speak to her child in Arabic. If Vilayat Khan catches her, he beats the language out of her. She speaks to him, her little boy called Taqdeer, in Swahili. The language is arabised enough for her to manage.

Often after his thundering slap has once again sent her crashing onto the mud floor of their hut, she considers returning to Zanzibar. She could reach Dar es Salaam through a sympathetic car driver, bargained bus ticket or even heavy foot. From there she could beg and pray for a dhow ride to Zanzibar. But she has no home there. And what of her infant child? She could write to her father. What will she say? Forgive me for I have sinned in my ignorance? What will he do? Undoubtedly his slap will be as hard as Vilayat Khan's, if not harder. He will issue her out the door. Her mother's compassion, even wailing, what will it accomplish in this world of male significance? Zahra is no longer the daughter of a wealthy and influential merchant, she is the wife of a coolie. She must remember that she chose this fate. Zahra will stay. Their fates married in blood that flows in the child's veins. She will breathe twelve lives for him. They will speak Swahili and Gujarati, but not know a word of Arabic. They will pledge allegiance to the Imam of the time. They will wear the mask of Khoja. But hair will shine golden like the Egyptian sun, skin will glitter like moon-kissed dunes in the Sahara. Despite herself, Zahra loves Vilayat Khan. He has not beaten it out of her.

Zahra met more Indians, some of whom now distinguished themselves as Muslims, uttering that still premature identity: Pakistani. She embraced them. She embraced the Africans. Zahra embraced everything around her. She needed the return of her energy. She embraced to heal. She advised other women to do the same. They would gather, heat turmeric and heal their wounds. Zahra became their nurse, mother, leader, goddess. Zahra learns that her fate is not so exceptional. The women whom she embraces, when she shows them her scars, have ones to match. She refuses to drown in a pool of pity and despair. She learns to love, and to smile and heal. She reaches deep inside, digs for strength, and hands it around. The deeper she digs, the more she finds. Women from nearby villages begin to visit her. Africans and Khojas. They bring their sorrow, their illness, weakness, disease and hunger. She opens her door wide and they enter. She feeds them, hearing their tales. She soothes bruises, mends cuts, calms fevers, appeases scrapes and scars. She renews from despoil and disease their withering spirits. Zahra pours the burning fire of her beauty into them. She makes them beautiful.

She has no science, no philosophy, no theoretical injunction, only pure unwavering faith. Zahra healed with her conviction. She healed with the power of her spirit, passion, the strength of which sent her lover cowering into vileness. Zahra channelled her love, bitter pain, anger and confusion into a balm to soothe and heal those born into the world to be tempted astray. Kafirs, we, all of us Indian and Arab, African and European, Hindus, Muslims, Christians. All the while her husband worked, or sat outside the Jamaat Khana drinking chai and smoking bedis with the men.

She bequeaths to their children her regal breadth: her pronounced beauty will last into the second and even third generations. Her children become disciples of the moon. She bathes them in her love, nurtures their souls, teaches them to dream and above all to be free. She shields them from their father's anger but they witness his fury all the same. They watch as their noble mother bows under his crude thunder. They will see her blood on his brow. They will hate him, only to discover his blood in their own veins, loving him in the same breath. Zahra's children will carry the passion of Vilayat Khan, in hatred and in love, to death, both his and theirs.

When Ali was born, their twelfth child, a son, they did not have a name for him. Vilayat liked the English endearment "Jimmy" and called him this name as he held, rocked and entertained him. The rest of the household picked up the name and the baby boy was known as Jimmy, but he was clearly still unnamed. When he was three months old, while Zahra was meditating with closed eyes to her zikr, her eyes opened to see the baby cooing his own name: AaaaahLeeeeey. That evening she told her husband she had decided to name her son "Ali". He did not object. Julleh Laal.

Vilayat Khan tended the land with the help of his five sons ranging in age from six to twenty-two. Harvest came twice a year. The two eldest sons took coffee and cocoa beans into the markets of Moshi and Arusha, and traded them for British East African shillings. The youngest stayed at home with their mother, three sisters, two sisters-in-law, and two toddling nephews. These boys were older than Ali, but still too young for the farm. They were the offspring of the two eldest brothers, who had already married and brought their wives home to live on the land. They erected tiny hut-rooms behind the rickety wooden structure that Vilayat had provided as his family home. The bhabis and their subsequent children lived in the house with the rest of the family. Two sisters had also married. The eldest lived fifteen miles away in Arusha with her husband and infant son. The second-oldest had married into a Sindhi family and lived a foreign life in Karachi. She had already borne two children.

The young women of Zahra's household tended to the daily chores. Grinding dried grains into flour for bread. Harvesting, washing and preparing vegetables. Cleaning and cooking freshly slaughtered meats. Sorting, soaking and cooking rice. Lighting fires, and sweeping and mopping the rooms. Washing, hanging and folding laundry. Feeding, bathing and minding the children. Sewing and mending clothes. In the midst of this, Zahra, in her crowning role of supervising mother, sat with her tasbih, which she called sibah, counting out on its beads the recitations of her zikr and receiving the visitors whom she soothed and healed. Many stayed for lunch or tea while they waited, and the young women served them. The house was blessed with Barakat. Ali stayed always beside his mother. When they were alone, she gave him her breast and rocked him to sleep with stories of the seashore in Zanzibar, and a house framed by sycamore branches.

When Ali was four years old, Zahra died while reciting the second part of the holy heretic prayer called Du'a. Her heart stopped. Zahra, who had married Vilayat Khan at twelve years of age, died twenty-eight years later, having borne him twelve children. There were rumours that she had committed suicide, unable to bear Vilayat. But those who knew her denied this fervently. Zahra's faith was as strong and solid as a column that holds the dome.

But what of Vilayat? Two lakshmis in one lifetime, both lost. Zahra, beatings sustained, elevated his life. She brought him closer to heaven. Her smile, with which she woke him, was like a ray of morning sun. The flowers collected and placed in every room, in glass jars and tins, or floating in a pool of water held by a low wooden bowl. The scent of lemon or frankincense, rose, coconut, amber, sandalwood, perfuming every moment. The taste of fresh hot chapattis, sweet succulent rice, tender lamb roasted in its juices, ripe mangoes skinned and sliced for his consumption, tea always with cardamom, flavours like a symphony orchestrated for him. And her beauty, legendary as it became, even when she darkened under the sun. Her beauty was the testament to a smiling God, an emblem to Allah's gracious glory. How would Vilayat live without her? Make no mistake of it, she loved him, violence withstanding. And he? He loved her most after she died. Each day without her, he repented what he did when he was with her. She grew in his spirit like a goddess, the altar firmly lodged. Oh the children! How would the children get on? How would they survive without Mother? And Ali? Still a child, but just.

And I, Zahra's granddaughter, I deny it. I know the truth. It was told to me by Zahra's very own daughter.

Taqdeer, Zahra's first-born, was very ill. Twenty-six years old and married, he had been sweating with a fever for over a fortnight now. He was boiling red like chilli. And his wife, poor thing, could not cope. Not with the little ones running around, the housework falling to pieces and in her seventh month, big as an elephant. So Zahra, sweet mother-in-law, heart falling apart at the sight, went to Tadqeer's room and helped him through the night. She placed cold compresses on his brow, and dipped his feet in bowls of cool water, calmed with mint essence. She spoke to him, telling him stories. Whatever came to her mind she told him. She didn't care to censor. No, she told the whole truth. And late in the night, towards morning, when her strength was leaving her but the sun had not risen yet, she spoke to him, her son, in her mother tongue. How sweet the taste of freed vowels, and the crisp consonants that rolled off her tongue strumming like a dusty oud rescued from hibernation. What pleasure in hearing her own voice utter the endearments of her youth. Language, a sequestered and repressed rose, flowered like a revolution. She found her old self again, expressing to him those potent ideals and beliefs that had been stored away for so long. She gave free rein to her grief, released it without rationalisation, without diluting, masking and contorting it to make it palatable. To speak so easily, so freely, what an emancipation. But Vilayat finds her. He arrives already annoyed at her having spent four days away from his bed.

At dawn he comes into his son's room to find his wife by the bedside, whispering her mother tongue. Fury overcomes Vilayat Khan. Jealousy or rage we shall never know. Due to her absence or her betrayal of her Arabness, who can say? Due to her beauty that he resented, even while it continued to arouse him. He beat her, mercilessly. And Zahra, distraught at the death that she knows is coming to her son, so rudely woken from her reverie of liberation, is broken at last. She prays, enters a covenant with Allah. Take my life and spare my son's. Please, save him. Zahra's heart stops beating later that day, in the evening, while reciting the second part of the holy heretic prayer called Du'a. Taqdeer survives his fever. God keeps his word.

Fatimah and Karimah, Zahra's third and fourth daughters, raised Ali. He acquired his mother's breadth and nursed it in her absence. Incipient freedom. No one ever told him that his mother had died. They did not explain death. Only that she would never return. Where had she gone? Ali was robbed at an early age of that paradise which lies at a mother's feet, affectionately kicking us small distances into the world until we become accustomed to it, forgetting the early paradise yet longing for it always. Alas, few among us can name it.

Ali left Vilayat Khan's farm at the age of fourteen. He sought to carve his own fate. Vilayat Khan, in his bitter grief, engulfed by self-pity and unable to face the injustice of Fate, became ever more impatient. Often, he would explode, unthinkingly hurling his abuse at whatever or whoever was in sight. Ali hated him. He had witnessed his father's cruelty to his mother. It was the defining memory of his childhood. Ali intrinsically and perhaps even unconsciously blamed his father for the loss of his mother. He could not bear to stay and witness further evidence of his father's violent temper. He left the farm and laboured, on contruction crews, with the Africans. He lived in the jungles, became a friend of the Masai, and hunted monkeys to be captured, contained and displayed in English zoos.

When Ali was eighteen the East Africa Games were held on Zanzibar. Ali was on the Tanzanian national football team. He and his colleagues, ripe with youth, indulged in sport all day and all night. Ali was an excellent striker. His bronze curls, mint-green eyes, six feet of height and golden skin, thundered as he kicked the chequered ball. He remembered his mother's tales of barbecued fish and the bejewelled sea and sky. Look, the streets really did twist here and there, and palm trees hovered. Everyone and everything enchanting, kissed by the moon, and whispering her secrets. Ali only remembered his mother in things, moments, whispers. He could not know but only remember, see but never embrace. He missed her torturously. Sometimes the scarlet blood in his veins would ache for her presence, and then he would sit, in a Jamaat Khana, a courtyard, by the sea, under the moon, and he would call to her, losing himself in the vastness. Mother, where did you go?

Ali sensed his mother here as he had known her in his childhood. He indulged in short, quick, jarring memories of warmth and softness with the delicious scent of amber on her skin and jasmine in her hair, as she cradled him, comforting him from the darkness of his father's anger. He searches for the house which his elder sister Fatimah has described. It has a mesmerising courtyard. He knew not its name, nor the name of his grandfather. Zahra told them nothing of her family, but she recounted tales of a courtyard where the shadows of sycamore branches inspired patterns with which to contemplate the nature of divinity. He roams winding streets, stopping at the squares to ask about the house of Zahra, an Egyptian's home. He can feel her presence. She must have been here. Dusk is approaching. Azure sky is on the brink of exploding into scarlet. The scent of jasmine perfuming the air teases him. Ali comes upon a courtyard framed by sycamore trees. The sun blazing through its leaves. Red and green, just like our veins. His heartbeat, slow and heavy, tolls. He can feel Zahra here. Imagine her soaring spirit and golden smile frolicking between the trees. He wants to enter the courtyard but the gates are barred shut. He can hear European music, see European shadows. Ali stands staring at the house. He walks around it twice. The askaris are watching him. He asks who lives there. They ignore him. An old sheikh, returning from the mosque, stops, glances at Ali, recognises his spirit, approaches him.

"Jambo buona."

"Jambo Sheikh. Who lives here?"

"Mzungu. They rent from bigwig Alexandrine family with import-export business. People who think themselves fairer than Mzungu and holier than Muhammad."

Ali interrupts, "How many daughters were there? Do you remember their names?"

The sheikh ignores Ali. "I gave lessons to their daughters, once upon a time. Until the youngest one ran away with an Indian coolie. She went one afternoon to the sea and never returned. The mother went mad with grief. The man, Sultan, sent his men to look for her, even in the ocean. You know they say a dead daughter is better than a dishonoured one. Finally one of the Indians working on the ship blurted out that he had seen her on the shore. The men gave him a few thrashes and his tongue went loose. He said she had eloped to Tanganyika with one of the Indian coolies. Can you imagine the father's humiliation? He was furious. She was a real beauty, tall and fair with doe eyes. There were rumours of her marriage to the Sultanate's crown prince. The father said he would never look upon her face again. The men were to stop looking for her at once. 'Let her be free. Leave her to her Fate.'"

The sheikh shakes his head sadly. "I always knew she would go astray. She could never concentrate properly. She lacked focus. Zahra was her name."

The name! Ali has been listening for it. Tremors begin in his heart and pass through the diaphragm, streaming into his limbs. *This is my mother's home! She was Egyptian!*

The sheikh, emboldended by Ali's silence and thrilled at an opportunity to resurrect the scandal that had rocked Zanzibar, continues. "Anyway, the two remaining daughters were to be kept in line and sent immediately to Alexandria with their mother. They were married and settled in the city. Do you know it? You are Egyptian, no? You certainly look like them. So, the mother returned to Zanzibar and lived a lonely life without her daughters. Every year, she visited the two girls, left this ocean to arrive upon the shores of the Mediterranean. Finally, she couldn't bear the loneliness anymore, and now they have returned to Alexandria, and are renting the house to these Europeans. But you are Egyptian, no? Come, ahlan wa sahlan, I also speak Arabic. In fact, I need to practice. You must be from Cairo, the Alexandrines are such snobs. Come, my boy, that house is no place for your type. Come, have some tea."

Uncharacteristically, Ali weeps and runs, leaving the bewildered sheikh hobbling on the street.

Is it true? How could she? Why did she choose my father, a man who would batter her to her death, over a prince? Why did she defy her family? She was nobility and look where life took her. What logic, what justice lies in this? How can it be? Oh Mother, why?

Ali, at twenty-four years, goes to Aswan in 1958 to attend the Imam's burial. He leaves on a plane from Kampala airport, along with other notable members of the community. Enormous tents have been erected on the island to accommodate hundreds of the Imam's followers from all over the world—India, Pakistan, Iran, Nepal, Syria. Aswan: an oasis, faithful servant of the Nile at Egypt's bottom. Land of the Nubians, site of ancient pharaonic sacred spirits. Ali mixes with men forty years his senior. The next morning they are taken by felucca across the Nile to a small desert island, scattered with dry shrubs and low, smooth rocks where the Imam's austere mausoleum has been erected. At the shore of the island, below the mausoleum will sit the Begum's winter home. Every morning of her remaining years she will climb hundreds of steps to visit her beloved, and place a rose upon his tomb. Ali finds an indescribable resonance in this land. He will stay on after the others have left.

Ali visits Cairo. He strays lingeringly through the dusty old cobbled alleys of Fustat. He kneels at the shrines and mausolea of Sayyida Zeinab. He wanders through the Old City. He feels the excitement of wandering alone through the Khan el-Khalili, stopping to look at everything that catches his fancy. He strolls along the corniche of the Nile and watches the brazen sun sink into its waters. He hires a guide to accompany him through the bustling cafés. He spends a full lunar cycle in the heart of Egypt. He decides to visit Alexandria. He wants to glimpse the Mediterranean and to see his mother's homeland. He takes a train and arrives in Alexandria just as the sun is bidding its adieu. The city is filled, not only with

Egyptians and Arabs, but also Armenians, Greeks, Italians and Turks. British, German and French colonialists still lurk about, hesitant to return to their smoky grey skies. Ali cannot resist the temptation to find Zahra here. He has come armed with the name of her father and his family, which he learned, not without effort, through a few bribes in Zanzibar. He asked for the proprietors of the house in Stone Town at the edge of the Sultan's imperial estates, and he learned the name of Ahmed Sultan. He knows that there were no sons but two sisters. Fortunately Muslim women do not take the name of their husband but keep that of their father. The sisters were not difficult to find. The family was well known in Alexandria and Ali had only to ask a few shopkeepers and doormen, bawabs. He was led on foot by the friend of the bawab of his hotel to a house on the corniche.

The house is of European style and looks as though it was built in the 1920s. It is not the house of Zahra's childhood. His escort explains to the bawab that this man has come from East Africa and would like to visit Lutfia Sultan. The bawab guides them through the doorway and asks the servant to fetch his mistress. Ali and his escort are led to a salon. After several long minutes, an elderly woman just able to carry herself enters the room. She sees Ali and as she approaches him curiosity drops from her face to be replaced by shock. Her hands begin to tremble. Ali looks like Zahra. He has her face: the gaunt cheekbones, cool slanted eyes. Lutfia, Zahra's elder sister, is having trouble forming words. She stutters and then with the air of composing herself gasps, "Who are you?" The escort translates.

Ali, drowning in a sea of memory triggered by this tangible momento of his mother, replies. "I am Zahra's son, my name—"

"Zahra died fifty years ago!" Hearing her agitation, a maid comes to her assistance. Lutfia sits on a chair and requests Ali and his escort to do the same. Ali is dumbfounded. Bells ring in his ears. His head is swooning. He wants to run thundering out of the house, out of this city, this country, off this earth. Who is he? Indeed, who? Instead he sits.

"My sister Zahra, you look like her, but she died in Zanzibar. She drowned in the Indian Ocean. I remember it so well, the shock, the denial, the refusal to believe it. How could Zahra, so bursting with life, so astute, how could Zahra have drowned? Then the unbearable grief, our father's fallen face."

"But who are you?"

"I? I am an orphan." He lies, suppressing his emotions and regaining cold control. "I had hoped that perhaps your sister Zahra would be my mother, but it seems I was wrong. Tell me, please, where did you live in Zanzibar?"

"We lived on the Sultan's estates. My father was a merchant under the Sultan's engagement. We lived in a house by the sea, on the Sultan's estate. I believe some Europeans live there now, Germans perhaps."

"I am sorry to have intruded on your time. Thank you for your kindness. I am afraid I must leave."

"At least stay and have some tea."

Lutfia always suspected that Zahra had never died. As she sat with Ali in her salon, sipping tea and nibbling delicious Alexandrian sweets, she noted how much he resembled her sister. He even carried her expressions. But prudence silenced her: those lessons that teach us to bow under the hand of honour, to bury shame at all costs.

But just before he left, she sent her maid to fetch her jewellery case. She took out a pendant carved with the name of Allah and gave it to Ali. The pendant had been Zahra's. "May He watch over you," she said. "I hope you find your mother."

Ali returned to East Africa believing that his father had robbed him of not only his mother but also her lineage. He began his own life, separate from Vilayat Khan, on the bustling shores of Dar es Salaam. Ali began to work in the city. He wore clean pressed khakis and safari shoes. Drove European cars. Acquired a reputation. Ladies swooned at Ali's feet, workers straightened their backs when he entered the room. He was ruthless but generous. Proud. Most of all he was brave—but plagued by his scarlet blood.

In the evenings, seduced first by the glamour and later by gambling, Ali began frequenting Dar es Salaam's casinos. He was quick to learn, played well and often won handsomely. He became acquainted with Dar's informal economy, its Mafia. From them he learned the pleasures of luxury. He began to work for the Mafia. He smuggled diamonds with the Punjabis. He transported tanzanite, amber and rubies along the southeast African route from Cape Town. He was imprisoned, and released. He carried on, gambling in the drinking dungeons of Tanganyika. Amongst his friends were Indians and the newly named Pakistanis of all castes, faiths and walks of life, Gulf, Levantine and Maghreb Arabs, Africans from the military, the jungles and the universities, Germans, Italians and Englishmen. He was connecting, stretching his horizons. There was one problem: whenever he felt confined, the scarlet blood of Vilayat Khan erupted and with it, his raging anger.

VILAYAT KHAN

During Ali's second imprisonment, his father died. Vilayat Khan, his passions drained by time and the loss of two beloved wives, was dwindling away on the farm. He spent long days with nothing to do but complain and nit-pick over the household chores of his daughters-in-law. One fine day Vilayat Khan aged eighty-five walked tall and erect as a pillar to the newly installed toilet at the kitchen end of the house. His bronzed arms pushed open the door and he felt a faint pain in his chest. He took a deep breath and shifted his body to one side, in an effort to lean against the doorway. Instead he fell to the floor landing on his side.

Zahra comes to him. Her hair dipped in sunlight, and glowing, shines through her headscarf. Vilayat's heart leaps through his opened mouth into the air, meeting the sun's embrace and Zahra his mystic moon. His eyes fall back and a last breath leaves him. Vilayat Khan died of an instantaneous brain haemorrhage. His teeth, all thirty-two of them, were intact.

Taqdeer knew that Ali was in prison and got a message to him. Ali, with the help of his friends, escaped from prison to attend his father's burial. The funeral is held at the Jamaat Khana in Arusha. The ceremony is solemn, crowded with recitations from the Qur'an. It culminates in the performance of the chantah, where members of the family individually and the congregation collectively forgive the sins and misdemeanours of the deceased by washing them away with sprinklings of blessed water. Ali is apprehensive about his chanto for his deceased father. His conscience will not allow him to perform a fake or superficial chanto and so he must find it in himself to forgive the father whom he believes stole and betrayed his mother. Had his father not stolen his mother, he himself would never have been born—but he needn't have destroyed her. He didn't have to beat her with his own desperate rage. Why did he? How Ali would like to know why! Now it is too late. Anyway, how could he have asked such a thing to his proud, distant and silent father? Ali must find it in him to forgive his father. Alas, the Mukhi Sahib has announced his name and Ali rises towards the rug just in front of the altar where his father lies shrouded in a white cloth. He kneels before his father, behind whom sits the Mukhi Sahib with a small ceramic cup, a pyala filled with blessed water. Ali knows the ritual recitation that he must utter just loud enough for the Mukhi Sahib to hear and respond "ameen," but his mouth is dry as the Sahara. The Mukhi Sahib looks at him expectantly. Ali is on the verge of violent panic when he has an epiphany. He understands, finally. Ali comprehends his father's violence: it was born of panic, shame, self-loathing, that distinct inability to look oneself in the eye. A terrified desperate panic that burst out of its impotent shackles and struck that which was most precious. That gem whose dazzling glitter itself inspired the knot of self-loathing and shame to swell, bursting finally to release a lethal poison. Ali sees that his behaviour was unconscious and without intention. Ali cannot excuse his father, but he has understood him and this like a balm softens his tight mouth enabling the utterance of a prayer of forgiveness, and so he begins, "Yeah Shah Banday Gune Gaar..." and the Mukhi, relaxing, dips his fingers into the water.

While Vilayat Khan was buried in the muslim cemetery, the women at the Jamaat Khana recited tasbihs. After the funeral more than two hundred people returned to the farm house to mourn the passing of a patriarch, and to be fed with kheema, rice, daal, tea, pound cake and naan-khathai shortbreads. They stay till the evening. The men linger in a formal receiving room at the front of the house, some seated on sofas and chairs, others on white sheets that have been spread across the wooden floor. They discuss the great life of Vilayat Khan. How he came to East Africa a mere coolie aboard a ship, married a poor, nevertheless beautiful and graceful orphan, and left the world having amassed not only land but also respect and integrity within the community. The women congregate in the back of the house, near to the kitchen. They remember Zahra and lament the passing of the man that tortured her. Vilayat Khan is remembered merely as Zahra's husband and indeed their talk more often than not centres around pleasant memories of teas sipped in the same house in Zahra's luminous presence. Some of the women wonder if Allah will forgive Vilayat Khan's sins and send him to paradise or punish him in hell. If he goes to paradise will he meet Zahra there? Surely Zahra is in paradise, where else would she be? In the evening at prayer time, they all pray together and the Jamaat Khana is empty but for a few desolate unsociable souls.

The family will mourn the loss of their father actively for ten days. On the tenth day a majlis is held at Jamaat Khana to commemorate the passing of the first ten days of the soul's journey towards eternity. They will mourn passively for another thirty days, fulfilling the Islamic obligation of forty days of prayers, donations, charity and offerings. The blessings will be received by the soul of the deceased, helping it in the arduous journey from the known world. The women will wear white and steer clear of extravagant jewels or makeup. The men will wear old clothes and humble, sullen faces. Everyone will attend evening prayers at Jamaat Khana for the full forty days, partially to pray for the soul of the deceased and, partially, so society can see that they are praying for the soul of the deceased.

Ali is the sixth son and twelfth and final child. He does not return to prison. He returns to the farm to start a new life. With a combination of his skill and charm and Taqdeer's connections, Ali landed the cherry-pie job of managing Riddoch Motors for the Arusha region. Three of his brothers, Taqdeer the eldest, Mustafah the third son and fifth child, and Zulficar the fifth son and tenth child, lived on the farm with their wives and children. Taqdeer was married to Zeenat and they had three daughters and no son. Mustafah was married to a high-born, soft-minded beauty named Khayroon who gave him four sons. Zulficar was unmarried like Ali and desperately trying to escape East Africa to England. Shiraz, the second son and fourth child, had married a Ugandan woman from a once wealthy but increasingly penniless family and lived with her and her family in Kampala where he managed his father-in-law's dwindling estates. Hakim, the fourth son and seventh child, was named after the mad Caliph, became the insurgent of the family, proving truly to be his father's son by running off with a Bantu woman to Kisumu and becoming a cotton farmer. No one has seen him since. The sisters lived with their husbands in Arusha, Dar es Salaam, Nairobi, Kampala and Pakistan. Mumtaz, the eldest daughter and second child, had been married by Vilayat Khan into a well-to-do family of Gujarati businessmen who migrated to Karachi after partition. Mumtaz in turn had arranged for the marriage of her younger sister Sherbanu, the fourth daughter and eighth child, to one of her husband's cousins also living in Karachi, thereby securing both a good marriage for her sister and a companion for herself amidst Karachi's bewildering society. Fatimah, the second daughter and third child—her mother's favourite—had stayed in Arusha and married a humble man with a good heart. Laila, the third daughter and sixth child, was married off to a wealthy merchant trader from Dar es Salaam. He was twenty-two years her senior. Karima's marriage was arranged by her brother Shiraz in Uganda. The fifth daughter and ninth child, she married Shiraz's wife's distant cousin and settled two blocks away from him in the green hills of Kampala. Lastly, Kulsum, the sixth daughter and eleventh child, Ali's childhood companion, just shy of six years at the death of her mother and raised like Ali largely by Fatimah but also by a rotating retinue of parenting relatives and friends, was married by Taqdeer to the promising son of a Nairobi textile family.

In 1964, the year following Vilayat Khan's death, Tanganyika is granted independence by the British and Nyerere becomes Prime Minister. The land becomes free. It is granted to the sons whose hands have nourished it. After three tumultuous years of courtship, Tanganyika and Zanzibar marry to form Tanzania. The Indian and African subjects become the keepers of this new identity.

When Ali was four years old his mother Zahra died while reciting the second part of the holy heretic prayer. Two weeks before Zahra died, an infant was brought to her from nearby Moshi. She was asked to bless her and to pierce her ears and nose. Something Noor, the child's own mother, could not do. The girl was unnamed. Four-year-old inquisitive Ali had been overjoyed. Zahra named her Ghulshan because her cheeks held the pink colour of damask roses. I am Ghulshan and Ali's last daughter. My name is Zahra. I am African, at the juncture of India and Arabia. An orphan of the sea.

Thet
Canada

NOOR

Outwitted by Zeenat and cheated by Hussein, I escape London to Ghulshan and Ali's Canadian refuge. Between the mountainous zones of East Africa and Western Canada, some details have changed. The peaks of the Rocky Mountains hover above us in place of Kilimanjaro, and the blue glacier stillness of Lake Louise replaces the sweet troubled waters of Lake Manyara. We still take day trips, and watch the roads for deer instead of zebras. We snack on roasted corn seeds and peanuts. We stop by the lake to picnic on mishkaki kebabs, wrapped now in toasted, soft, white disks of tortilla breads instead of naan. Curried potatoes have become paprika- or barbecue-flavoured chips, and mangoes and papaya have changed to honeydew melon and nectarines. Unchanging spirits, new avatars. This is the lyric of my refuge.

Noor lives with Ghulshan and Ali in their townhouse that overlooks rolling green hills, a highway and a plaza. Noor's health is failing. Her tears have filled her heart and she must take pills to drain it, lest her spirit should drown. I visit her at the hospital. She wears dark sunglasses, having undergone a cataract operation. After a couple of days post-op, Noor returns to Ghulshan and Ali's home.

The doctors have informed us that Noor must rest. She used to glide on the balls of her feet, her calves and knees in supple obedience to her wishes. She walked stiff and upright into her eighties. But things are different now. At last her body has betrayed her. Her bones ache and rattle in their skin. Her limbs seem to argue in stubborn refusal every time she wishes to move or to gesture. Noor's eyes have sunk into their sockets, discoloured by the misty film that covers them. It will take her time to recuperate. However, the day after her release from hospital, my chronic curiosity and Noor's immortal brightness lead us to her trunk. Here, she stores the relics of the momentous journey of her life that took her from Gujarat to East Africa to exile in England fifty years later, and now to Canada. Noor has crossed four continents and six seas to come to Calgary. She has survived her husband, two sons, one daughter, one grandson and one granddaughter. She has outwitted tragedy by entering new lands. Her tongue has learned to twist three ways. It can swing from the familiar high-pitched vowels of her native Kutchi-Gujarati to the foreign but now familiar accents of Swahili, and then switch to the new cadences and unfamiliar consonants of English. This colossal Devi, this giant of human will, is my fragile, shivering, sometimes confused grandmother.

Her trunk has remained unopened since she left East Africa. I solicit my father to force open the lock. The key is lost. He recognises in me that childhood nuisance that sweeps the dust off sleeping graves—accepting it as the twin of my presence, he complies. He steps gingerly into Noor's room, announces his presence to her, and settles himself cross-legged before the steel trunk. After much frantic, frenzied, harried activity with a hammer and a pair of pliers, and a couple of curses in my direction, the lock is struck open. I am loudly ecstatic, bestowing upon my father the praise that he deserves and needs to hear. Something has lit up Noor's face. Even Ghulshan wants to know what secrets lie inside the trunk, but she announces that dinner is ready and hot on the table.

We dine on fluffy chicken pilaff, plain yoghurt and a salad of cucumbers, tomatoes, white onions, carrots, cilantro leaves and green chillies all diced into minute cubes and tossed with lemon, salt and a hint of red chilli powder. We eat with our fingers, scooping the rice with forefinger and middle finger, holding it in place with the thumb, raising hand to mouth with the tips of fingers just touching the edges of the lips, then in one swift and final motion, by flicking the rice into the mouth without wetting the fingers. We savour droplets of yoghurt and chicken juice that stick to our fingers. The flesh of the chicken is split from the bone using again the forefinger and the middle finger. We eat always with only one hand, the right, and only two fingers and one thumb. Anyone who eats with more than two fingers we consider uncouth. Ghulshan has sliced oranges into quarters. We eat them after the pilaff. The meal is not relaxed. My mother and I begin to clear the table while Ali is still toying with a slice of orange. His teeth are no longer what they once were. Uncharacteristically, Ghulshan leaves the dishes dirty in the kitchen sink. I make a pot of tea. Noor fills, wraps and folds paan leaves. We stuff paan into our respective mouths, leave Ali in his armchair watching *Jeopardy* and retire to Noor's room.

Ghulshan and Noor settle themselves on the bed, each with a mug of tea in hand, and I kneel on the floor before the trunk with my tea beside me. Noor recites the Bismallah as I lift open the lid. The smell of time fills the air, dry and dusty. We are faced with a sheet that was once white but has aged to yellow. It is the mantle for Noor's treasures. Sitting on my haunches I reach my hands into the trunk and gingerly lift the sheet passing it to my mother who examines it briefly and passes it onto her mother who holds it, dust and all, in her lap. Here at last is that for which I have been pining: a history to connect me to the world. An emblem to lend me a sense of belonging. An invitation to come in from the cold. I have found it in my own home.

Beneath the shroud is more cloth. It is also white, but finer and embroidered. "What is it?" Ghulshan asks, elongating her neck like a swan.

"A white sari," I reply, lifting it out. It falls from my hands to reveal a fine sheer cloth embroidered in white silk with tiny pearls in a cashew design. It unfolds the scent of a bride, rose and sandalwood.

"Pir Shah, yeah Khuddah," exclaims Noor as I carry it to her. It is a wedding sari. Not Noor's but Ghulshan's. Celebration abandoned for mourning as she left the altar for her father's grave. I am unaware of this as I stupidly hand the sari to my grandmother, assuming it belongs to her. She calls again upon Allah, the prophet and his descendants, praying for protection from the curse which killed three of her children and brought one to her father's grave instead of her husband's bed. Noor looks at Ghulshan who is silent. She places the sari on the bed and Ghulshan fingers it with misty eyes. I can no longer bear the sight of tears in my mother's eyes. Her cheeks bloom red, putting roses to shame. Her lips quiver and shine. The skin, still porcelain. I cannot believe how beautiful she is, my mother, sixty years old. So fragile yet unbeatable. I do not understand why she is crying. Tell me Mother, how else will I know. But she doesn't. Neither she nor Noor speak. My voice has choked. I decide to ask at another time. Ghulshan folds the sari and puts it aside. I return to the trunk.

I sit before the trunk and let calmness descend upon us. After several minutes I pull out a bundle of dusty Gujarati books. They are quite small and thin. I look through the titles. They are mostly religious books. A history of the Imams. A collection of the Farmans of the previous Imam. A book of Ginans. An account of the life of the Prophet, peace be upon him. A moral guide. And then, a sewing book of patterns. A book of designs for embroidery. And a romance, *Romeo and Juliet* translated into Gujarati! We were colonised to the bone. I show the books to Noor and she tells me that Razak bought *Romeo and Juliet* for her. There are more saris. A thick red silk one that she wore to the Diamond Jubilee Padramani in Dar es Salaam and one of green chiffon that she wore when she was Mukhiani of the women's majlis. There is a coin folded into the first one. A large gold coin. It is Razak's medal for voluntary service, presented to him at the Diamond Jubilee. I find several ankle-length frocks with v-necks and elbow-length sleeves with matching chiffon and cotton pachedis. The pachedis are quite large and bordered with bands of multicoloured embroidery. At the bottom of the trunk is a black box made of cardboard but with a rosewood veneer.

I snap open the box. It is lined with a scarlet velvet. Inside is an assortment of passports, a wedding certificate, coins, photographs and a small red pouch tied with a green string. I carry the box to the bed and Noor, Ghulshan and I sift through the contents. The passport is Noor's. It certifies her as a British subject, allowing her to cross the Indian Ocean from Gujarat to East Africa. Dated 1922, it gives her birthdate as August 20, 1910. Noor does not know when she was born. The date is fictitious. What Noor knows is that she was born at the time of Divali. The coins are priceless. There are ten. Silver shillings of the British Empire dated 1901 with the hook-nosed profile of Queen Victoria. Noor's father had slipped a fistful of coins into her hand at the quay, between her tears as she boarded the ship at the Gulf of Kutch. She would never see him again.

There is a yellowing, muted photograph of Noor, Razak, Ferial and Qassim standing at Mombasa harbour with the Mukhi Sahib. I cannot believe my eyes. Noor is tiny and frail, but imbued with grace. Thinned out from the journey, gaunt-cheeked, shy, Noor stretches her pachedi over her face, standing a foot away from her husband. Razak stands proud but timid, gazing at the shyness of his wife. The ship looms above them. Behind them is a flurry of activity. This is their wedding day, the second one. An emaciated Noor is floating in her wedding clothes, looking terrified. Ferial is smiling heartily, Qassim standing close to her. The white sari is not there. Noor is wearing a frock-pachedi that looks like it might have been white with gold or silver embroidery. I look up at Noor. The light has left her face. I cannot see her. She seems masked by a canopy of time. Her eyes are vacant, clouded with sadness. I have seen women weep until their chests heave like the ocean storm. But I have never seen Noor weep. I ask her why there is no white sari. I cannot help myself. I want to know. I want to share her sadness. Noor's hands reach for the photograph. They are trembling as they often do these days. Her whole body—face, neck, shoulders, lap—is shaking. I am afraid she is going to die. Ghulshan is rock-still, staring at her mother. I climb onto the bed beside Noor and put my arms around her. I hold her with all the strength that is in me. Ghulshan leaves the room. I know she has gone to cry privately. Ghulshan cries a lot. Years ago the doctors gave her anti-depressant drugs. They didn't work. They unbalanced her. She was unbalanced for a decade. She is better now. But she still cries. Noor has stopped shaking, but her hands are still trembling. With an unsteady finger she points to herself in the photograph. "This is me." And so she begins her tale, so that I can end mine.

NOOR'S TALE

Yasmine, the mother whose womb had housed and nourished me over nine moons, died soon after the birth of my brother Sher Ali, her third son. I had just begun to speak in finished sentences. My elder sister, Ferial Massi, had to carry Sher Ali because he was just an infant and I was still small. We were sent to Chachima's home. She was the wife of our father's younger brother Nasir Virani. My father was not there and neither was Nasir Chacha. Ferial was inside the house taking care of Sher Ali and helping Chachima. I was outside, loitering a bit and also playing with my cousins. Our elder brothers Shamsh Ali and Karim Ali had also disappeared. I knew they would be with my father so I was not worried. I felt safe at my Chacha's house but I felt troubled. Finally my elder cousin Tamiza came up to me and screamed, "Ha ha Noor, your mother is dead. No one to look after you now!" In the evening, even after we had said our prayers, I decided to ask my Chachima. I went to tug at her cherou and said. "Chachima, Chachima do you know where my mother is? Tamiza said that she was dead. She is not dead is she?" I was teary-eyed. My Chachima must have felt pity for me.

She said to me, "Of course your mother has not died. She has just gone to hospital. She will be back soon. Tamizaaa?" She called. Tamiza came to answer her mother's call. "Why did you tell Noor that her mother has died?" Tamiza looked at me. She looked at my tears and looked down. She did not say anything. Chachima said "naughty girl" to Tamiza and dismissed us. That night I knew Tamiza had not been lying. I knew my mother was dead. The cowardly Chachima had lied to me, to soothe me, as she would again many moons later.

Five years we lived with Chacha and Chachima, Ferial, Sher Ali and I. We saw our elder brothers and our father only on Fridays when we all went to mosque and ate together. Our Chachima treated us as she treated her own girls. We helped her with the household chores. We were not sent to school, but she taught me how to embroider and sew. Sher Ali was reared among all of us. My mother did not come back.

Our father at last managed to release the memory of mother, to accept a new wife. When I was about eight years old, I was told that my mother had returned and I could go home. Ferial who has always been wiser than me had already deduced the facts. She did not share them with me. We each held the hand of our little brother and returned to our home with Ferial leading the way. I was dressed in my best pink frock, and my brother Sher Ali in a white bush shirt and navy shorts. Our two elder brothers came running to greet us. They were almost men now. But, "Where is Ma?" I wanted to know.

A woman ten years younger than my mother had been five years ago emerged from the wooden doorway of our mud and brick house. She embraced Ferial first, and then my brother and then me. As she bent at the waist, allowing the head and shoulder of her sari to fall— as I inhaled her scent—I decided this was not Ma. That evening I started my lifelong conversation with the sun, the moon and the stars. I asked where Ma was. For four years, Ferial, our younger brother Sher Ali, and elder brothers Karim Ali and Shamsh Ali and I lived with our father and recast mother. She was as kind as her nature allowed, but not more. She had her reasons. Her husband could not bestow upon her the gift of motherhood until the children of her predecessor were safely settled. He denied himself the pleasure of her nightly warmth lest it bear fruit. Perhaps it did not occur to him that he was also denying her. Seven mouths however, are already plenty to feed. So Shamsh Ali, Karim Ali and even six-year-old Sher Ali found work either carving or cleaning and carrying wood. With the blessings of that same Mukhi Sahib who had arranged my stepmother's marriage, suitors were found for her skilful stepdaughters. So it was, as you already know, that she entered the room where Ferial and I slept to whisper secrets of good tidings and long journeys. But she forgot to smile.

As Noor weaves her tale, recalling occasionally the patterns of her stitchwork, Ghulshan returns. She places her heavy head on a pillow and drifts to sleep. I am wondering how and why Noor endured. How did she reach this eighty-two-year-old heart-troubled state? What force convinces her to take her twelve multicoloured pills every day? Why, having named her first-born daughter and granddaughter after her beloved mother, and losing all three Yasmines, does she still believe? Noor, O enduring lightness, why do you still pray every morning and every evening?

Holding my mother's gaze, waking her from her sleep, Noor sketches upon a pillow, with her bony finger, a pattern of cashew paisleys and crescent moons. She tells me this is the stuff of life: the contemplation of meaning, the desire for form. These paisleys and moons, recurring forms of her pattern, are the Yasmines, the prayers, births, deaths, smiles and tears of her small life. One could recount the history of India, or of my grandfather, by recalling the drinking of cups of tea and their changing moments. The same act, new locations, same form, new position: unchanging spirit, new avatar. If you must ask why, then you must seek your answer in those eyes belonging to your sister, Fate. You cannot wrench from her your blind destiny. She will grant, and you will see in your own way, at your own time. Naseeb. Even if, until the new moon, your beauty does not flower at the edge of the seashore on this night, even if the heavens are blind, you will see. When Fate beckons, you must follow.

The other photographs from her trunk are memories of the dead. There is a photo of Razak. He is young and handsome, wearing trousers and a bush shirt. There is a photo of Noor Ali and Ahmed Ali, the two sons that drowned. The next photo is of a two-year-old Yasmine, Noor's deceased daughter. It is accompanied by a photo taken on the farm. There were four of us: Yasmine, Ahmed, Sultan and me. But Noor has cut Sultan and me out. "The living must not be buried with the dead," she says. Yasmine looks like Noor. I have never noted this before. They have the same face, the same small frame.

My mother, still stone-faced, is sitting on the bed looking at the photos of her father, her brothers, her sister, her son and her daughter. All have died, all are buried together in Noor's trunk of memories. I can feel my heart sinking. I don't want to think about this. I want to forget. Allah, please allow us to move on. Forgive our sins. Have we not repented? We women, we suffer together, sharing our pain. The men, Ali and Sultan, they suffer separately. They bury their sadness only to dig it up and wallow in it. I reach towards the red pouch that sits alone in the box. As it shifts, I hear a tiny jingle, like that of bangles on a woman's arm. The green string has been tied into tight and enigmatic knots.

My mother has gone to join Ali in sleep. Sitting on Noor's bed while she recites her midnight tasbih, I have unravelled the knots of the green string. The red cloth opens. Inside lies a tiny pair of gold hoop earrings. I fiddle with these, sliding them onto my pinkie. Noor finishes her prayer and I show them to her. Her face lights up. "This is what I wanted to find, sweet Zahra," she tells me. "These are Ghulshan's hoops from babyhood. Earrings given to her by that other Zahra whose spirit lives in you. The angel who pierced your infant mother's ears and filled them with this gold. These are for you. You must keep them for your daughter. Inshallah, you will be blessed with a daughter. Without daughters, we cannot survive. Our daughters create and nourish, as we once did. These are our secrets. We must keep them, follow them, remain loyal and teach them to the ones who come. Come here, let me put these earrings into your ears."

Noor prepares for sleep while I heat some milk with saffron and bring it to her. She removes her teeth and places them in a bowl filled with water and denture-cleaning salts. She covers this bowl with a white doily with beaded tassels around its edges. She slides under the many layers of blankets into her bed. I lie beside her. At half-past three, two hours before dawn, Noor wakes up. She shuffles to the adjacent bathroom and washes. When she returns, she wraps a shawl around her shoulders and sits crossed-legged on the floor, lips moving, silently chanting her zikr. I do not move, lying in that familiar state between dreaming and wakefulness.

A woman enters the room. She does not notice Noor but comes to me. She sits on the bed and strokes my hair, bringing me calmness. This woman is me. I recognise my face. Older, lined, scarred, but still mine. Are you Zahra? She speaks in Egyptian amiyah, her Arabic that I miraculously understand. She is telling me to let go. It cannot be. The house cannot be my house. It was never hers. She fled from it. It will harness and suffocate me, as it would have her. I must be free, accept that which is painful. Freedom is the Siamese twin of exile. This is my destiny. Accept it. Release these handcuffs. Zanzibar will taunt you. It is a curse. Let it go. Defy the evil eye. Do not covet. You cannot deny your nature. Freedom is your drug, accept your fate. Learn to be free.

I awake to the sounds of my mother and her mother preparing lunch. The sun is shining through the blinds, glittering on the gold that fills my ears. I continue, as I have since that fateful day when Fatimah-Fui oiled my hair, and perhaps even before, to imagine myself in Zanzibar. I glimpse the sea. I inhale the scent of barbecued fish. The night stole her beauty from the sea. I stole mine from the moon. Now, we are both disciples, the night and I. Of the sea and the moon: unearthly goddesses.

LONDON

After I returned from my visit to Ghulshan and Ali and Noor, newly enlightened by the tales which Noor had spun, and with Zahra's gold filling my ears, I thought I could forgive Hussein. Sipping coffee in the court of the Victoria and Albert Museum café, I pull out that luxurious implement of our technological age, the mobile telephone. I press the power button, enter "directory", "one" and ring my office. The receptionist informs me that Hussein has called twice and left a message. I am to meet him at the hotel at six o'clock. It is half past three and I am starving. I buy a tuna and sweet corn sandwich. As I bite, chew and swallow, I think about how I will confront Hussein.

Quarter-past six, he is waiting for me in the lobby. I have dallied in the shops along Knightsbridge, seeking refuge in buying power and instant gratification. I have bought an assortment of fruity grooming tools from the Body Shop and a minty green silk cardigan from Anvers, the colour of his eyes. I arrive in style in a cab and with shopping bags hanging from my arms. In the lobby, he greets me with a single fragrant magnolia, unburdening me of my bags. It is difficult for me not to melt.

How does one reintroduce bitterness and scrutiny, after having spent two long, sweet, blind nights together?

I consider inviting him to my cottage in Barnes where I would be more comfortable, surrounded by my things and by faces of my spirit that he has not seen. Zahra standing naked and scared. Can you look? What if disaster strikes? Where will I run? Should I boot him out? I should, I probably should but I can't. This is not the weakness of cowards it is the strength of lovers.

We are sitting at the bar. I have not touched the tea that he has asked the barman to place before me. He is watching me, quiet. His fingers caressing the sweaty rim of his glass. I have not spoken yet. He reaches for my hand and uncurls the fingers. I cannot face him.

I cannot turn my head and look at his face or into his eyes. I will melt, my coolness will slide.

"Zahra, are you all right?"

My mouth is dry, tongue is stuck, lips will not move. I can only look—stare out at him—allowing my eyes to spill their thoughts.

"You want to know about your grandmother's house?"

No, actually we can skip that uncomfortable, nasty, disgusting, evil bit, you stupid, senseless, womanising gigolo! I wish I had said this. Instead, I said: "Yes." And he said: "Okay."

"I have bought your grandmother's house from your Aunt Zeenat."

Well, at least he knows a square when he sees it. The man who declares he is a bastard is already halfway towards salvation—I did it for you"—but not when he blames the victim. Why can't men just apologise?

"You wanted to save me the agony of having my grandmother's house? Why? So that I would never have the opportunity to collect my scattered selves? To rob me of my last vestige of hope?"

"No, Zahra! Stop! You are such a dreamer. Does every detail of your life have to have meaning? Fit into some grand scheme that you've imagined? Anyway, that house would never have been yours if your brother had bought it. It would belong to him, to his wife and to his children, never to you, or to Ali."

"It would have belonged to my family and that would have been enough. You don't even know my brother! How can you speak that way about him? This has nothing to do with Ali, it has to do with me."

"Zahra, you are so naive—"

"Shut up. Stop. I am sick of your bullshit," I scream. The barman is politely ignoring me; Hussein appears shocked. How typically stupid. I run out of the bar, through the lobby, into the ladies' toilet. What else am I supposed to do? I sit here for a while and I cry.

When I emerge into the lobby of The Gore Hotel, eyes inflated, nose scarlet and cheeks pallid, Hussein is waiting for me. He is on a sofa smoking a cigarette. He gives me half a smile. I take my seat beside him. In the end he comes with me by taxi to Barnes. But I still have not forgiven him. He does not come in, instead he returns to his precious hotel room. Separation, that necessary medicine. Madad-e-Sina, the help of Ibn Sina. His flight to Zanzibar leaves tomorrow morning. He has said he will be in touch. If I marry Hussein, I will be mistress of Zahra's house. I know this. I thought of it long ago.

Hussein telephones to inform me of his safe return. He does not call again. I spend lonely, dull grey days in London's rain, waiting. In the beginning I find solace in his promise to remain in touch. It colours the contours of my world that are otherwise dull with defeat and confusion. Several months pass. As I wait, the silence of the telephone, the emptiness of the post box dilute my solace. But it is still there. I clutch at its frail form and weak hues. Eventually, after six, eight, ten months, solace eludes me altogether. It is replaced by bitterness and anger. I begin to remember him as a man who makes promises he cannot keep.

NAVROZ

At Amir Uncle's Navroz luncheon, Abdel-Aziz Zamakhshari, recognising Ali Khan immediately, pulled him aside to have a chat.

"What a coincidence and pleasure, Mr. Khan," he exclaimed. My ageing father, who had also recognised the ageing lawyer, was perplexed. For over a decade he had crucified himself under the burden which Zeenat had bequeathed to him. The burden of his brother's blood spilled in place of his own. It was not just imparting Zahra's house to Zeenat that had destroyed him. It was the whole haunted tale. Zeenat and her deceptions. Zeenat and her murders. Zeenat and her cold green blood. Ali's broken heart and wounded pride. Ali wanted to protect Ghulshan. He wanted to protect Sultan and me. He knew that all three of us, had we known of Zeenat's secret tryst with the Tanzanian militia, would have killed her. But Ali also feared our judgement. He lived tormented by the idea that we might judge him. Had he been a coward? Should he have killed her himself? Should he have refused to surrender the house? These questions, like daggers, cut Ali's spirit. The truth was Ali had been afraid. Fearless, brave, Ali stricken by the grief of his divided family, perishing with the knowledge of his lost son and daughter had been afraid. Of Zeenat. He could not take her on, could not fight it out. His spirit had sunk like a drowned fire. He chose to flee into safety with at least half his family intact. How would we judge him? Ali Khan, a lion of Kilimanjaro, became a refugee. In England and then in Canada, he lived humiliated, as an ordinary man. A man without power.

Abdel-Aziz Zamakhshari knew the whole story. The lawyer had been present in that airport room where Ali had impugned Zeenat. Ali had confronted and accused Zeenat of sending him into exile with her vicious tongue, of burning down the farm with her black heart and killing his children with her green venom. "You really have gone mad Ali. How could I, a poor widow manage all that?" she had exclaimed. "I suppose I understand. You have lost everything, and now this. But I must ask this of you. I have no other choice. You are a man, you have a son. I have nothing. And all because of you! You think I don't know? I know everything. My husband died in your place." Ali had begun to weep. He was ashamed of breaking down like a child but could not stop himself. He hurled abuse at her, gave her the details of the story the colonel had told him, the servant-soldier, the loaded information, those dark tricks. The colonel had spared neither Ali nor Ghulshan. Ali was red in the face. Red, red, his scarlet blood was throbbing. He almost attacked her. Mr. Abdel-Aziz Zamakhshari had stopped him. Now this man Zamakhshari, greeting him like a chum. That young lawyer was his son. Ali should have known.

Abdel-Aziz Zamakhshari has taken hold of my father's arm. "Shall we go for a walk, Mr. Khan? It is a lovely day. The sea is whispering to us. We shall greet her." Amir Uncle lives in front of the Aga Khan Mosque. Not far from Zahra's house. Abdel-Aziz, hobbling a bit, leads the way. They walk towards the sea but then he turns right. He leads him down a narrow street. It seems familiar to Ali. He sees it, recognising it easily from the street as the only empty-looking grand house in a cluster of neglected buildings that are otherwise used or occupied by the poor. There is a gate at the road. Mr. Zamakhshari has a key but the askari lets him in. He leads Ali to the courtyard where they sit on a bench under the shadow of a mango tree. "This is your mother's house." Ali is not weeping but tears are rolling across his wrinkled cheeks. Silence is his refuge. "Your daughter was looking for this house. She has found it. My son is helping her. She wants to buy it from your sister-in-law." Alarm invades Ali's face.

"No. No. Absolutely not! Never. My daughter must not know! She must not negotiate with Zeenat! Please, please. I am once again at your mercy. This is not our house. It does not belong to us. It never belonged to my mother. My mother left it. She chose my father over this house. Whatever her reasons, we must respect them. We must live by her choice, and that of her family. They abandoned her. They preferred her death. I must honour my mother. I and my children, we must honour my mother. They know nothing. Perhaps I should have told them. But now, now it is too late. The tale has been spun. We cannot rewrite what has passed. We must live with it. Please, I beseech you. Do not let her buy the house." Ali's pride has vanished.

Abdel-Aziz Zamakhshari has noted that Ali Khan is a changed man. He is perhaps a broken man. Fallen. Twisted at the hands of Fate into a bent old man. There are still signs of the stature he once held, but only to the knowing eye. "Mr. Khan, I give you my word. Your daughter shall not buy this house. Mr. Khan, I must tell you something. These things are difficult to tell and quite complicated as I am sure you know. But, ahem, you are my kin. Yes, yes it is true you are my kin. We are related by blood. Your mother's father Ahmed Sultan was my uncle, my father's younger brother. My name is Abdel-Aziz Zamakhshari Sultan. Your mother was my cousin-aunt. She was the daughter of my father Sayeed's brother's son Ahmed. Ahmed was like my father's own son and our elder brother. His children were our siblings. Your mother was like my elder sister. She was to become the bride of the Sultan's son Khaifa Ibn Harub who was to be Zanzibar's last Sultan. Alas, it was not her destiny. We all live whatever path is chosen for us, I suppose. These things are difficult to make sense of. Zahra's mysterious tale has lived like a myth in our family. We, all of us, remember her, recounting to our children her magnificent beauty and glorious spirit. Sometimes we just have to accept Allah's will and have faith that He is doing what is best for us. I always knew she didn't drown in the sea. She couldn't have, the fire in her was too strong. So you see, I am your uncle. You are my nephew. It is late for us now. We are old. But our children, our children must know. We must end this silence. I shall leave you now for a while. Will you find your way back?"

Ali grasps his hand. He embraces his uncle and then watches him shuffle towards the street. He remains seated on the chipped bench in the courtyard. His mother, her spirit, it has come again. She is pleased with him. This is not her house. Her son understands this. As Ali, a thin, silver-haired, wrinkled old man with a broken heart sits alone on the bench outside the house that belonged to his mother's father, he allows himself to weep long, cold, silent tears.

As he walks back to Amir Uncle's, Ali understands something else, that his daughter, Zahra, the one he named after his mother, is looking for roots. A home to call her own where she is not the "other", not a minority. A place where they can belong, from which no one can evict them. She has not lived enough to see that such a place lives only in your own heart.

ZANZIBAR

Zahra's house by the sea, abandoned for almost half a century in decrepit Stone Town, has fallen to neglect. Zahra's house is empty, vacant, like a ghost. It faces the sea, looking for its memories of life.

Crafty Zeenat sold whatever furniture and carpets she found in the house. The sales were boosted by the mysterious story of the change in ownership that had become notorious in Zanzibar society. Zeenat did her best to pass off all contents of the house as Omani or Arab antiques. She struck a deal with the city mayor to convert the house into a storage facility for the government in exchange for a monthly rent to be paid in foreign currency into her London bank account.

Hussein's wife who has heard the gossip surrounding the house sets out towards Stone Town with high hopes of glamour but arrives at the gates to be disappointed. She walks around the withering garden and crumbling benches, her head cocked to one side in dismay. She eyes the cobwebs dripping from the windowpanes. A greyish layer of dust and grime veils the wooden floors. Clear fluorescent light pierces the room from the eastern windows and her heels staccato into the kitchen which is now rotting. In a rage of disgust she leaves the catacombic stench of Zahra's house. She takes a taxi to Hussein's office where she barges into his morning. She refuses to occupy the house until it has been cleaned up and fully refurbished to her exact taste. The venture of the house by the sea has proven increasingly complicated, not to mention expensive, and Hussein wonders why he allowed himself to get involved in this mess in the first place. Ambitious soul, he has not yet recognised Fate's invincible, obstinate will.

His wife furnishes the house in a classic decadent style characteristic of the third-world upper class. A style that still postures towards the ghosts of colonial vogue. The rooms are littered with plush sofas upholstered in florals and checks, dark woods and glass tables. White walls are adorned with elegant landscapes. Finally she transports her things and moves her self and their infant son into Zahra's house. She leaves her father-in-law asleep in his study.

Hussein returns to Zanzibar from London to live with his father. His days at the office stretch into evening and night. He is lost in a farrago of his emotions. His lively demeanour is replaced with a dry, stiff bearing and brief, curt remarks. People gossip. They divine his separation from his wife as the spell behind these moods. Eventually, and without much difficulty he finds another mistress. She is a teacher at the government primary school, from a good family of mixed Arab and African origin. They meet in the late afternoons after school and spend hours until dusk in a rented room at a second-class hotel. She is twenty-one years old. He drops her off in the suburban neighbourhood where she lives with her elderly father and four siblings and drives back to Stone Town. He visits his estranged wife and child at the house by the sea. One evening during the season of the rains, after a long and busy afternoon at the courts, having missed his rendezvous at the hotel, Hussein takes a walk to shake the buzzing fog from his mind. He strolls through muddy streets, skipping over potholes full of rain and almost slipping on the cobblestones. He reaches the harbour and shields himself from the roaring waves behind an abandoned dhow. He squats on his haunches and lights a cigarette, savouring the smoky dry nicotine. Cold and wet, he makes his way to Zahra's house to see his wife and their son, whom he misses. His wife is in a state of disarray. She has not been out of the house in three days. The household help is ill and the ayah who minds their son is away. Anisa has been tending to all the housework herself and to her infant child, alone. The house is cold and damp, filled with ancient drafts, the sea seeping through the walls. He thinks of London. His wife offers him something strong to drink, a whisky perhaps. He accepts it. They sit on the veranda, wrapped in blankets, watching the rain. Then Hussein tells his wife about the house in which she is living, and about me. He tells her he bought the house because he had sworn to his father that he would not allow me to buy it. He did not add that his father in turn had sworn to Ali that me, Zahra, his daughter, would not be allowed to purchase the house in which my grandmother lived for less than a year.

"Well, I would have never suspected her, so plain."

That night, his wife seduces Hussein. They sleep in their matrimonial bed. He feels comfortable there. It is not so difficult, no; it is soothing like a familiar habit.

NAVROZ

Back at the house of Amir Karmali Abdel-Aziz Zamakhshari takes his son aside and asks him to take him home. Hussein whispers an excuse into Amir Karmali's ear and escorts his father to the yellow Mercedes. Something must be amiss. This is strange behaviour for his father who loves celebration and the company of people. While Hussein drives, his father sits in silence, hands locked together, resting in his lap. They return home and Abdel-Aziz asks his son to come inside with him. They settle into the living room. Hussein finds himself a scotch and faces his father.

"My son, what do you know of this girl, Zahra Khan?"

"Very little I'm afraid."

"Why is she interested in this house in Stone Town?"

"She believes it was her grandmother's house. I guess she feels some kind of sentimental attachment, some affinity for her grandmother, and wants to purchase the house to feel closer to her. I don't really know."

"Sit closer, Son. I have more to tell you, things I did not want to say the other day when you told me she was looking into the house. The story of how her Aunt Zeenat came to own it is only part of the tale. It seems you young people just will not let sleeping graves lie."

ABDEL-AZIZ'S TALE

An Egyptian merchant sailed to Zanzibar and fell in love with the Swahili coast. His father was a pasha, but the merchant was the second son and so he did not inherit the title. He was my uncle, Ahmed Sultan, my father's younger brother. Their father had given him a house in Alexandria, and he had married a fair-skinned beauty from the new wealthy class. While he was here in Zanzibar, he wandered in the markets where his cotton was sold, and was especially liked by the British who bought most of it for their linens and for export. They invited him to their clubs, where he was a guest among English, German, Italian, Indian and Arab ladies and gentlemen. He watched them dine over candlelight and muted conversation, and then dance the foxtrot accompanied by a roaring orchestra of coloured men who mixed Europe's melodies with a touch of their own throbbing rhythms. Eventually, he received an invitation to the court of the Omani Sultan Sayyid Barghash. The Sultan found himself at ease with a fellow Arab, although Egyptian.

After a year, he returned to Alexandria to convince his wife to migrate to East Africa. The family settled predictably into their new life, with one shining exception. Zahra—yes, another Zahra—was wild and free, her spirit could not be confined, especially not by her haughty mother. The Sultana, impressed by her beauty, had chosen Zahra to be the bride of her son. His mother was looking for a woman fit to be queen. Alas, Zahra's spirit overtook her. It led her away, astray perhaps, or to her own Right Path. Who knows? We are not fit to judge such things.

The story we heard was that she had been kidnapped from their home and drowned in the harbour. Tongues wagged. Her mother blamed the evil eye. The servants were severely interrogated. She believed it was jealousy that her daughter would become queen. This in the end became the accepted tale.

Some of us, however, my father chief among them, knew better. She was not the sort of girl to allow someone to kidnap her without causing a colossal fuss. But what in the world happened to her? A second story began to circulate. The girl had been sighted at the harbour. Some Indian coolies confessed that she had run off with one of their lot. But this was too unbelievable. It was laden with shame, the kind that good families cannot face. The tale of her death was much more palatable. Indeed it became the official story, even for her sisters.

I do not know how Lutfia Sultan, Zahra's sister, learned of Ali Khan nor how she found him, but she did and she knew he was Zahra's son. Her marriage to our cousin had failed tragically. He would not leave his mistress and she, unlike most women of her generation, refused to look the other way. They divorced after two years of marriage and she moved back to Alexandria. I don't think the marriage was ever consummated. In fact, they didn't have any children. Since Zahra had never claimed the house in Zanzibar that Ahmed had secretly, and with vain hope, left for her, he bequeathed it at his death to Lutfia. They had a tacit understanding, however, that the house was Zahra's and if she ever appeared it should be made hers. I had just begun to practise law at that time. There had been much turbulence in Zanzibar. A lot of land and money changed hands between the Omanis, the Germans and the British. Ahmed Sultan, my uncle, had recommended me to Sultan Khaifa Ibn Harub. In less than six months I was put in charge of legislating the imperial estates. Therefore it was natural that I should transfer the house in Zanzibar from the name of Zahra Zamakhshari Sultan to that of Lutfia Zamakhshari Sultan.

Hussein has finished his scotch. He has smoked all his cigarettes. Something is beginning to dawn on him but he is not yet quite sure what it is. Hussein is not sure he can believe his father. The old man after all is pushing ninety. Perhaps he is losing his senses. His father has paused to catch his breath. He is coughing from exertion. Hussein asks a servant to bring some tea. His father clears his raspy throat and continues.

In the summer of 1969 I received a letter from Lutfia who was in the shadows of death, as I am now. She asked me to leave the Zanzibar house in the name of an Ali Khan. Of course I was surprised. However it was her dying wish. I decided to make some enquiries and learned that this Ali Khan and his brothers were some bigwig coffee farmers in Arusha. This was even more perplexing. Had Lutfia accrued a debt? I could help her. There was no sense squandering family property on some unknown Indians. I sent one of my men to Arusha to investigate the man. We found that Ali had had some dubious involvement with the black market. He had even been to prison. However it seemed that the man and even the family were in good standing. I felt even more confused. Who was he? I began asking questions among the Indian community in Zanzibar. Our Mr. Amir Karmali was in Zanzibar on holiday at the time with his wife and young daughter. I invited them to lunch.

Your mother prepared a feast for them, right here in this house. Then I invited Amir into this room for a smoke and an afternoon drink. I asked him about Ali Khan straight out. And he knew him! Can you believe that? Yes, he laughed and told me they were child-hood friends.

"What do you want to know about him?" he asked me. I wanted to know who he was, you know. Who was his father? Who was his mother? What kind of man was this? Amir Karmali launched a long speech about the honour and good character of this man. And then, then it came out.

"His father," he said, "was a man of high temper but hard-working all the same. You see he came to Africa a pauper and became a rich man. It was the coffee. He had struck gold. Probably a combination of luck and industry."

Amir Karmali then told me. "Ali's mother is a bit of a mystery. No one really knew about her roots. Her name was Zahra. They said she was an orphan from Zanzibar. Came over to Dar es Salaam with him on one of those dhows. He married her. She was a great beauty. You can still see it in Ali and his sisters."

After Amir Karmali left I mulled his words around in my head over and over again. Lutfia's strange request drove the whole thing home. How could she possibly know? How did she know about the relationship of her sister and this man, this Khan? I never asked Lutfia. How could I shame her in her dying days? It became a little secret between us, and it will remain a mystery.

Hussein's father smiles in satisfaction. "Somehow it fits doesn't it? That this girl, this new Zahra is looking for her house. The poetry of Allah, I say..."

Abdel-Aziz gazes at his son who is no longer questioning his father's sanity. And then, for the first time in ten years, he becomes impassioned. "Oh, no! No! Yeah Allah, please no? You love her? Well it cannot be. No! Never. You are married! Moreover, we must respect the past, do you understand? Secrets must lie buried, that is their nature!" He is scowling at his son. "Oh, you foolish man."

He looks at his hands. "Son, I have just had a word with Mr. Ali Khan. You know, he is your cousin."

"What?"

"Well, Auntie Lutfia. He is the son of her sister. The son of my father's nephew's daughter. But we have always been one family, so my cousin's son. Your cousin."

"Hmmm. Yes."

"Son?"

"Yes?"

"You must not allow her to purchase the house. Not under any circumstances. I have given my word to her father, your cousin."

"Why not?"

"Because better the past lies buried."

"Can't you give me anything more substantial than that?"

"I was there, Son. I tell you, I saw how the transfer of that house took place. It was under the devil's own shadow. It is loaded with baggage and emotion, confusion and bitterness. A symbol for the son of a mother he didn't know. And for a woman, a token of wealth to protect her future. All because of a spontaneous marriage. Love that was not wise. This, Son, is why we advise you to marry your own kind. At least the children will know who they are. These children, look at them, born in a black continent with bronzed skin and a tethered history. How could they possibly know where they are going? No foundation, not even a nationality. They have been split across three continents. Bastards, they have become orphans of the sea."

ZANZIBAR

For six months, Hussein lives in Zahra's house with his wife and child. Ghulshan receives letters from Mrs. Karmali informing her of the couple's separation and their blissful reunion. Eight months later, we hear that the elder Mr. Zamakhshari has passed away. My father is grieved. He wanders around their Calgary home with an inexplicably long face. No, he will not attend the funeral, nor send a card. Guardians of the truth, our twisted tales, soon they will all vanish deep into the murky earth, taking with them their burdens.

My mother keeps me abreast of Zanzibar gossip, courtesy of Mrs. Karmali. They have separated again, Hussein and his wife. This time they will definitively divorce. Amir Uncle visits Hussein at his office to try to convince him to keep the marriage alive. His wife visits Anisa, who swears that her husband will never set foot in her house again, that he has told her so. And she will make damn certain, move heaven and earth if necessary, to ensure that the house will be hers. Then she tells Mrs. Karmali a little secret. "You know who it was, don't you? That little whore, Zahra Khan. And while I was carrying his child!"

I am anticipating the wrath of God, a shower of stones upon my head. But it does not come. Mrs. Karmali did not believe her.

"Zahra still wears her father's shirts and malapas for God sakes," Mrs. Karmali mutters to herself. Several months later Ghulshan informs me of their divorce and Anisa's possession of the house. "She certainly got her lot," my mother says, mischievously. Neither Ali, nor I, nor Sultan have mentioned Zahra's house to our beloved Ghulshan. And she shall live in oblivion.

Dhi, Thi, Thi
England

LONDON, AFTER TWO YEARS

Sultan phones me at my office to inform me that Zahra's house has been returned to its original splendour and turned into a bed-and-breakfast for the discerning traveller. I am not shocked. Later that year, in the summer, I am sent on an evaluation mission to study primary schools in the Dar es Salaam vicinity. While in Dar, I decide to take a three-day detour and visit Zanzibar. Some fires never subside.

I do not stay at Zahra's house, now the Stone Town Guest House, managed and owned by Hussein's wife who, I must admit, I had totally underestimated. It has fifteen rooms filled with Zanzibari knick-knacks and boasts a romantic garden café serving an amalgam of Arab, Indian and Swahili delights. I receive an affordable rate at the refurbished Serena Inn, in the crescent formed by Shangani Street. I am blessed with a room overlooking the sea. It is the off-season as summer in Europe translates into the rainy season here. Zahra's house is a ten-minute walk away. I decide to have lunch at Anisa's little café. Who would have thought? My nemesis, Elektra, I feel your pain. We who have bowed to the sins of the flesh, must fall. Heaven and hell are both on earth. I pray before setting out for lunch.

A placard on the gate, painted Ottoman yellow, reads "The Stone Town Guest House". Vines have been woven through the gates. African violets, fuschia roses and crimson birds of paradise line the newly tiled path that leads to the magnificent front doors which now stand open. At the entrance lies a guest book and a deep clay pot with floating lotuses. The man who ushers me in is wearing a white kanzu over cotton trousers, leather sandals and a kofia hat. The woman standing behind an impressive carved wooden table is wearing a short sleeveless dress made of a kanga. She gazes at me with a smile. I declare that I do not want to check in. Rather, just to have some lunch. The handsome kanzu man leads me to the garden café. "Is this your first visit to Zanzibar, Madam?"

"No." I must make an effort to be more civil. I look up at him and smile. "I have been here before." He sits me across from the fountain, under the mango tree, now trimmed to half its breadth. I receive a complimentary glass of cool coconut water and some sliced mango. No juices streaming down your fingers. Of course I have thought of phoning him. I have not done so. If heaven helps me, I will not do so. I choose to eat cassava fries and a fish mishkaki. Then I wait: I have an apology to make. Heaven help us.

I hear her before I see her. She waltzes in with her head cocked to one side. "Oh my goodness! Zaaahrahh?" She has changed her look. Hair is flat and long. Blow dried. She wears neutrals with a hint of pastel. Understated elegance. Effortful effortlessness. "Well, you have some nerve. My, my. Look at you. Haven't you changed? Cut off that hair I see. Short hair, umph. And tailored clothes, tch tch. Impressive. His Highness must be paying you well! Oh and the bag! How could I have missed it? Hermès. And in red."

Mercifully my food arrives. "Prompt service," I say.

She looks at me through her lower lashes. "You know, everybody is welcome here. We don't kick anyone out. Stay as long as you like and come tomorrow." She leaves abruptly, clutching a copy of this month's *Cosmopolitan* magazine.

The food tastes bitter. The fries are soggy and the fish is foul.

I leave the Stone Town Guest House and amble along Sukokuu Street toward the harbour. I have reached the sea once again. I remove my expensive sandals and walk along the sand, which here is not soft and lovely but rather rocky. Yet the smell of the sea imbues me with memory.

I hear footsteps running behind me. "Zahra!" Not the office, please. Lazily I turn my head. Hussein. He stops running, catching his breath, he waves his arm and pulls it down. He stares at his hands as he walks towards me, like a mischievous child that has been caught. He comes and stands beside my sandals. I look up at him. I can only smile. He sits beside me and smokes a cigarette.

"Want to go and have some barbecued fish?"

"No."

"Why not?"

"I'm not hungry."

"Okay."

He doesn't move. He doesn't go away. I stare at the sea.

"I have a story to tell you."

"Looks as if it might rain."

"Will you listen to my story?"

"Yes."

"Come inside then."

We walk to the Floating Restaurant off the edge of the harbour. What story could he possibly have? Some jangled tale, pleading excuses. What could possibly excuse him? And me? What excuse have I got? I will listen to him all the same.

"Zahra, would you like something to drink?"

"A cup of tea."

He orders a cup of tea for me and scotch for himself. Little changes it seems.

"Will you come to Alexandria with me?"

"What?"

"Come to Alexandria."

"Are you out of your mind?"

"That is where you will find your grandmother's home. Not here."

"Hussein, please. I am not interested in a game. Really. No more mystery. If you have something to tell me, then tell me. Otherwise leave me. Let me be. I'm getting on with things, no more twisting waves."

"Then you are not living."

"For God's sake."

"Trust me. Please. Come to Alexandria and I will explain everything."

"When?"

"Tomorrow morning."

"No." I want to get up and walk out but I don't. I remain sitting. Waiting for him to insist, to explain. Something.

"My father has passed away."

"I know. I'm sorry."

"I was going to marry you so you could have the house."

This time I stand up and I leave.

He comes running. "Don't go away. Not like this."

"How would you prefer me to leave?"

"After Alexandria."

"Why on earth should I come to Alexandria?"

"Zahra, your grandmother. She was not Zanzibari, nor Omani but Egyptian, from Alexandria."

I'm falling into the sand. Who can stop me?

ANGELS

My body rotting away in the Saharan dust. Away, away, rotting. From now until tomorrow. Blood tomatoes and olive oil from the trees of Palestine. The Nile caressing the tongues of the Mediterranean. Spitting slowly into a pit of darkness, from then until eternity.

The telephone won't stop ringing but it is never for me. I am in the Sahara spitting slowly into a pit of darkness.

Arms hovering overhead, they reach for Moses on Sinai's peak. Green eyes, finding only empty Coca-Cola bottles. Winding down the twisting waves of her tresses, the words of the Qur'an—to protect and guide the child who falls into the valley.

CAIRO

I have packed my bags. I have spun a long winding tale to my office, was granted a week's leave. I arrive at Zanzibar airport at nine in the morning. He is late. I wait outside on the curb drinking coconut water straight from the shell. So, she was Egyptian. Alexandrian. Am I surprised? No, not really. It puts my affinity for Egyptians in a new light. Presumably, Ali knows this. It rather explains his youthful trip to Egypt, doesn't it? Not just for the Imam's burial. Why didn't he tell me? Why must I rely on strangers for grains of truth?

He arrives with apologies. The people on the curbside begin to notice me now that I have been met by a golden boy descending from an expensive car. He picks up my bag in addition to his and we scramble to the KLM check-in. We are flying first-class to Cairo. His passport is Egyptian. Why first-class, I want to know. It's a special occasion, he explains. Experience teaches me that men become gallant knights the moment you lose interest in them. I am determined to remain unimpressed by first-class. In the lounge we have a choice of ten exotic drinks but I choose water. He laughs. Then orders two freshly squeezed mango juices. One for him, the other to rest in my eye's gaze. He looks at me, noticing perhaps for the first time the absence of my mane.

"I cut it off."

"Why?"

"To avoid men like you."

"Ouch."

"My pleasure."

"I'm still here."

"Congratulations."

"My pleasure."

"We are flying to Cairo?"

"Uh, yes. My family is there. We have a wedding. Just two days. Then I will take you to Alex."

"A wedding! You expect me to come to a wedding with you!"

"I didn't ask you to come to the wedding. Cairo is a fascinating city. If you choose not to accompany me you can amuse yourself elsewhere."

On the brink of informing him that I have been there, I hold my tongue. I look away. Absorb, Zahra. Stop engaging. Just listen. Look and you shall see. There is a grand design. It all falls into place.

In Cairo he waits while I go through non-domestic Customs. A driver appears and collects our bags. We climb into an old black Mercedes. Ah, Cairo—Misr. Those familiar smells, the sounds of Egyptian dialect, 'amiyah. He asks the driver to stop at a kiosk around the corner and runs out to buy cigarettes. The driver smiles. We make small talk. Hussein returns.

"Such a long time since we have seen you, Ustaz Hussein, but you always come with a beautiful woman." He winks at me in the rear view mirror.

"Be careful," Hussein tells him. "She is my wife."

"Really? That's not what she told me."

Hussein looks at me. "What do you mean what she told you. How? She doesn't speak—" He stops. Looks at me again.

"Of course she speaks Arabic, Egyptian dialect. You can't hide an Egyptian from me." The driver chuckles.

Shock value. There is nothing quite like it. I have been dumbfounded in his presence on many an occasion, but this is his first time. His head has not moved. He looks as if he might fall off the car seat and sink into an abyss.

"I studied at the American University in Cairo," I explain.

"When?" he asks.

"Seven years ago."

Smile. He reaches out and takes my hand.

We arrive not at a hotel but at the Garden City residence of the Zamakhshari family. It has changed, of course. The family no longer occupies the entire building. The apartments of the west wing are let out, mostly to diplomatic staff and visiting professors to the American University. I have been here before. Martina, my Post-Colonial History professor, used to live on the first floor. I tell him this. He looks at me enigmatically.

"Maybe God exists after all."

"Of course."

In the startling mid-afternoon light the amber in the limestone gleams from the steps and façade of the building. The doorman in a crisp baby-blue galeibeya and white turban rises off his worn wicker chair, stubs out his Cleopatra and greets us. He motions towards our luggage. Hussein stops him, insisting that we are not staying. We have just come for some tea and to see the family. It strikes me that I am the second East African-Gujarati girl that he has brought home. This unnerves me somewhat. He takes my hand and leads me to the door. We stop in front of a wrought-iron contraption built in the 1930s by the Germans, and faced with wooden doors by the Egyptians. He presses a golden knob and we hear the gates click on the upper floors before the lift embarks on its slow descent. It drops before us. The gates clatter before locking into the ground floor. He opens the wooden doors, then unlocks the gates with a key and we climb in. He reaches out to shut the wooden doors first, then the iron gates. He pushes the golden-edged number 4, the top floor. The lift drops and clicks again before ascending.

"Who are we meeting?"

"Om Habiba, my father's sister."

We exit the contraption and arrive at a flat marked 4A. He rings the buzzer. A woman opens the door. Grandchildren emerge from behind her, running and shrieking at their "uncle". I think of his son. Two-and-some-odd years old now. He doesn't introduce me to the children. A four-year-old girl with cascading locks that ripple like the sea floats into his arms.

"Tanta," he calls. She is sitting, in that half-reclining way that children and the elderly possess.

"Hussein, ya habibi, wein intah?" Her face lights up when she sees him, the apple of her eye perhaps. I look at her face. I cannot miss the resemblance. She looks like me.

Tanta, I would like to introduce Zahra."

She stands up, comes closer to inspect me. She walks with difficulty. Her spectacles come off and she squints at me.

"What kind of fool do you think I am?" she asks her nephew.

I am beginning to understand.

"Who are you?" She speaks to me in Arabic.

"No," Hussein says, wishing her not to answer.

We both turn to look at him.

"My name is Zahra. My father's name is Ali Khan. I was born in Nairobi, Kenya. I have a Canadian passport. Until yesterday, I thought I was Gujarati."

"From India?'

"Yes."

"Yeah Allah, innaka 'alaa kulli sha'in qadir." She embraces me. Her eyes are teary. I can feel her bones tremble. "We cannot tell the family."

Hussein is furious. They argue. I collapse on a chair and take refuge in silence. She insists. There will be shame and scandal. After all these years. A lie. It must be buried.

"We are honourable people!" his aunt exclaims.

I have never seen him so violent, so upset. "You and your cobwebbed world! When the truth comes, when light pierces darkness, you run scurrying like rabid dogs to hide it before the world can see. All in the name of shame. Pride, that tongue that licks the dust on the ground. Kafirs, you are." He storms out, taking me with him.

In the rickety lift, he is seething. He cannot look me in the eye. Outside, we hasten to the car. He takes the keys from the driver. We drive out of the city towards the pyramids. There is a hotel there. At the foot of the Sphinx, the Oberoi. He checks us in.

"I want to be alone." I walk past the parking lot, past vendors, hustlers, children and camels, into the desert. I haven't got Egyptian pounds to pay the entry fee into the pyramid complex. I walk around it. The Sahara is sprawled before me like a sea. Harmonious. Monochromatic. Like caramel, smooth. Never-ending. Rippled. I rent a horse from a stable, swearing by the golden amulet of Sur'at al Khursi strung around my neck that I am a guest at the hotel and I will pay them tomorrow. They award me a black stallion. Smooth, sleek, strong. Thank God I gave up my project to be chic and am wearing jeans. The boy holds the horse while I mount. I give the stallion a soft kick and we trot past the traffic of the stables. The desert appears, flat and uninterrupted. I sit up, lock my knees, push into the stirrups and whack the horse. He shoots off. Fast, faster than I have ever ridden. I have to hug his neck to stay on. The wind comes like a force, straight at me. The sand stirs up, wafting around us in clouds. And we run, unstoppable. Angels, dear God, the One and Only, how could this be a coincidence of spontaneous combustion?

ZAHRA

I am sitting on the veranda of Zahra's house on the northwestern coast of Egypt. I am gazing at the Mediterranean Sea, eating figs from the trees behind the house. Here in the old city of Alexandria, on the corniche.

Hussein, my cousin, has given me a house by the sea. Meaning. Resolution. That is what I have wanted.

The house is not in Zanzibar, not on the Indian Ocean, which I will always call a sea. It does not face Gujarat, does not even face east. Rather, it faces west, towards Europe's lofty head, overlooking the Mediterranean, that melodic sea which bridges chasms between Europe and the Orient, uniting to divide. A sea which gave birth to those channels which linked mysticism to science, the Tartars to the Kabbalah, Islam to mediaeval Latin alchemy. This house is my house, I will make it Zahra's home. It is not our house, not mine and Hussein's, just mine. I know this seems terribly selfish, even childish. So be it. I have longed for a house by the sea, for a place where I can escape from the world and everyone in it. I have not found it myself, as I thought I would. Hussein has given it to me. A gift. Of love? Repentance? Guilt? I have accepted, all the same.

Here comes Hussein. Returned from the garden with cherry blossoms. I accept them gracefully. I am as naive as the world believes me to be. I have refused to marry him. I will not become wife when I can be so much more.

I know this house is not mine alone. I haven't even seen the papers. I do not know how long he will stay here by my side. But for now, he is here with his crescent smile and I will embrace him. Angel, do you hear me? The world will not dilute me. I am and always will be Zahra. Wherever I live. Whatever I taste. However I clothe my limbs. Whoever I see. I still dream of Yasmine. I remember mangoes and the peaks of Kilimanjaro. I embrace Ali and kiss Ghulshan. I dance alone. I speak soliloquies. And I still cannot meet my mother's gaze. Her eyes shine.

Hussein will leave for London next week. He hopes to start a practice catering to business from the Gulf. I will stay here. Make this house my home. I dream of bringing Ghulshan and Ali to Alexandria. I will convince them to join me for a lengthy holiday. I hope they will forgive me, the adultery with the gigolo lawyer, the lack of a husband. Perhaps Sultan will come with his wife and children. And perhaps we will share some resonance of that cacophonous laughter which crackled amidst the coffee branches at the foothills of Kilimanjaro.

Here, I will stop. I have run too far, for too long. Now, I will rest. This niche is mine. A breath of life. Reality is whatever we imagine it to be. I no longer need to escape.

Ali had a spirit that soared the heights of Kilimanjaro. He has bequeathed it to me. Ghulshan has nourished it, dutifully. This is the story of Ghulshan and Ali. Take heed, dear one. The blind do not see their labyrinth, but we do. Blind, blind king, how will you hold Ghulshan's gaze?

I love him again. Not like I used to but more. I must marry him. I know this. But not just yet. In spite of it, of everything: betrayal, tragedy, all those tears, I love him, still. The choice is not mine to make. When She beckons, I always follow.

CAIRO

Around midnight I return to the hotel. The doorman is dubious about letting me in until I speak loudly in English. I fell off the horse. Jeans are ripped at both knees, scraped and bleeding, face is scratched and bruised, ankle twisted. I am hobbling, covered from head to foot in sand. Glamour, ha ha. I can hear the shadows chuckling. Worse still I have lost the horse. Have prayed that he has returned to the stable. Otherwise, fifteen thousand pounds, minimum, sterling, that is. I limp through the grand lobby of the Oberoi Hotel. All eyes turn to me. The women with disdain, men with pique. The concierge comes hopping along. I know better than to speak to him in Arabic. I wait until he switches to English, then French. Always the best bet. I explain that we have a room. Hussein Zamakhshari. A name, that is all I need.

"Oui, oui Madame, but he has been searching for you all evening. C'est un truc ça. We sent a team into the pyramids. Mon Dieu! Are you all right? Attendez, don't take another step. Hassan, bring a chair for the madame."

A chair appears, I am lowered onto it. Two porters carry me, aloft on my throne, into the carpeted lift. On the seventh floor, we arrive at room 706. They knock at the door. He opens it. The look on his face is priceless.

A half-empty bottle of scotch stands open on the coffee table. He lifts me off the chair and onto the bed. Settles the tip with the porters. I wonder how much fifteen percent of me is. He shuts the door, then walks to the bed and sits down beside me. His face is grim, pupils are red. Uncontrollably, I start to laugh. He is not amused.

"Where in the world—What on earth—Are you out of your mind? Barking mad! Do you have any idea how I worried? My God. What were you thinking? One minute we are checking in, the other you have disappeared into thin air! Do you ever think about anyone but yourself? I have never in my life met such a selfish woman!"

"I said I wanted to be alone."

"When, when did you say that?"

"While you were checking in, I know you heard me."

"I did not hear you, nothing of the kind."

He gives me a bath. Cleans my wounds. Phones the reception and asks for a first-aid kit. He disinfects and bandages my cuts. Gives me a shot of scotch. Orders soup and bread for me from the room-service menu. Tucks me into bed and lies down beside me. In a man, even more precious than good manners is the ability to nurture.

"What happened?" He has returned to his scotch.

"I went for a walk and decided to go for a ride."

"What kind of a ride?" He is indulging me, like a child.

"On a horse." I lisp.

"You decided to go for a horse ride? Just like that."

"I didn't dream it up, there are hundreds of stables around the pyramids."

"Yes, yes there are. They are for tourists. To ride in daylight with a tour guide."

"The desert invited me."

"Oh, did it."

"Yes."

"How nice."

I tell him about the stallion, about my foot caught in the stirrup and the fall, about being dragged by the horse.

He is standing now. Hands on hips. "The horse DRAGGED you? But just for a bit. A stallion."

"I hope he went back to the stables." Silence.

He is pacing now. "You hope—" He waves his words away. "How did you get back?"

"I walked."

"At night?"

"Yes."

"Through the desert?'

"Yes."

"Without a flashlight."

"Yes."

"Zahra!" Hands are running through hair which is peppered white now. "Do you have any idea what could have happened to you? I mean, this is Egypt. Egypt, okay. Not London, not Canada, not some golden field."

There is a knock on the door. He opens it. My soup has arrived. The attendant smiles sheepishly. He walks to his jacket that hangs over a chair at the desk. He shakes the jacket, locating several pound notes and tips the attendant. He closes the door. He pulls a chair up next to my bed. Carries the food tray and places it on the chair. Sits me up, puts a pillow on my lap and serves me the lentil soup and flat bread. My back is killing me. He knows this. Asks me if I want another shot of scotch.

"No." I respond with mouth full, bruised cheeks tingling slightly. "But I would like some chocolate."

I am drifting dreamily to sleep with a full tummy when a thought wakes me. I push myself up with my arms. My eyes open. He is not sleeping. There is a small lamp burning. He sits hunched in a chair, cigarette with long ash in hand. He is reading something, it must be Arabic. At least the book opens the wrong way.

"Hussein?"

"Yes."

"What are you reading?"

"Rumi."

"In Arabic?"

"No, he wrote in Persian."

"Where did you learn Persian?"

He closes the book, stubs out his cigarette, exhaling smoke. He looks up with a smile. "At Al-Azhar."

"What?"

"I studied at Al-Azhar. Wanted to be a Muslim thinker, like those great mediaeval philosopher poets."

"What happened?"

"This is not the age for it."

"Why not?"

"Because. The doors of ijtihad are closed. The Muslim mind is closed. The lock has been turned twice. Once by the essentialists, who dirty Islam with their temporal political agendas. A second time by the fanaticism of the western media. We live in the reign of the ego."

"So you just gave up. You quit like a coward?"

"Yes."

"No. Look around you. Islam is alive still. That spirit which unites everything, allowing you to see One in All and All in One. The principle of charity, of equality, tolerance. How can you give up?"

"You live in a fantasy."

"No. Look at us for example. How else would we have met, if it wasn't for that uniting breath. What else could possibly have brought Egypt to Zanzibar?"

"Trade. Money. Political interest."

"What about Zahra, my grandmother? She went and lived in a community where the only thing she knew was their God. He was the same as hers."

"Not in all opinions."

The thought that woke me comes clamouring back. "Hussein?"

"Yes."

"How are we related?"

"Zahra and my father were cousins. Second cousins."

"So that makes you..."

"Your father's cousin."

"And my uncle?"

"In an eastern sense. Yes."

"How do you know this?"

"My father told me."

"How did he know?"

"Lutfia, Zahra's sister, before she died left the house in Zanzibar which she had inherited from her father in your father, Ali Khan's name."

"How did she know about him? We never had any contact with them, with anyone. I've only just found out that my grandmother was Egyptian."

Hussein stops to consider my question. "Baba couldn't figure it out either."

Then I remember. "My father did come to Egypt, sometime in the late 50s. Nasser's time. Do you think they met?"

I can always tell when I have caught his full attention. He stops in the midst of a gesture and looks at me, as he is doing now. "Of course. They must have met. How else could she possibly know about him?"

"You think he just rang her up and said, 'Hi, I'm your sister's son'?"

"Not exactly."

"And why didn't he keep in touch with her then, and she with him?"

"Maybe they did keep in touch. How do you know they didn't?"

"Oh for God's sake, surely we would have met her then."

"Maybe they decided not to complicate things. You know how they think. Anyway, why don't you just ask your father?"

"My father does not talk about the past. He would not. Never, ever. It simply is not done. When he came to Zanzibar we had one conversation about the house, consisting of two sentences."

"Did he know you were looking for the house?"

Silence. He looks away, melancholy again. But I want to engage him. This man who knows my tale. "I wonder how they met."

"Who?"

"Zahra and my grandfather, Vilayat Khan."

"At the harbour, perhaps. She saw him across the sea and her heart melted." He smiles.

"Or she saw the vehicle of her escape."

"From what?"

"Monotony."

He chuckles. We breathe silence. He smiles again. "Zahra?"

"Yes."

"Would you consider marrying me some day?"

"What does Rumi say?"

"He says, 'Why do you stay in prison when the door is so wide open?'"

Early tomorrow morning he will send out the footman with fifty dollars to pay the stable and inquire if the stallion has returned. I will sleep until noon and wake to a big black moon on my face.

The room is empty. The smell of his cigarettes still lingers in the air. I rise with difficulty from the bed. My right ankle is bright red, like a large mango. Both knees are scabbed, the right one has lost a leaf of flesh. My abdomen burns. My back feels stiff, as if knotted together to keep it from falling apart. I manage to reach the bathroom by holding onto furniture strewn along the way. I take a long hot shower standing on one leg. I am thankful for my short hair. Cannot imagine washing a long tangled mess at this juncture. When I hop from the bathroom, I find him in the room. He extends his hand to me and I use it to propel myself towards the bed where I can have a seat.

"We are going to the wedding," he announces.

"What? In this state?"

"I want you to meet your family."

"Let us understand something. I have a family. They may be spread across the globe and embroiled in petty, egotistical feuds, but I do have a family. This, these people, they are not my family. They can't even acknowledge that I exist out of fear and shame!"

"Zahra, you're not being fair. It's a natural reaction. People are provincial."

"I don't care if it's natural. It doesn't excuse it. These people are your family. Yours. Purebred. Belonging to one land, one place. Not infiltrated by foreignness. Unbastardised."

"For God's sake! Why are you so angry?"

The room is losing focus. Emptiness washes over me. "I'm not sure." I miss my sister Yasmine.

THE DESERT

The zephyr is chilly and dry, lacing through my short hair. A west wind blowing in the east. This is the Sahara. But no longer an undulating monochrome landscape basked in the sun's golden hues. It is dark now. A cool, black night enveloping the sky. I have fallen into the desert. I am shrouded from head to foot. The scent of the desert is like dry musk. Silence. The lush green rain of the tropics bequeathing to its flora the dazzling hues of a jewel. That moist scent, the rhythm of water. All are absent here. Africa, where are you? I am lying in the Sahara. Must stand. Stand and walk. I am blind. I am walking through the Sahara, blind. I am listening. My heart beats like a drum. I am indulging that need for heroism, imagining the footsteps of those mediaeval men who stormed the desert. I am alone. A solitary figure in this vastness. There must have been women, too. We just never heard of them. I am a woman walking alone through the dark Sahara.

Allah, guide me to the Right Path. I can taste the sand. The knee is throbbing. Forehead to the sand. Allah, guide me. Truly then it is the tongue of pride that licks the dust. Forgive my sins.

Walking now, again, I am walking. I can see light. I am walking towards the light. A mirage hovers around me. Steaming water, warm and moist. Here. Just to the left. Come. But there is no light. Where is the light? Straight ahead, darling. It is seven hours walk away. Where shall I tread?

Angels, where are you? Yasmine, is that your face? Is that your face etched into the night? Why did you go? Leaving me all alone to court the desert like a pilgrim.

THE WEDDING

I am wearing a blue sari. No makeup, it just accentuates the bruises on my cheek. I have become acclimatised to the enquiring gazes that pass judgement even before they have turned away. He is behaving rather admirably. Introducing me as his "friend" Zahra. Women pass knowing looks and men chuckle. Indian, no? is the obvious response to the sari. Oh and there sits Om Habiba, presiding over her vast family. She does a double-take upon seeing me. Surprised at my presence or my state? I wonder. A thin smile passes her lips. Hussein, affectionate despite eastern decorum, plants a kiss on my head.

The wedding is his niece's. She is four years younger than I am. Marrying a young professional boy from a good family. Doctor or lawyer. I can't recall which. She has graduated from the American University but doesn't plan on being employed. Roasted pigeon with moulukhaia and French delicacies collide on my palette. The air is resplendent with the smell of perfume and expense. Little Rapunzel whom I did not meet at the flat yesterday appears and tugs at Hussein's trouser leg. He lifts her onto his lap. What of your child? I wonder. His brother, father of the little doll, comes by with second child in tow. He stands to greet his brother. They embrace. He motions towards me. This is Zahra. His brother's name is Khalid. Khalid looks at me and then looks at Hussein. Then he pulls him aside. They return with the sister. Her name is Ghada. She is blonde and thin. She is graceful, and looks at me benignly. They are going to congratulate the bride. Off they go. Hussein asks if I would prefer to sit comfortably. Of course I would.

A very old woman makes her way towards me. She is clearly not from these classes. A loyal servant perhaps. She approaches me somewhat hesitantly. All smiles. I smile back. She comes nearer. Sits down next to me. She is frail, looks as if she might crumble.

"Ahlan," I welcome her.

She takes my hand, puts it to her cheek. Her movements shake. The mouth always swallowing in that manner peculiar to the elderly. Her eyes are watery, have faded into a grey. Hair also is grey, and thin, almost mossy, swept into a knot the size of a coin. Her face can be read. A canvas of the suns and moons she has seen. My hand sits in her lap now. She pats at it. Then swallows vigorously, squeezing my fingers in an effort to collect her scattered strength.

"I am Fattheyah," she announces to me, her eyes shining with expectation.

I am trying desperately to relate some meaning, anything, to her words, her name. Meanwhile, her eyes crinkle, the corners droop.

She sucks her lips in and then nods for a while. Then she looks up again. She makes me feel like a robust giant, a newborn babe, in her presence.

"Do you know who you are?" she whispers.

"I am Zahra."

"Yeah Rab." Her eyes turn upwards.

We have an audience of Om Habiba, Hussein and his siblings. I try to ignore them all. "Do you know me?" I prod her gently.

"Yes. I know. I know who you are. God bless you. May He protect you from evil and envy, Amen." She pulls me closer to give me a kiss. "My Zahra, you must be free. Do not come again. You are not of their kind. They will harness you, like a donkey. You will be enslaved to their modes and tastes. Be free, dear one. Be free."

"Fattheyah."

"Yes. I am the one they always blame."

"Tell me how she was."

"She. Why, she was you. Just like you. She did not bow to the whims of society." Hussein is approaching from across the room. I am not sure I want him here, now. But he will come all the same.

"Zahra," she smiles. "Zahra. You came back, just for me to see. Al humdulillah, I am thankful to the Great One. My heart has peace now. I always knew. You ran away. I could see it in your eyes that day. When we woke for tea and I didn't find you in your bed I knew you had gone. Oh my. There was such a fuss. Your father searched high and low.

"'How can you promise a bride to the Sultan and then lose her?' your mother shouted! 'How can you lose my daughter!?' your father growled."

"They were never the same again, your mother and father. Always bickering. Your father never recovered from your loss. In our hearts we all knew you were alive. He blamed himself. He should have found you. I think in his old age he finally understood what you had run away from. It was the same thing that kept him from finding you. They call it honour. But it is not. No, it is fear. Fear rooted in the cowardly conceit of pride. Oh look! He is your man? Yes, yes of course. Abdel-Aziz's son. From our very own blood. You really did come back. But take him, and go. Do not stay Zahra; do not stay." She rises respectfully to Hussein.

"Fattheyah, why are you standing? Sit, let me listen to your tales."

"No, no. My tales have been told. You have heard them all, many times over."

I stand on my one foot to bid her farewell. Bending to reach her crumpled cheek, I find it wet, before I plant my kiss.

Hussein escorts her back to her chair. Then he joins me. "She must be at least a hundred years old," he laughs. "She's been around for as long as I can remember. Dear old Fattheyah."

"She was my grandmother's ayah?"

"Yes. Yes I think she was."

"Can we go now?" I ask him. I am ready to leave without him.

"All right." I can feel him compromise. "You must be tired. Just wait here while I fetch the car."

He leaves me again. I want to join Fattheyah in her lonely seat beside the grand old dames. But I don't think I can. All eyes are on me. Their tongues must be wagging. Ghulshan would die of shame if she saw me now. Limping heavily and awkwardly, like an old beggar woman who must carry her load across the street. Then magically, almost miraculously, Fattheyah, the hundred-year-old woman rises to help me. Everyone else remains seated. Watching. Their eyes glassy like a serpent's. As Fattheyah cups my elbow in her fist, I bend to her, catching her eye. Laughter dances there, mischievously. We laugh out loud. She has aged beyond judgement, and I have learned not to care.

ALEXANDRIA

We drive to Alexandria in his rediculous fifteen-year-old black Mercedes. We leave the hotel early the next morning. Annie Lennox sings to me. I sing along at the top of my lungs. He makes good sport of not minding. We drive north, past Heliopolis and Giza through the desert for about an hour. Then we take a detour eastward, around the Mediterranean. He stops the car by the water, driving almost up to the shoreline. I roll down my window to feel the happiness of the sea. The scent of the Mediterranean is pungent.

Its colour today is an icy blue. Where the sun shines the water is tinged with a marine green. Light dances on water. I wish to swim but satisfy myself by hobbling along the shore and immersing my hands. We stop for some dark, sickly sweet tea at a tin kiosk, where the men share their Cleopatras. He pulls me away. Leading me back to the sea. His eyes are clear, fiercely clear. The sun shines through him.

"That spring you came to Zanzibar with your family. At Navroz, do you remember that Navroz? At Amir Karmali's house? My father went for a walk with your father. He took your father to Zahra's house. It was perhaps insipid. But he told him everything. He promised Ali. My father promised your father you would not have that house. I kept his word. Perhaps that makes me a coward."

Dear darling. I am tired of this.

"I tried to keep the house through the divorce. I did everything in my power. I'm so sorry, Zahra. Anisa had figured it out. Actually, I think I told her. She knew what it meant to me, perhaps even understood what you meant to me. She used the house as her weapon."

I have sat down. Surely people don't live like this. How could they? And this man with whom I have spent the total of a fortnight, dispersed over the space of two-and-some years, why does he affect me so?

"Zahra. Are you all right? Don't cry."

"I am not crying."

He kneels down beside me, and speaks to me as if speaking to a child. "I have something else for you. A house. The house, here. Lutfia, Zahra's sister, didn't have children. And Mouna, her children live in Cairo. I will keep my promise. Zahra, look at me."

We drive on awhile and then enter Alexandria, passing the famous lighthouse on our way into the city. Hussein does not stop for lunch. He drives straight to the house of Ahmed Sultan. We drive through Alexandria's narrow serpentine streets, into the old city's affluent neighbourhood by the corniche. He parks the car on a hill and we walk a block and a half to the house. It sits perched on the corniche, the gardens sprawling, facing the sea.

Sikeena Karmali

ESPLANADE
Books

THE FICTION SERIES AT VÉHICULE PRESS

www.vehiculepress.com